ALLIE PLEITER

ONE SHARP STITCH

KENSINGTON PUBLISHING CORP.
kensingtonbooks.com

KENSINGTON BOOKS are published by

Kensington Publishing Corp.
900 Third Ave.
New York, NY 10022

All Kensington titles, imprints, and distributed lines are available at special quantity discounts for bulk purchases for sales promotion, premiums, fundraising, and educational or institutional use. Special book excerpts or customized printings can also be created to fit specific needs. For details, write or phone the office of the Kensington Sales Manager: Kensington Publishing Corp., 900 Third Avenue, New York, NY 10022. Attn. Sales Department. Phone: 1-800-221-2647.

KENSINGTON and the Kensington Cozies teapot logo Reg US Pat. & TM Off.

First Kensington Hardcover Edition: April 2025

ISBN: 978-1-4967-5201-7
First Trade Paperback Edition: March 2026

ISBN: 978-1-4967-5202-4 (e-book)

10 9 8 7 6 5 4 3 2 1

Printed in the United States of America

The authorized representative in the EU for product safety and compliance
is eucomply OU, Parnu mnt 139b-14, Apt 123
Tallinn, Berlin 11317, hello@eucompliancepartner.com

Praise for *One Sharp Stitch*

"Shelby Philips is an irresistible, gutsy new heroine with a heart as big as her needlepoint projects. *One Sharp Stitch* and its wonderful cast of characters kept me reading and guessing and second-guessing until the surprising finale in this well-crafted and enjoyable mystery." —Sally Goldenbaum, *USA Today* bestselling author

"Plenty of quirky characters lead up to a surprising denouement in this promising series kickoff." —*Kirkus Reviews*

"Allie Pleiter has stitched together a delightful, clever, and well-written mystery that introduces Shelby Phillips, a memorable heroine who learns to embrace her artistic abilities and her new role at the Nimble Needle, a charming little needlepoint shop at the heart of the community, in order to solve a puzzling murder." —Darci Hannah, author of *Murder at the Lemonberry Tea*

"Secrets, sisters, and scandal! A delightful cozy mystery, One Sharp Stitch introduces appealing characters and a humorous local tradition in a lakeside town set in North Carolina. Readers will love the perfect mix of murder, family, needlepoint, and charm." —Krista Davis, author of *The Diva Poaches a Bad Egg*

Books by Allie Pleiter

ONE SHARP STITCH

TWO PURLOINED PILLOWS

Published by Kensington Publishing Corp.

For Jeff

CHAPTER 1

"Here they are, Shelby, the keys to the kingdom." Mom handed me the shop keys with all the pomp of a coronation.

This wasn't my idea. My brilliantly devised "achieve success by thirty-five" plan did not include the loss of my dream job. Or a move home to play kingdom sitter to my mother's needlepoint shop.

Seeing as how this gig came with a rent-free apartment above the shop, however, I found myself unable to fend it off.

And my schedule was alarmingly empty.

I stared down at the set of old-fashioned brass keys that unlocked the doors to Nina's Nimble Needle. "Don't you think Jessica would be better at this?"

Of course Jessica would be better at this. Jessica was better at *everything*. I'd spent most of my life trying to get out of the shadow of my big sister's effortless perfection. Ambitious "success by thirty-five" plan—Exhibit A.

Mom frowned. "You know she's too busy for this."

I didn't agree. All this would come as second nature for Jessica. And it wouldn't matter that she already had two kids and a part-time job writing columns for a decorating magazine, because that sort of plate-spinning was Jessica's native language. We both knew she could run the shop better than I could without breaking a sweat.

Which left only two real explanations: This was a pity gig. Or a shameless attempt to pull me back to Gwen Lake. And into the crafting world my mother adored and where my sister already excelled. More likely all of the above.

"She's said she'd help if you needed it," Mom offered with a weak smile.

"Yeah, well . . ." In my view, the only thing in all of North Carolina worse than *needing* Jessica's help would be *having to ask* for it. She'd be so gracious I wouldn't feel the sting . . . at first.

"You won't need Jessica's help. You'll take to this like a fish to water. You're Shelby Phillips. It's in your blood." Mom closed my fingers around the keys after delivering this benediction. "You've got all that business sense. Just put it to work for the shop. I even bought that new retail software you've been hounding me to get."

Surprise dropped my jaw. "You did?" She was right. I had been hounding her to computerize her sales records. And telling her she could double her business with even the simplest of upgrades to her website. For a woman who sold needles, Mom clearly knew how to bait a hook.

She nodded. "You can install it and get it up and running while Dad and I are out on the road." She strung the last four words out like a rock star announcing a world tour. I suppose for her it was. For all the time she and Dad talked about this crazy dream of "going nomad," I confess I never thought they'd really go through with it. My parents love each other, but I can't quite see the logic of piling them into a smallish motor home for four weeks. Good marriages seem to need a lot more space than that—not that I would know.

I looked around the shop, trying to see it with new eyes. The Nimble Needle—we never called it Nina's Nimble Needle, because she was Mom to us, not Nina—had been part of my life for so long, it was hard to see it as a business venture. It was what Mom did. Everybody in Gwen Lake, North Carolina—

and probably in nearby Asheville, as well—knew Mom as Nina from the Nimble Needle. It was an inseparable part of her identity. I suppose that was why I couldn't quite wrap my mind around her wanting to leave it—in my hands, of all places—for a whole month.

I cast my gaze across the shop floor, over to the wall of mesh squares and rectangles needle pointers know as canvases. And *canvases* really was the right term, because these were painted like artwork. Paging through the collection of large canvas-filled boards that swung from the wall on hinges was like walking through an art gallery. A feast of possibilities met the eager shopper's eyes: canvases ready to become mountains of pillows, large and small, from simple to ornate. Others ready to become little signs and ornaments, wall hangings, bags, and eyeglass cases. Still more ready to become luggage tags and belts, coin purses, coasters and, of course, Christmas stockings. An art gallery of gorgeous images waited to become decor and accessories in the right hands.

The opposite wall held the means of that transformation. Thread, floss, fiber—there were different names for the small twisted skeins and smaller cards of colored thread—all meant to fill those canvases. I suppose I became a graphic design major because of my life among all this color. There was never just blue in the world; there was ocean blue and sky blue, lapis and cerulean, royal blue and turquoise, peacock and electric blue. There wasn't just red; there was poppy and cardinal and vermilion. Green, yellow, orange—I could name twelve versions of any of these colors as if I walked through life with a box of 120 Crayola crayons (of which I owned three).

In the middle of the shop were three tables. One displayed all kinds of tools and notions, one had a specialized display of holiday things or other seasonal items, and the third one, a large table, was where stitchers gathered either for classes or merely to socialize.

Gathered around that table were four women who were

practically aunts to me: the NYAGs. The NYAGs were all women of Mom's age and had long ago christened themselves "Not Your Average Grannies." And they were not your average grannies, to be sure. While each of them was an accomplished needle pointer, most of them debunked the stereotype of the rocking-chair granny with a vengeance. While Faye, Livvy, Tilly, and Dot were each in their sixties, none of them were anything close to "old." Mom had only barely escaped the tattoo two of them had gotten last year—a threaded needle, of course—because Jessica had talked her out of it.

Can I really do this? I waffled between doubt and determination on a moment-by-moment basis.

Technically, I *could* do this. I had run the administrative functions of Batterson Graphic Arts Design as office manager for two years. I knew the commerce of art and the strategies of sales.

Right up until that fateful meeting a month ago, when Dave Batterson had called us all into the Savannah, Georgia office and had announced he was selling the business to some large corporate firm. One that was not interested in "retaining existing staff." It had taken us all of thirty seconds to realize we'd just been let go. And if we hadn't caught on, the envelope with a pitiful severance and a written order to clean out our desks by the end of the week would have made things crystal clear.

If only I had actually followed Mom and Dad's advice to stash some away for a rainy day. I had honestly thought I was Dave's right hand in the business. Indispensable, in fact, and dancing on the edge of a personal romantic relationship.

As it had turned out, I was neither indispensable nor on the brink of an office romance. The way Dave made his quick goodbyes had told me I wasn't on the brink of any romance at all. Ouch. On any number of levels.

"Your biggest challenge will be Saturday," Mom was saying, dragging my thoughts back to the present.

"What's Saturday?"

"I told you, that's the trunk show. We do a trunk show the first Saturday of every month, so you'll only have this one to manage. Dad and I will be back before the next one."

Trunk shows are where one designer or vendor sends over a huge selection of his or her work so that customers can shop. They get to know the artist. And there are snacks. It's basically a retail party. "Okay." I'd organized enough client events to give me a shred of confidence that I could pull this off. "Who's the vendor again?"

"Your old friend the scissor gal."

I racked my brain for the name that fit this description. "Huh?"

Mom walked over to a glass display case by the cash register. "Gina Katsaros. She creates the most beautiful needlework scissors now. You didn't know?"

"No, actually." I peered into the case to see half a dozen intricately crafted small scissors. They were closer to silverware or jewelry than to standard scissors, fashioned as birds or flowers or delicate, ornate shapes. Needle pointers are notoriously picky about their scissors, and it wasn't hard to see why these had gained popularity. Mom had always had a great eye for artistic talent.

"She sharpens knives and such, too, but it's mostly the scissors that are the draw on Saturday."

"Kat makes these?" I asked, rather shocked. My eye caught the Kat's Kutz label, which I'd missed until now. "Kat from school?"

Gina "Kat" Katsaros was a year behind me in school and not someone I'd expect to have such talent. Kat was a misfit of sorts, quiet, and awkwardly geeky. The sort of person who fades into the woodwork in the wild drama of high school.

"I don't know why you're so surprised. Wasn't she artsy when you two were friends in school?"

I knew Kat, and Kat knew me, but we weren't friends in the way Mom seemed to think we were. "Sort of, I suppose."

Kat was always nice to me, but it was in a needy way. She would call me on the phone and sometimes trail behind me down the hall like a lost puppy, but we never hung out together. I never called her or invited her to anything. To be honest, I tolerated her—and, if I was being totally honest, it was a cold, weary toleration. More acquaintance than friendship.

Ah, but now she was evidently a successful art entrepreneur, and I was an unemployed office manager, ignoring any artistic talent I might have. Turnabout can be humiliating, can't it?

"So now you two can get to know each other again. But I should warn you, there is something a bit . . . sticky in her visit." Mom rubbed her hands together with a nervous twitch. "It's why I scheduled it for while you're here, actually."

"What do you mean?" I didn't like the sound of this. Faye's frown from the NYAG table wasn't helping, either.

"Gina has been hinting—rather broadly—that she'd like to take over the shop. When I retire." Mom never did take to calling her Kat.

Wait . . . retire? Was this "going nomad" not just a vacation but a *trial retirement*? All these new facts made me feel as if the shop floor was shifting under my feet.

"*Are* you retiring?" She hadn't said she was. Was I going to get a phone call from Nevada to tell me they'd decided to make this trip a permanent departure? That possibility landed like a rock in my stomach.

"No," Mom was quick to reply. The alarm must have shown on my face. "Well, not yet," she went on. "Not for a while, I think." Mom leaned in. "But the point is, I don't think Gina is the one to take over the Needle when it's time."

Her answer made me feel better. Slightly. I would certainly expect Mom to be picky as to who took over for her. "Why is that?" This was treading out onto some very thin familial ice, because I knew one of the reasons had to be *I'm expecting one of my daughters will take the reins.*

Now the timing of this trip and the scheduling of this trunk show were starting to make a calculated sort of sense. Despite Mom's assurances, I began to realize this wasn't just a stint of shop sitting. I'd been unwittingly lured into a full-scale apprenticeship.

"Mom . . ."

Mom waved me off, having misinterpreted my misgivings to be about Kat, aka Gina, rather than this first mention of retirement.

"Why don't you think she would be a good fit? She's obviously creative, and she was always sort of sweet in a quiet way."

Tilly, another of the Not Your Average Grannies, looked up from the canvas she was working on. "I think she's interesting."

"Chester uses her because she's convenient, coming to the butcher shop and all, but honestly, I find her rather . . . odd." Faye snipped off the thread she was working on. "Intense, and not in a good way."

All four of the NYAGs were working on what looked like pillows with sayings on them—a needlepoint mainstay if there ever was one. Mom must have owned a hundred. Her house was full of them, and she brought a new one to my apartment every time she visited.

Dot, who was always the rebel and who wasn't even a grandmother, let alone your average one, was working on a pillow with a pirate and some startlingly salty language, which I won't repeat here. "I'm with your mother. She's not the one. The talent is there, but not the people skills. And . . . well, you'll see."

All the other NYAGs nodded, that uniquely Southern "Bless her heart" expression on their faces. What was everyone going out of their way not to say?

Mom put on her own "Bless her heart" expression, which I

recognized as her "customer service" smile. The soft, slightly forced smile that was usually at odds with whatever she was really thinking. "You should never judge a person by how they dress."

Dress? Kat was so unmemorable, I couldn't remember how she dressed. Just that she was always there, bumbling around the outer edges of my life and always trying to get in, like a fly on a summer porch screen.

Even if she'd gone from neutrals to wild Lilly Pulitzer patterns, I couldn't see how any of that would render Kat Katsaros unsuitable to run the Needle. *Think of it as a second chance to be nicer than you were*, I told myself. I looked around the room. I liked all these ladies, but I could use a few friends my own age to get through this month. I'd been terrible at keeping up with childhood and high school friends in college and beyond, so sure I was moving on to my snazzy new life in Savannah. Maybe I could get along nicely with Kat, get past the shop friction. But, I admit, I fought the urge to pull out my cell phone and google her name to see if I could pull up an image. How much could one person change in the years I'd been in Savannah?

Livvy, who oddly enough was your stereotypical grandmother but still counted herself among the NYAGs, leaned over in her chair to peer out the shop's front window. "Speak of the devil, she just pulled up."

"Good." Mom headed for the door and motioned for me to follow. "I thought you two should get in a hello before Dad and I say goodbye. Just know she's a bit . . . different . . . than you remember."

The look in Mom's eyes didn't inspire comfort as I got a glimpse of a large white van with KAT'S KUTZ emblazoned on the side in bold black letters. The van boasted a logo—an enormous cleaver and a giant pair of scissors overlaid in skull-and-crossbones fashion—surrounded by sharp, jagged lettering.

Zigzags of black and purple covered the van, with the words *Artisan Scissors* and *Mobile Knife Sharpening* appearing several times in white diamonds.

In all honesty, it made me a little nervous to see what sort of woman would get out of the van. I didn't think she would bear much resemblance to the Kat I'd known. The Kat I'd kept only as a lukewarm friend, if that. You never really know someone, do you?

My jaw dropped as she got out. Or at least the person I had to assume was Kat Katsaros got out. I stared at Mom, then back at Kat.

Mom's "a bit different" was the understatement of the century.

CHAPTER 2

The van should have been my first clue.

Here I was envisioning the quiet wallflower Kat Katsaros—someone who looked exactly like a needlepoint shop owner. I now understood what Mom was trying to put so delicately. Tilly's description of her as "interesting" came up rather short. Faye's description of her as "intense" hit closer to the mark.

In fact, *edgy* was the word that came to my mind. Kat's formerly unremarkable brown hair was now a choppy black bob with a streak of purple on one side. It took me a minute to reconcile the eyes I knew with the ones now framed in bold black eyeliner. When she turned to retrieve a bag out of the back of the van, I saw that her black leather jacket also bore the Kat's Kutz logo. I had to admit, the woman knew the definition of *on brand*.

Now, don't get me wrong—I have no problem with people who dress on the edgier side of things. My shock came from the total transformation Kat had made and the fact that I couldn't quite picture the woman in front of me pressing Mom to hand the reins of the needlepoint business to her. Unless that van was decked out in expletive pillows (and believe me, those do exist in the needlework world), the contrast was too much of a reach.

"Shelbyo!" Kat called as she walked in the shop door and headed straight to where Mom and I were standing. Her use of an old nickname for me proved it really was her. "I heard you were back."

I couldn't tell if the faint undertone of disappointment was just my imagination or a hint that she really did see me as an obstacle. "I am," I replied as I strove to keep the shock out of my voice. "For a while, at least."

Kat held out a hand sporting black fingernail polish and thick, chunky rings to shake mine. "Wow," she said. "Look at you."

"Look at you," I wanted to say but didn't. If I ever needed evidence that you should never judge a person by how they were in high school, it was standing right in front of me.

"Hiya, Nina," Kat said, giving Mom a chummy little punch in the arm. She'd always been super-polite, calling my mom Mrs. Phillips, if she spoke to her at all.

"Hello, Gina," Mom replied. She flicked a split-second *See what I mean?* glance at me before saying, "I'm glad I got to see you before we head off."

"Ah, the lure of the open road. You may never come back, huh?"

It was an awkward thing to say given the circumstances. I heard a murmur coming from the NYAG table, as if those women weren't in any hurry to welcome Kat into the fold, no matter how gorgeous her scissors were. Which was funny when I thought about it—women so intent on bucking the stereotypes of "grannies" shouldn't be so bothered by a woman who bucked the stereotypes of needlework enthusiasts. In fact, Kat dressed like half the creative staff at my old firm. It was just the juxtaposition between the Kat in front of me and the Kat I remembered that threw me.

"We'll be working together on Saturday," Kat said, giving me the same odd buddy-buddy arm bump she'd given Mom.

"What do you think of that?" Again, there was just the tiniest note of challenge in her voice.

"I'm glad to be hosting the trunk show," I replied. I nodded in the direction of the glass display case nearby. "You do amazing work. Where did you learn how to forge metal like that?"

"Oh, it started at the Renaissance Fair. I had a thing for one of the blacksmiths there. He gave me private lessons." She gave the last words a flirtatious edge, which let me know Kat really had come out of her shell since school. The Kat I'd known could barely talk to boys without reaching for her inhaler. "And I'd always wanted to make jewelry. I just sort of put the two together."

Kat abruptly switched gears and walked over to the NYAG table. "Hiya, gals! Whatcha working on?"

She worked her way around the table, oohing and aahing over the projects and making comments about each woman's work. I suddenly realized what felt a touch off to me: she was trying too hard.

And there was the Kat I'd always known. Lingering just outside the social circle, not realizing her overenthusiastic attempts to fit in just pushed her further out. Mom used to call her "the darling little misfit," and despite the leather and ripped jeans, it still applied. I didn't know quite what to do with that.

Kat swaggered back to Mom and me. "So, am I in good hands this weekend?"

"You most certainly are," Mom said, putting her arm around me.

"Imagine that," Kat said. "Who'd have thought we'd be here, Shelbyo? Life is strange, huh?"

Oh, life had proven strange lately, that was sure. "Never a dull moment at this place," was all I could come up with to say. For no good reason, I felt embarrassed that I'd been given run of the shop when Kat so clearly had wanted it. "I'm looking forward to Saturday. Mom tells me you sharpen knives like your dad used to do at the hardware store, too. Pretty clever business combination."

"Dad stopped doing service at the hardware store when I took it mobile. I've even got an app. Cal told me it would never work, but I proved him wrong, didn't I?"

I tried to picture Kat's big, beefy brother and what he must look like now. "What's he doing these days?" I asked, just to make conversation.

Kat tucked the purple strand behind her ear, revealing earrings that were tiny dangling pairs of scissors. On one ear, that is. The other had a tiny silver meat cleaver, so together the earrings were just like the two parts of her logo. "On brand" down to the last detail. "Not much. Not enough. Dad's not sure he'll ever amount to anything. Me neither. Of course, now he plays around with wanting to help me with the sharpening side of the business, as if we're partners or something. But you know Cal. You can't really depend on him."

Two years older than Kat, Cal Katsaros had been a dark and grunting gorilla of a guy and had been just as fumbling as his sister when it came to social interaction. I had done my best to ignore the crush he had on me—I hadn't wanted to deepen any connection with that family, and he'd been far from my type, anyway. I regretted that perhaps Kat and her brother felt I had looked down on them. I'm ashamed to say it was true. In high school you think you know all the answers and just how life is going to work, don't you?

"Some guys are late bloomers," I said, just to be supportive. "We had a guy at the office who was a total mess until he figured out he was brilliant at animation software. Now he's really successful."

"Cal's not a *total* mess." Kat smirked. "But he is kinda close. You can judge for yourself. He told me he's going to stop by the trunk show and say hello."

So now I had to juggle not one Katsaros on Saturday, but two. When Mom had said she believed in jumping in with both feet, I guess she'd meant it.

Nina's Nimble Needle sat on the lower floor of a tan brick building and was fronted by a big display window shaded by a bright blue-and-white-striped awning. Above that awning sat the bay window of my current living quarters, accessed by a side stairway with a small balcony. Dad knocked on my door at the top of those stairs an hour or so later, huffing from his walk up.

"Forgot how steep those stairs are," he said as I let him in the door. "You settled in?"

"As much as I need to be." I'd cleared out my Savannah apartment and unpacked myself here as much as I dared. I wanted to send the message that this wasn't a permanent placement, but without seeming ungrateful for a welcoming place to land. "Thanks for talking Mom into this."

"You need your own space." Dad had wisely convinced Mom that I could keep an eye on their house without having to move *into* it. No one needs to plant themselves back into their childhood bedroom at thirty-one. There was still a twin bed in there, for goodness' sake. I was amazed my five-foot-ten frame had fit in there when I was eighteen, and I had vivid memories of cramming myself into it on college breaks.

"But that doesn't include dinner," Dad went on. "Everybody's coming over tonight for a send-off. Your mom evidently needs a final fling in a full kitchen."

That came as no surprise. Mom is one of those food-is-love people. I was convinced her never-ending supply of goodies brought into the Nimble Needle was an effective—if accidental—marketing ploy. Between Mom and the NYAGs, no one ever went hungry at the shop. "Jessica, Hal, and the boys?" I asked, wondering about the guest list.

Dad nodded. "They're excited to see you. I bet you're excited to see them, too, huh?"

That was half true, to be honest. Time spent with Jessica was a bittersweet pleasure. My older sister was a lovely person. She was just excruciatingly perfect. At everything. And given the state of my personal and professional affairs at the moment, that was a bit hard to swallow. Jessica's texts and social media posts showcased her achievements, nutritional goals, effortlessly perfect hair, gorgeous decor, and superhuman organizational skills. I was sure she had flaws—I just never saw them. Neither, I expect, did the rest of the world. I worried the face-to-face version of Jessica might prove more trying than the electronic one.

Plus, I worried about the whole *I'm running the Needle and you're not* dynamic. Mom might view Jessica as far too busy to mind the shop, but Jessica was also fiercely competitive. Anything that seemed to put me above her—in any respect—would bug her. I worried how it might come out in our interactions.

Still, she was my sister. I loved her and her boys. They'd just chafe a bit until I got my feet underneath me. And a full family send-off was certainly in order, not to mention that I hadn't yet filled the apartment fridge for any decent meals on my own. "What time?"

"Late. Seven or so. The boys have soccer practice, and Jessica's got some sort of pirate-y exercise class."

I chuckled at Dad's take on the word. "You mean Pilates?"

Dad pointed a finger at me. "That's it. You know Jess. Fit as a fiddle."

"Yep." I mentally went through my closet, in search of an outfit that would hide the pounds I'd added from self-indulgent cheesecake as things were falling apart at the office. Jess probably considered a tablespoon of peanut butter an indulgence, whereas PB was nearly a side dish in my world.

Mom had taught us all good manners, so I asked, "Can I bring anything?"

Dad surprised me by pulling me into a big hug. "You brought you. What else do I need?"

I loved the warmth in his voice. "You really gonna do this thing? You and Mom in there all over the place for a whole month?" I tried to keep my voice playful, despite the load of doubts I carried about the success of this adventure.

He smiled. "Sure are. I can't wait. Your mom and I going anywhere we want in the Nimble Nomad without any set plans. How much fun is that?"

I laughed. "The Nimble Nomad?"

Dad shook his head. "You know your mom. I figured that motor home was going to get a name at some point. Turns out it took a day and a half before she christened it the Nimble Nomad."

Raising an eyebrow, I commented, "Could've done worse. I have a friend who currently drives Milton the Mazda."

He laughed, and I decided this was a good time to get a little background information. "Hey, what do you know about the whole Kat thing? Did she really tell Mom she wanted to take over the shop? I mean, I'm not one for stereotypes, but she hardly strikes me as the needlepoint type." Then again, some people might raise an eyebrow at Dot and her foulmouthed pirate. The great thing about art is that it should be for everyone, in any way they like.

Dad tucked his hands in his pockets. "Kat's a bit of an odd bird, I agree. She tends to rub some people the wrong way— and not just with the purple hair. She's mouthy. But she's become a regular customer, and Mom says she does fine work. She just tries a bit too hard." He gave me a knowing look. "And your mother has always had pretty firm ideas as to who she'd like to take over the shop."

I leveled a serious look at Dad. "Not me."

He shrugged. "She'll take some convincing of that."

That had become clear. "So maybe you could help out with that while you're roaming around the country in the Nimble Nomad? I'm not saying it should be Kat, but I'm pretty sure it shouldn't be me."

Dad pulled his hands from his pockets and clapped them together in a *That's enough of that subject* gesture. "How about we leave that as a future problem and just have a nice family dinner?" He leaned in. "She made your favorite. Caramel-walnut brownies."

Nutrition could wait one more day. Even if Jessica stared down her low-carb nose at me while I ate some, Mom's brownies were worth it.

CHAPTER 3

"Aunt Shelby!" I was nearly tackled by a tandem of boys as I pushed open the front door just after seven that evening. "What'd ya bring us?"

"Boys!" Jessica scolded. "Manners, please."

Ah, the bluntness of grade-school boys. Still, a couple of years ago I had figured out the fast track to "cool aunt" status: sports jerseys. And with a Brit boasting good soccer contacts on our staff at Batterson Graphic Arts Design, I had been able to score big points with the boys.

I took a moment to enjoy the hefty dose of nephew enthusiasm. I fixed the pair of them with a confused look. "Was I supposed to bring you two something?"

Their "I'm disappointed, but hopefully, she's kidding" looks were adorable. "Well, you always do," Taylor said with a sheepish look.

I ruffled my nephew's neatly cut hair—the same blond shade as my dad's and Jessica's. "Yep, I always do. It's in the striped bag in the hallway."

Without a moment's hesitation, Taylor and his twin brother, Chaz, barreled down the hallway to where I'd stashed a pair of pint-sized jerseys from what my guy assured me was this year's hottest team.

This left me in the front room with Jessica. My sister looked exactly as I expected. Tanned, with stunning blond hair in a stylish bob; cheekbones I had envied every day of my teen years; a cute brightly colored print skirt showing off lean, fit legs; and gleaming teeth. The only feature Jessica and I shared was our mother's hazel eyes. Her whole family always looked as if they'd stepped out of a catalogue. I'd worn what I thought was my most stylish casual outfit and still somehow felt under-dressed. My less remarkable honey-colored hair never quite made the dial down from frizzy to wavy. Long days behind the desk at Batterson had left me pale. Most days the five-year gap between us felt about so much more than age.

"Hi, sis. Sorry about the boys." She gave me a quick hug and something just short of an air kiss. "They adore you."

They adored the stuff I brought them, but with grade-school boys, that's about as close as you can come to true affection. I shamelessly nurtured my most-favored aunt status. They were, for the most part, great kids and fun to be around.

Hal came through the front door a moment later, practically hidden behind a casserole dish in one of those monogrammed thermal carriers and a large gift bag. "Hey, Shelby," he said with a nod as he peered around the items. "Good to see you in town." He turned to his wife. "Where do you want this, Jess?"

She lifted the gift bag from atop the casserole. "Dish in the oven, and I'll take this."

Hal's arrival brought Mom out of the kitchen, wiping her hands on a dish towel. "Hello, honey." She accepted a quick kiss from Jessica and one from Hal. "Oven's ready for that," she told him, pointing back toward the kitchen.

Of course Jessica had cooked something. I'd asked and been told not to by Dad, but maybe this was one of those situations where I should have brought something, anyway. There always seemed to be a secret code for that sort of thing, one I'd some-how never quite mastered.

"What's this?" Mom asked with an undisguised glee worthy of her grandsons.

Jessica presented the bag to Mom with a flourish. "Just a little going-away present." I tried to ignore the matching tissue paper, expertly tied ribbon, and what I was sure was a homemade gift tag. Taylor's and Chaz's gifts were simply tucked into the plastic drawstring store bag I'd received them in, but boys don't care about that sort of thing, right? Had I even remembered to cut the price tags off?

I don't know why I was surprised when Mom pulled a gorgeous needlepoint sign out of the bag. *The Nimble Nomad* was stitched in letters the color of Mom and Dad's new van. Next to it was an illustration of the van heading away down the road, complete with the correct license plate. Tiny puffs of exhaust floated out of the tailpipe and turned into stars as they rose toward a rainbow sky. Across the bottom it read, *All who wander are not lost.*

"Oh, darling, it's perfect! Look at this, Shelby. Isn't it amazing?"

"Sure is." And it was. Beautifully stitched and clearly custom designed. For a woman who was always so busy, she'd found the time to stitch it up. Mom and Dad had owned the van for only a month, and this looked like ten weeks of stitchwork, easy. That was Jessica—always excelling beyond expectations. The antique compass and leather-bound atlas I'd bought them now paled by comparison. I know comparison is the thief of joy, but I'd feel much better if I didn't always, *always* fall so short of Jessica.

The rest of the dinner send-off was a mix of family news, excited listings of places Mom and Dad planned to go, awkward questions about my future plans, for which I had no ready answers, and buckets of good food. Jessica even "indulged" in half of one of Mom's famous brownies. I ate two. Maybe three . . . I wasn't really counting. Finally, the evening wound down as Mom and Dad claimed they wanted to get an early start.

"Last night in a big old bed for a while. I want a full night's sleep," Dad joked, stretching his arms and giving Mom a grin.

It struck me at that moment that they really were going to do this thing. Tomorrow morning the Nimble Nomad would pull out of their driveway and head on this wild adventure. I still had doubts that this was a good idea, but watching their excitement, I found myself rooting for them. Dad seemed energized in a way I hadn't seen in a while. Mom seemed to relax from her nonstop management mode.

I chose to see her unwinding tension as confidence in me. She felt she was leaving the Needle in good hands, even if I wasn't sure I could pull it off. After all, she wasn't expecting me to pull off garden-variety store management. I had this trunk show with Kat Katsaros to pull off in two days' time. That felt rather like baptism by fire, especially with all the emotional baggage attached. I yearned to be able to call her on Sunday with a report that Saturday's event had been a great success. To prove her confidence in me was well placed. And, maybe, just to show Jessica up a tiny bit since Mom had put me in charge. Don't judge. If you have a sister, you know exactly what I'm talking about.

"You're really going to do this," I said as I hugged Mom at the end of the evening.

"Your father's wanted to do this for ages," Mom said as she handed me the stash of leftover brownies wrapped up on a paper plate. "It'll be fun. I haven't ever taken four weeks off from the store. I bought a whole stack of books to read."

I enjoyed her grin. "And how much needlepoint?"

Mom's eyes took on a twinkle. "None."

That was a shock. "What?"

"We're going to visit a few shops along the way, and I'm going to buy whatever suits my fancy. And just because I like it, not for any store promotion or to make any vendor happy." She looked like a kid with a blank check in a candy store. Or like Jessica given free rein in the fancy yoga pants boutique. Or maybe like me after having won a lifetime of free coffee drinks. Just plain happy.

"I think that's a great plan." I rather liked that I was helping to make that possible. Life had handed me precious few wins—i.e., none—since the office collapse, and this felt good.

Mom took both my shoulders. "You'll be great. I'm leaving the Needle in good hands. I'm so glad you're here."

"Kat's going to be a bit tricky," I admitted, just in case my Sunday phone call didn't turn out to be a 100 percent win.

"It's nothing you can't handle. JanLi and Leona are solid staff people. And you've got all the NYAGs as backup to boot. You've always had good people sense. Just ring up the sales and enjoy yourself. Maybe find a project you'd like, hm?"

I had thought about it. Lots of what was in the Needle felt too "cottage chic" for my taste. I'm not a throw-pillow or wall-hanging kind of gal. But a small clutch purse kit had caught my eye. And if I was going to spend the next month embedded in the needlepoint world, I ought to take the craft back up.

"After the trunk show, I'll pick out a project for myself," I promised. "I'll come down and see you off in the morning."

"Don't," Mom said, putting a hand on my cheek. "It'll just make me cry. Just let us slip out quietly, and I'll text you a pic from our first stop."

I raised an eyebrow at the teenage smartphone wording.

She puffed up with pride. "Taylor and Chaz gave me text lessons the other day. And I'm on FaceSomething Kids Messenger with them now. I'm learning to be a digital native."

I didn't bother to correct her terminology—she was definitely a digital immigrant rather than a native, but I appreciated her sense of cyber adventure. I appreciated her sense of adventure, period.

I gave Mom one more big hug, found Dad in the driveway, finishing up the packing, and waved bon voyage to my newly minted nomad parents.

* * *

Maybe it was all the sugar. Maybe it was the tiptoeing through family subtleties all evening. Maybe it was the full moon or the owl that seemed to be three feet away or the fact that my entire life had been upended in the past three weeks.

For any or all of these reasons, I lay staring at the ceiling, still wide awake at one thirty in the morning. Every effort to shut off my brain's pointless spinning had met with failure. And maybe it had been counterproductive to get up and have a glass of milk with two leftover brownies, but I probably would have eaten them for breakfast, anyway.

Yawning and weary, I got up and tossed a Savannah College of Art and Design sweatshirt over my pajama top and returned to the kitchen for no real reason. It wasn't that chilly a night, so I suspect I chose the sweatshirt on purpose—a declaration that I did possess a business degree with a design minor from a school as prestigious as SCAD. A tangible reminder that I was, in fact, qualified to do this thing that seemed to scare me for no good reason.

After padding to the door that led from the kitchen out onto the apartment's small balcony, I touched the big brass keys now hanging by my door. *I have the keys to the Needle. I'm in charge. Mom's entrusting me with the Needle.* I could almost feel the shop looking up at me from under the floorboards. Looking to me to keep her up and running. All my affirmations ground to a halt at the thought *And I can't let her down.*

I pulled open the door, suddenly finding the air in the apartment close and warm. The particular scent of a North Carolina spring evening—a mix of clay soil and pine trees and azaleas and the tang of lake water—met my deep inhale. Home is a powerful thing, good or bad. Failure or soft landing, step forward or back, I couldn't say yet. I yearned to feel more comfortable in both where I was and what I was doing here, but I knew that would take a while. The only weight I was under was the pressure I'd put on myself. And, perhaps, the glare of Jessica's watchful eyes. Or the challenge in Kat's.

Or the surprise in the pair of yellow-green eyes I suddenly caught a glimpse of at the far end of the balcony. A small cat sat on the railing, staring at me with a *Where did you come from?* expression.

"Hello," I said. For no good reason, I added, "Come here often?"

The cat swayed the tip of his—her?—tail in a thoughtful sizing up of this new inhabitant, who made bad jokes in the middle of the night. Silver-gray striped fur stretched over what seemed to be rather thin ribs. No collar graced the cat's neck, giving me the impression this cat was likely a stray. I confess I felt a bit like a stray myself.

"Hungry?" I asked. Did I have anything a cat would want to eat? The brownies were long gone, but I did have a box of cereal and the carton of milk Mom had foisted on me as she emptied out her fridge. I held up a finger. "Hang on. I'll be right back."

I half expected my balcony companion to be gone when I returned with a small bowl of milk and Cheerios. He still sat carefully on the railing but leaned in when I set the bowl down on the balcony floor. "Not much, but it's all I've got at the moment," I admitted as I sat down a good ways away from my offering. "Help yourself."

I really wanted him to. Weird, but I suppose I felt so much like I was taking from Mom and Dad—room, board, opportunity—that it felt good to give something away. Still, I couldn't suppress a smile when he jumped down and sauntered over to inspect the bowl. With a last dubious look at me, he nosed around in the Cheerios and then began to eat.

Devour, actually. My new feline friend polished off his meal so quickly I was tempted to go back and get more. "You're a hungry fella, huh?" He looked male. Or at least I thought he did. I wasn't going to ask him to roll over and show me his anatomy to confirm this.

He stared, licked his chops with an almost comical relish, and offered a long musical meow. *Thanks for the vittles, ma'am.* He sat beside the bowl, twitching his tail in a way that told me he wasn't going to come any closer, but he wasn't going to leave, either.

"I work here for now." I couldn't bring myself to say, "I live here." It sounded too permanent for my short managerial gig. "I guess now I have two cats to contend with, huh?" The irony of a Kat and a Cat almost made me laugh.

We stared at each other for another minute or so, and then the cat made a wide circle around me as he walked to the other side of the balcony. With one more meow, he effortlessly leapt back up onto the railing.

"How about I have something a little more cat appropriate tomorrow night?" I offered, not quite sure where my sudden commitment to stray cat welfare had come from. I liked him. He seemed like a no-nonsense kind of cat, an easy companion. I could use something that felt easy.

His tail curled in a slow *I'll think about it* gesture. I appreciated his careful consideration. After all, Dave Batterson had fed me a host of lush, fancy, "Let's take things beyond the office" dinners before pulling the rug out from under my heart and career. Cat and I both knew a bowl of Cheerios could be as much bait as any act of benevolence.

"Y'all come back," I called in a voice that mimicked Livvy's Charleston twang as the cat leapt silently off the railing and into the dark branches of a nearby tree.

I gazed after his exit, amazed and impressed at how he had disappeared without a trace. "Strays ought to stick together," I said softly as I gathered the bowl and closed the balcony door behind me.

CHAPTER 4

Friday at the shop was blessedly ordinary. Uneventful. Even after I did everything I could think of to get ready for Saturday, I had time to spare. I spent some time getting to know Mom's two shop staff, Leona and JanLi.

Leona was one of those people who seemed to have mastered every craft, from needlepoint to cross-stitch to knitting and crochet. She was a hearty, curvy woman with salt-and-pepper hair and a generous smile. Leona freely shared the wisdom of her seven decades and seven children, not to mention her gift for making anyone feel encouraged to tackle something new in their choice of projects.

JanLi, on the other hand, was a perfectionist and a consummate organizer. Petite and energetic, with thick black hair and intense eyes, she could solve almost any problem with a customer's needlework. JanLi knew the thread catalogue of each of the shop's vendors practically by heart and had a great eye for colors.

Both were enormously supportive of my taking the helm of the shop. They piled on the compliments all day long and went to great lengths to talk me up to any customer who walked in.

In short, things started off just about as wonderfully as I could hope.

Which is why it took all of us by surprise when things didn't go nearly as smoothly on Saturday morning.

JanLi gave me a panicked look at 9:45 a.m. "We're supposed to start in fifteen minutes," she whispered. "Where is Kat?"

Livvy had shown up the minute the shop opened. "Not very responsible of her," she pronounced as the three of us scanned the neighborhood street. "People are already here. She should have been setting up half an hour ago."

I pressed my lips together, fighting my own rising sense of panic. "That's what we agreed. She seemed enthusiastic. Something must have happened."

Despite the fact that JanLi had been on staff for two years and, I suspected, Livvy knew the shop even better than I did, both women looked to me to solve the current crisis. After all, I'd been placed in charge. And while yesterday the shop had run smoothly during my "maiden voyage" of a day, it was starting to look like today might go badly. A cold weight landed in my stomach. I did not want to fail Mom in the first forty-eight hours. It was soon enough that she might try to convince Dad to turn the Nimble Nomad around—and no one wanted that.

"Maybe she got caught in traffic?" I offered with a weak smile.

Livvy gave a derisive grunt. "She lives ten minutes away."

For one irrational second, I wondered if Kat was more upset about being passed over to run the Nimble Needle than Mom realized. Would she be the type to pull a no-show just to make me look bad? Even Kat's new, edgier self didn't seem capable of something like that.

"Where's Kat?" Dot asked as she walked in the door. "Shouldn't she be here?"

Livvy planted a hand on her hip. "She most certainly should." She looked at me as if I'd just been declared spokesperson for my demographic. "What's happened to common courtesy?"

The silent "With you young people" came through loud and clear.

"We have to do something." JanLi's whisper was pitching higher. "What are we going to do?" As if to make her point, the front door opened and three more customers walked in.

We had had enough absent-minded artistic types on staff at Batterson Graphic Arts Design that I had developed a solid arsenal of good stalling tactics. "She's an artist. They're notoriously bad at keeping track of time. Set the coffee and goodies out and help people look around the shop. Grab a skein of something and let them try out the few pairs of Kat's scissors we have in the case." I grabbed my jacket. "I'll just go take a look outside."

I wasn't sure a walk to the sidewalk would accomplish much, except that it would buy me a few minutes to come up with a plan.

It couldn't be a weather delay. While an ice storm can wreak havoc in the foothills of the Blue Ridge Mountains, those were mostly behind us, and it was, in fact, a gorgeous April morning. I pulled in a deep, cleansing breath of air—blissfully devoid of Savannah's oppressive humidity—and scanned the few blocks that made up Gwen Lake's quaint downtown. On our side of the street, parking spaces and the shop's tiny side lot were filling up with customers coming for the trunk show. Kat's telltale van, however, was nowhere to be seen.

Mentally calculating how much stock I could give away in an improvised game of needlepoint Bingo, I walked to the end of the block to peer down the side of the street in both directions. No van.

Just as I was turning back toward the shop, I caught a flash of purple between two trees a block or two away. I stopped in my tracks and turned to look more closely. The color I saw was too unique to be anything else but Kat's logo. Sure enough, on one of the side streets, in what I remembered was the driveway into the park by the lake, I spied what had to be the back of her van.

A last-minute nap? Knife-sharpening emergency? Whatever was holding Kat up, I needed to head over there and get her underway to our shop. I picked up my pace to a light jog and dialed the shop from my cell phone.

"Nina's Nimble Needle, here for all your stitching needs. How can I help you today?" came JanLi's greeting in a tone of tightly forced cheer.

"I found her. The van's parked down by the park near the lake. I should be able to get her up to the shop in a minute or so."

"What's she doing there?" JanLi said something in her native Mandarin. "They've started into the cookies already."

"It'll all be fine," I said. "Just a small snag. Needle pointers know how to fix those, right?" My first needlepoint joke of this managerial stint! I'd endured enough of Dave's artistic hissy fits at the office that I felt confident I could coax Kat into the store and get our event underway.

The van was tucked far back into the parking lot. It was a miracle I'd seen it at all. She hadn't slept here last night, had she? When I got closer to the van, I heard a machine sound and rock music coming from the interior. Maybe she had to fix something at the last minute for the trunk show and had lost track of time. I knocked on the side of the van. When that brought no response, I ducked around to the driver's side and peered in the window. The driver's seat was empty, although I could see piled on the passenger seat a clipboard and a handbag with half the contents spilled out.

"Kat!" I called, rapping on the window. "Hey, Kat, it's time for you to be up at the Nimble Needle!"

A pair of teenagers stopped playing basketball on the nearby court to stare at me. I suppose some strange lady yelling at a van does attract a bit of attention.

"Has this been here all morning?" I called.

"Dunno," one said. "A while, maybe."

No help there. I took a breath and tried the handle. The door was locked, obviously from the inside. Still, I could hear music blaring and machinery running in the back. I pressed my face against the glass, not caring if that looked stalkerish to my basketball audience. No matter how I tilted my head, I could not see into the van's cargo section, where Kat must keep all her machinery to run the mobile sharpening shop.

I banged on the side again, right under the giant pair of stylized scissors painted above KAT'S KUTZ. "Kat! Are you in there?"

The same steady machine hum and harsh music vibrated in my ear and under my hand, but no response came from inside. Maybe she couldn't hear me over all that racket?

With the image of two dozen needle pointers milling impatiently around the shop flashing through my brain, I ducked around the corner of the van and grabbed at one of the two back-door handles.

With all my might, I yanked. The door gave way easily, nearly knocking me backward. There was an oily smell to the air, and the whirring, slightly squeaky sound of a large machine came from one side of the van. A loud, wailing guitar and relentless pounding drums emanated from the van's stereo, and drops were running down the van wall farthest away from me. It took me a second to recognize that the dark figure in the corner shadow was Kat, peering down at whatever she was working on. Her face was blocked by her thick black hair.

Only she wasn't moving. Who falls asleep with all this noise when they should be making a promotional appearance? I shook my head, biting back a muttered comment about impossible artists, as I stepped onto the bumper to lean inside.

My motion rocked the vehicle just enough to send Kat tilting out of her chair and slumping to the floor.

I let out a yelp as Kat tumbled flat onto her side, one limp hand flopping to the van floor and nearly reaching my feet.

It was then that I noticed the blood. A lot of it, oozing dark and thick down her arm and onto the floor. What I'd smelled was not oil.

"Kat!" I grabbed at her and was momentarily shocked by the slickness of the blood smearing my hand and the deathly cold of her skin. "Are you all right?"

I admit, not the brightest of questions under the circumstances, but shock tends to blunt your common sense in such a situation. I couldn't imagine what sort of grisly accident might happen to someone who sharpened knives, but it was clear this was no minor mishap.

I jammed my free hand into my jacket pocket for my cell phone, but my hand shook so hard, I dropped it onto the asphalt. I bumped the van again as I scrambled down to fetch the phone, and the vehicle shifted just enough to send Kat rolling onto her back.

There, glinting in the clear April sunshine, was the largest knife I'd ever seen. Surrounded by a pool of red where it lay embedded in Kat's chest.

This time I didn't yelp. I flat-out screamed.

CHAPTER 5

I had no memory of dialing 911. The minutes following that initial shock were a blur.

My next memory was of standing in the parking lot, next to Kat's van, surrounded by what must have been every one of the half dozen squad cars in Gwen Lake. Someone had silenced the blaring music and the industrial knife-sharpening machine, leaving the chilly, sunny day blanketed in an eerie quiet.

I was trying hard to keep myself together and not exactly succeeding.

"Did you touch the knife?" A man who had introduced himself as Chief Evan Tallen asked me this with sympathetic persistence. I was having trouble forming sentences as he pressed me with questions I barely knew how to answer. My throat constricted as I watched them remove Kat's body—Kat's *dead* body—from the van.

"No." I couldn't imagine reaching for that knife. I'd barely remained functional enough to dial my phone. Kat. Dead. In a van. And I'd been the one to find her. My brain couldn't process the information.

"Expensive knife—the Bour du Chef brand, which my wife wants. Did you touch anything or move the body in any way?"

I replayed the gruesome tumble of Kat's body onto the van

floor. "No. She sort of . . . fell . . . when I knocked up against the van. I didn't see . . . the knife . . . until that happened."

Chief Tallen turned the page in his notebook. "Terrible shame. I've told her a dozen times to be careful with that stuff. Anyone around here who might have seen when it happened?"

"No. I mean, the guys playing basketball told me they'd seen the van here, so you can ask them." I looked up at the chief, who was astoundingly tall, nearly half a foot taller than me. "She wasn't supposed to be just parked here like this. She was supposed to be up at the Nimble Needle, having a trunk show."

"That's right. You're Nina's girl."

"Girl" is a bit of a stretch for a thirty-one year-old, but now wasn't the time to quibble over small-town semantics. "I'm running the shop for her while she and Dad are on vacation."

"I'd heard they were taking some time off. Did you know Ms. Katsaros?"

Suddenly that felt like a complicated question. "We went to school together. I suppose we were friends then." The thin nature of that friendship chafed my conscience again. I knew she had considered herself my friend. I had tolerated her presence. Did that mean I knew her? Could you really call such a lop-sided relationship a friendship? Guilt pricked at me for a dozen different reasons. I couldn't quite sort the true feelings from the utter shock of Kat's horrible accident.

Chief Tallen scratched his chin. "And now?"

"Like I said, she was scheduled to do a shop event. I hadn't talked to her in years before Thursday. I didn't even know Mom had scheduled her for the event until then."

He took my elbow and walked me away from the van. The chief then gave me a fatherly look. "Don't trouble yourself. I'll take care of things from here. I'm sorry you had to be the one to find her. Are you okay?"

His question hit me like a cold wind. "Not really. What do you think happened?"

He stared back at the van and blew out a breath. "Near as I can tell, it looks like her grip slipped and the machine spun the knife back at her. George always worried about her, said she took all kinds of risks and never was much for safety measures. She wasn't wearing safety glasses, and even I know you ought to have those on when you do this sort of thing."

Still, I thought, *that shouldn't kill you. Should it?*

"I'll have the coroner's office over here, but it seems clear enough to me." The chief shook his head and swore softly. "I was always worried an accident like this would happen. All those knives. She tossed them around like toys. George could never . . . Well, a father worries, you know?" He put a hand on my shoulder. "But try not to worry yourself. I've got what I need from you for now, and I'll call you to come over and sign your statement later today."

He had a gentle tone, which helped me calm down. "I thought it was weird that the driver's door was locked, but the back doors were open," I offered. "And it smelled funny," I added. "I thought it was oil—like a machine burning out or something—but I think it was the blood."

He gave me a "Bless your heart" look of his own. "She had been dead a few hours from the look of it. Enough to bleed out, that's for sure."

I grimaced at the term. *Bleed out*—it felt so gruesome.

"I'm sorry you had to see it," Tallen said, consoling me. "Do you need one of my guys to take you back to the shop?"

"No," I replied. "I think I could use the walk and the air." A kind police officer had given me something to clean the smear on my hand—after putting a swab of it in an evidence bag—but I didn't feel clean. A two-hour scalding shower wouldn't rinse off the grisly way I felt right now.

A disturbing surge of uncertainty and angst poured over me.

What do I do now? I was sure there were several crucial things I ought to be doing, but they all seemed to loom just out of my grasp. I had called JanLi and told her to cancel the event. That had sent her into a full-scale frenzy, but it couldn't be helped. It also meant news of Kat's death would be all over town within minutes. Nimble Needle customers were a lovely bunch, but they were insufferable gossips. Given that this was likely to be the biggest thing to happen in Gwen Lake in months, if not years, I could almost hear the tongues wagging from here.

And Mom. How many minutes before this reached her? I was trying to wait until I could achieve—or even fake—some sense of calm before I called her. That was a lost cause. She'd probably heard from multiple customers, if not JanLi or Livvy. My phone had gone off repeatedly in my coat pocket, but I couldn't bring myself to answer it. This was so far beyond a worst-case scenario that my panic over not knowing what to do had dissolved into near paralysis.

Which wasn't acceptable. I had to kick myself into some kind of gear and take charge. This was awful, but the only thing that would make it worse would be for Mom to turn around and come home. I had to convince her—somehow—that the shop could weather this and keep going. After all, the shop wasn't connected except by Kat's scheduled appearance. Nothing related to needlepoint or scissors had led to this dreadful accident. It was knives. Or just one very large knife. I just had had the supreme bad luck to be in the wrong place at the wrong time.

"Do you want me to call your mom?" Chief Tallen asked.

That grade-school question woke up a fierce determination in me. I was a fully grown, responsible, intelligent woman. I was an adult and, up until two weeks ago, an administrative executive. I did not need anyone to call my mother. I was going to handle this. And handle it well enough that Mom would have no reason to regret leaving the Needle in my hands.

"No," I declared. "I've got this under control."

I didn't—not in the slightest—but all those needlepointed quote pillows must bear witness to the truth that declarations have power. I straightened my back, shook Tallen's hand with a manufactured confidence, and reached into my coat pocket for my cell phone as I walked away from the parking lot.

My phone showed four calls from Mom. I didn't need to worry about who had called Mom—she was already frantically calling me.

I probably should have called Mom back right away, but I knew better than to do that until I had my wits about me. I had to walk the delicate balance of having enough time to settle myself without taking enough time for Mom to already be turning back east on the turnpike.

Near as I could figure, that meant I had about twelve minutes. Mom is not a patient woman, and Dad's persuasion could hold her back for only so long.

I took deep, long breaths as I walked back up the hill. I pulled the shop door open to a sea of wide-eyed, shocked faces.

"Oh my gosh, oh my gosh, oh my gosh, are you okay?" came JanLi's gush of concern as she rushed up to me. "Of course you're not okay. How could you be okay? It's just horrible."

Control. I needed to show control, even though my insides felt like a bomb had gone off. I couldn't imagine the sight of that impaled knife ever leaving my mind. I felt weirdly hollow and filled with cement at the same time. *Is this what shock feels like?*

Leona, ever the motherly type, walked up and took my elbow. "Come on over here and sit down."

There were still quite a few people in the store, and every one of them was staring at me. Mom had encouraged me to make my mark on the store, but I don't think this is what she had in mind.

I resisted Leona's tug toward the table. "Thanks, but no. I need to call Mom."

"Did she reach you?" JanLi asked. "She called here a bunch of times."

"I was busy with Chief Tallen." That was true—mostly. I'm sure he would have let me take her call, but I knew better than to talk to Mom before I was ready. Well, a bit more ready than I was down in the parking lot. My current state of "could probably fake control" would have to do.

"Of course you were," Leona said. She hovered next to me, as if she needed to stay close should I faint.

I was not going to faint. I was not going to do anything except handle the situation. And, really, after loss of relationship and loss of apartment and loss of job, this just took things up a few notches to absurdly, sadly epic. I fought the odd, incredibly inappropriate urge to babble hysterically.

Instead, I spoke slowly and clearly. "I'm going to go into the office and call Mom."

JanLi nodded. "Got it. We'll handle things out here." She nodded to Leona. "We've got it covered."

I managed what I hoped was a grateful smile. "Thank you." I turned toward Mom's small office in the back of the shop, thankful it had a door and no window. My steps felt forced, as if I had to choreograph them. Just before the doorway, I turned and gazed into all the stunned faces. "Thank you all for coming. I'm so sorry things turned out the way they did. I'll be sure to let you know when we figure out what to do next."

Murmurs of agreement hummed around the room as I stepped into the office, pulled the door shut behind me, and sank into Mom's office chair. I felt the weight of her faith in me as I did, like some small princess climbing onto the queen's throne. I realize what an overstatement that is, but my emotions were bouncing all over the place.

I took two more deep breaths before I clicked the icon on my phone to return the last of Mom's listed calls.

She didn't even bother with a greeting. "I'm coming home right now."

I shut my eyes. "Don't do that. There's no reason for you to do that."

I heard Dad's belabored sigh in the background, telling me that he had already been trying to talk her out of turning the Nimble Nomad around and heading for home.

"What are you talking about? Poor Gina is dead. And you found her. Oh, mercy, hon, that must have been awful."

"Yes, it was pretty awful but, Mom, Kat's accident is not a reason for you to stop your trip." I forced that manufactured confidence back into my voice. "Everything's under control. It doesn't have anything to do with the shop. She wasn't even near the shop."

"Still—"

"No, really," I said, cutting her off. "This doesn't have anything to do with us except that we were on her schedule. Her dad and Cal . . ."

That was the wrong thing to say. "Are they there? They must be devastated." A sob interrupted her words. "So young. Such a terrible accident."

"Yes, it's awful. Kat's dad is out of town on some weekend hunting thing, but I think they found a way to reach him."

"Poor, poor man. And Cal?"

"No one seems to know where Cal is. I'm sure they'll find him, or Mr. Katsaros will. We just need to let the police do their jobs and try to get on with things."

"Someone has died, Shelby. There's no just 'getting on with things' after something like that. I think I should come home."

"Please don't, Mom. There's no reason to, really." I looked at the closed door, imagining the faces staring at it from the other side. "I don't want you to lose your vacation over this."

"Not lose, just postpone. I mean, we should be there for the funeral, shouldn't we?"

I heard Dad groan in the background. "No one knows when any of that will happen just yet, Mom. Everyone will just worry more if you come back, and that won't help anything. JanLi, Leona, and I really do have this under control."

"I don't know . . ."

"Listen to your daughter, Nina," came Dad's frustrated voice. "She says she's got it under control." He was getting ready to put his foot down, I could hear it.

"Give me three days," I said, scrambling for any way to keep that van heading west with both my parents inside it. "If things haven't settled a bit by then, we can talk it over more."

"In three days we'll be in Utah," Mom retorted.

Exactly. "Utah's not the end of the earth, Mom. Things will have calmed down, and we'll have a better idea of what to do. But I don't know that anything needs doing at all. It just means the trunk show is canceled, but we can deal with that."

Really, what was there to do? Kat had died, the police were handling the accident, and we all just had to find a way forward. That was going to be a bit harder for me, granted, but I didn't relish the idea of Mom rushing home to save me.

"You're sure?"

"I'm sure, Mom. I'll keep you updated, but I want you to promise me you won't come home. You and Dad deserve this trip. Give me the chance to let you keep on it, okay?" I pitched a familial Hail Mary. "I'll call Jessica if I need any more backup. But I won't. I'm okay." I gave the last two words all the force I dared, considering they were bald-faced lies.

"If you're sure," Mom said.

"She's *sure*, Nina," came Dad's reassurance. Somehow I suspected I might get a call from Dad at some point when he was out of Mom's earshot.

"All right, then. I'm so sorry this happened to you, sweetheart. It's just terrible. I feel terrible for you."

She was wavering again. "I'm fine, Mom. I'm going to go

take care of things in the shop now. I'll call if I have questions, but I think we'll be okay." I felt as if I couldn't repeat that enough. "I love you, and I want you to try to enjoy yourself. I promise I'll call if I need you."

"I'm here if you need me," Mom repeated.

"I'm sure Shelby knows that," Dad said. "Take care, honey," he called to me over Mom's phone.

"Goodbye for now, Mom," I said.

"Okay, then. I love you." Mom was stalling. I could practically hear Dad reaching to take the phone from her hands.

I clicked to end the call and rose from the chair to face the world.

I was reaching for the doorknob when the door opened on its own and Jessica burst into the office. "Did you talk to Mom yet?"

I wasn't really ready for Jessica, but there wasn't much I could do about it. "Yes."

"She's already called me. Twice."

"I'm sure she has. I've got a ton of calls from her on my phone, but I was busy with the police. Near as I can tell, it's under control." I didn't want to give my sister any reason to doubt I could handle this. I didn't want her swooping in to solve it for me. There wasn't anything to solve, anyway.

"So everything's okay?"

Well, no. But I said, "Yes," with all the conviction I could muster.

"Well, good. The last thing we need is you giving her any reason to turn that van around."

"I didn't."

"She and Dad need this vacation. They deserve it. What happened to Kat is terrible, but it doesn't really have anything to do with the Needle."

I could have used a bit more empathy from my sister, but I'd be a fool to expect that from Jessica. "I agree. I think Dad and I convinced her."

"Have you got her on the friend-finding location app on your phone?"

I had never seen the need to keep such close tabs on my parents. Then again, it wouldn't surprise me to learn the twins had been GPS tagged. "Um . . . no."

"Put her on. We need to make sure she isn't heading back east. And if she does, we intervene. Agreed?"

Wow. Mom and Dad were grown adults. I didn't want her coming home, but I didn't see the need to get that tactical in making it happen. "I'm not sure we need to go that far." Still, I made a secret note to myself to add Mom to my app list and check in on her location every once in a while over the next few days. Without telling Jessica.

I walked past my sister out onto the shop floor, where everyone was staring at us. "Relax, ladies," I said in my strongest office-manager voice. "We've got everything under control. The police are handling the accident, and we should all keep Kat's family in our thoughts and prayers."

Tilly, who was sitting with Livvy and Dot at the large gathering table, cocked her head. "Do you think the yacht club will do a salute for George? They did when Walter's son was killed in that awful car crash."

I blinked, having totally forgotten about one of Gwen Lake's oddest quirks—the yacht club. Gwen Lake, the lake from which the town took its name, wasn't large enough to host even the smallest yacht. Yet somehow, the town had gone and declared its model boat club a "yacht club."

"A salute?" I asked, almost afraid to know what they'd dreamed up now.

"They lined up the whole fleet for Walter's son," Livvy explained, as if it were perfectly logical. "The one guy who's got a cannon on his boat fired it off. It was sweet, really."

A burial at sea from toy boats? I thought but didn't dare say. A hobby's a hobby, and Dad would argue that a hobby had helped put Jessica and me through college.

"I'm sure they will," Jessica said. "It'd be a lovely gesture." Her gaze traveled to mine. "And remember what I said," she continued with a finger not so gently pointed my way. "Don't let Mom turn around and come home early."

A chorus of "Oh, nos" and "Certainly nots" rang out from around the table as Jessica headed out the door.

Leona's and JanLi's expressions told me they recognized just how tall an order that might be.

CHAPTER 6

Sleep eluded me that night, which wasn't much of a surprise. Hard to wind down after a day like I'd had. I'd gotten multiple offers of dinner—Leona, JanLi, and even Jessica invited me over—but I found I wanted to be alone to process everything.

Just after midnight I was pleased to hear a meow from the window that looked over the balcony. My feline friend hadn't shown up again since his first visit Thursday night, and I was extra grateful for the company this evening. I happily opened the door, with a dish into which I'd spooned a tin of one of those fancy cat foods. He sniffed, paused, then cautiously entered. My brain refused to stop replaying those awful moments in the van, and I welcomed another presence in the empty-feeling apartment.

"I missed you last night," I admitted as I sat down on the kitchen floor. "Thanks for coming by." Jessica might lecture me on the wisdom of letting a stray cat in, but I didn't care.

The cat gave me one long, yellow-eyed stare before digging into his dinner with an enthusiasm that told me my cereal snack might have been his last good meal. It felt nice to make someone's day better after all the crisis management at the shop.

"I can't keep referring to you as 'Cat.' It's a bit awkward, given the circumstances," I explained as he ate. "You're going to need a name."

He looked up at me with an aloof expression that seemed to translate to *If you feel it's necessary.*

As he polished off his dinner, I racked my weary brain for a suitable name. Everything I came up with felt too cute or too common. Finally, I remembered a specialized needle in the shop for fixing stray strands of thread. Time to fix this stray with a name. "How about Nabbit?"

He walked over and nudged my toe. It was just a soft, inquisitive touch, but I felt a small assurance all the same. An *I could live with that* gesture—or at least I chose to take it that way.

"Nabbit it is." The declaration made me feel a tiny bit more settled. The knots in my shoulders eased up, and I managed a small smile. I grabbed a scrappy old needlepointed heart pillow—one of my younger attempts at the craft, which I couldn't believe Mom had kept. It was faded and frayed around the edges, marked by dozens of mistakes and several rows where the stitches went in the wrong direction. It wasn't my first project, and it surely wasn't my best, so I found myself a bit stumped that she'd kept it and that Dad had delivered it here when he brought some other household supplies.

It was, however, just small enough to serve as a cat toy. Why not? I needed something lighthearted after the day's heavy events, anyway. "Are you up for a game?" I waved the thing in front of Nabbit's curious eyes. "Catch." I flicked the stuffed heart across the kitchen floor and was delighted when Nabbit raced across the linoleum to pounce on it. He swatted at it, sending it skidding back toward me.

The small laugh that escaped me felt healing. I flicked the heart toward him again, and he pounced even more comically, then rolled with the thing as it tumbled. We went back and forth for a few amusing minutes, until the mistake in the stitching snagged a stray thought in my brain: *the direction.*

The mistake stitches were tilted in the wrong direction. All the correct stitches were on a diagonal to the right, which made the incorrect rows stand out, because they leaned to the left. *The direction is wrong.* I realized that was what had been bothering me about the way I found Kat. It seemed like such a freak accident for someone skilled with a grinding stone to have it hurl a knife at them. Not even someone as reckless as Kat would set up the machinery incorrectly. The grinding stone would have been rotating away from her, wouldn't it?

"It doesn't make sense," I declared to Nabbit, miming the motions I imagined Kat had used to press the blade to the grinding stone. I'd never seen her do it, nor could I remember anything but the whining whir of the stone when I pulled the van door open. "Wait here," I said, holding up one finger while I rose to head to the living room, where my laptop was charging.

Nabbit, in the defiant way of all cats, did not do as he was told. Instead, he raced beside me into the living room and looked around, as if to scope out the place and consider how it would feel to live here.

"Back to the kitchen, mister. You're not moving in yet." I was surprised how the "yet" had slipped into my statement. I was a temporary resident in Gwen Lake, and I wasn't in the market for a roommate, four legged or otherwise.

After booting up the computer, a search on YouTube produced a video of someone using a grinding stone to sharpen knives. It probably would have been even faster had Nabbit not taken great delight in pawing at my screen, trying to sit on the keyboard, and generally getting in the way of my typing. I found one man with a nineteenth-century foot-pedal grindstone, and he warned me always to make sure the grindstone was rotating *toward* me. "Well, that supports Chief Tallen's theory," I said to Nabbit.

Only Kat didn't use a crude mechanism like that. She used a big, industrial machine with multiple discs. Was there a difference? I searched for a video with an electric machine and watched a few of them closely. Those rotated *away* from the user. That meant Kat's machine had most likely rotated away from her as she sat in front of it.

And then I remembered the wet van wall behind the machine. These devices all used water to tamp down the sparks made from the metal's contact with the grindstone. So if her machine had flung water away from Kat onto the van wall, that had to mean the stone rotated away from her. All that seemed to make it nearly impossible for the machine to have flung a knife *toward* her, even if she did lose her grip. "It'd have to have practically ricocheted off the wall to come toward her," I announced to Nabbit.

This notion didn't sit right. The machine *had* to have been the thing that had propelled Kat's knife at her. Nothing else in that van could have sent it toward her with the speed and force needed for her to sustain such a lethal injury. And it had been running at the time of her death. I'd heard it; I'd seen it. But I couldn't remember which way the disc was turning. Even if the rotation of the grinding stone could be reversed, what would make Kat choose to run it the wrong way like that?

The scenario I hadn't wanted to contemplate, the one that had been dangling just out of reach all night, crystallized in my mind with a cold skitter down my back. What if the real question wasn't *what* had sent the knife careening toward Kat, but *who*?

No one wanted to consider that theory. Still, it was there, a chillingly possible explanation for the fate that had befallen Gina "Kat" Katsaros. Brutal, something no one wanted to think could happen in Gwen Lake, but possible. Suddenly I felt like I wouldn't sleep a wink until dawn.

What if Kat's death wasn't an accident?

CHAPTER 7

The next morning I needed far stronger caffeine than I had in the mere coffee grounds at my apartment. I threw on whatever clothes were nearby, dragged a brush through my hair, and headed out the door to the place where I knew far better coffee awaited: CHNO.

CHNO was a relatively new arrival on the Gwen Lake retail scene. Tourists stared at the coffee shop's sign, puzzled at the collection of letters, supposing it was an acronym of some kind. Locals knew CHNO was run by Deborah Newman, one of the few high school friends with whom I'd actually kept in touch. CHNO was a simplification of the chemical symbol for caffeine—a reflection of this brilliant chemist-turned-barista's blend of wit and science. Even back in the day, Deborah was always the smartest person in any room but was still nice enough that you were glad she was there. Valedictorian of our high school class and in possession of at least one PhD that I knew of, I gave her a ton of credit for having the guts to ditch her corporate lab job to come home and open Gwen Lake's best—and only—coffee bar.

I pushed through the door and found Deb easily, despite the subtle changes in her appearance since I'd seen her last.

"Shelby Phillips!" Deb called with an easy smile the moment

I pushed through the shop door. Always a driven type-A brainiac, she had the new, softer tone of someone who'd found her true niche. "You're back."

I stifled a yawn, despite it being well after nine. "For a bit, to watch the Needle for Mom."

Her smile faded. "Hey, I heard what happened. Gruesome stuff. She was a year behind us, right? You okay?"

I shrugged. "Guess that depends on your version of okay." The concern in Deb's eyes made me add, "I'm a bit rattled, but I'll be okay."

"A rather awful welcome if you ask me." She straightened. "Let me change that. Your first drink's on the house. What will it be?"

I yawned again as I peered up at the chalkboard list of drinks, all with clever chemical-sounding names. "What's the strongest thing you've got?"

"That would be the Azido," came a deep voice from behind me. I turned to see a man in a baseball cap, T-shirt, and jeans. I hadn't noticed him sitting at the table behind me. "It'll keep you up till Wednesday."

"Sounds good," I agreed. I turned back to Deb. "Azido because . . . ?"

"Azidoazide azide," she replied with a mix of clinical precision and entertaining pride. "Strongest chemical on earth. Highly reactive and highly explosive. It's so sensitive that it will explode in virtually any scenario—even when left completely alone."

Even to me in my weary state, that sounded a bit extreme. "And I want to put that in my body before breakfast?"

"I have two a week," said the man behind me. "Haven't exploded yet."

"I don't think Jake's a special case," said Deborah, "but I might recommend adding a scone just to be on the safe side." She gestured toward a covered cake plate with a delectable-looking display of scones. "I'll throw in one just for precautionary purposes."

"Deal." I decided in that instant to be a CHNO regular.

As Deb went about preparing her volatile brew, Jake stood up and walked over. He was tall and lean—easily six feet three, if not more—but not gangly. He had a ruddy complexion and that effortless muss of hair some men could pull off. I became instantly aware of how I must look—not at all the good kind of mussed. In fact, I hadn't even brushed my teeth.

He extended a hand. "Jake London. I was a couple of years ahead of you in school. You probably don't remember me."

If he had looked like *that* in school, I would have remembered.

"I gave your folks' motor home a tune-up before they went out on the road. I can't imagine my dad ever doing something like that, even though he's retired now."

My foggy brain connected the facts as I shook his hand. His fingers were clean but had the slight rasp of a man who worked with his hands. "London's Auto."

"Yep. I run it now. So I get the 'watching the shop for Pop' thing. Although, in your case, it's your mom."

"I still can't quite believe they're doing it myself," I said with a wobbly laugh. "She was upset about what happened to Kat. Jessica and I are having to work hard to keep her from cutting the trip short." I wanted that to come out with more confidence than it did.

Jake's eyes warmed. "Well, I'm sorry it was you who found her." He motioned to his table as Deb set a tall mug with a molecular chart on it on the counter beside a plate holding not one but two scones. "Want to sit down?"

Coffee and scones accompanied by a smile with some of the most disarming dimples I'd seen in ages? It didn't take a second's thought. "Thanks. I guess I will. Store doesn't open until noon on Sundays, so I guess I have time."

He seemed genuinely pleased at having my company. "Today's my day off, so I've got all the time in the world. Well, sort of. Promised my dad I'd tinker with his yacht this afternoon." He gave the boat terminology the smirk of someone who didn't quite know what to make of Gwen Lake's odd little maritime fleet. "I'm probably the only mechanic in the state who has a steady side hustle of fixing model boat engines. Your dad has one, too, right? Wasn't he commodore or something once?"

It's funny how I'd almost forgotten about all that. "Yeah, he was. Weird, isn't it?" You had to be careful who you said things like that to in this town. Dad "sailed" for fun, but some of the "yachtsmen" took their hobby very seriously.

Jake took a sip of his own coffee and sighed. "High-octane stuff. Best in town."

Deb laughed from behind the counter. "Jake's a regular and occasionally a one-man marketing committee. I like having the appreciation of people who really know their coffee."

We headed over to the table, and I settled into the seat opposite Jake with my mug and plate. When he nodded a silent *Try it*, I sipped the brew. It was strong—very strong—and sharp, but not bitter. The kind of marvelous, warming bite only a really good espresso could give. "Wow. You're right."

"Of course he's right," Deb echoed.

I had to ask. "Do you own one? A yacht?" I felt silly using the word and couldn't picture him getting into the regattas I knew the yacht club hosted on a regular basis.

He laughed. "Oh, no. I confine my passions to the four-wheel variety." He tilted his chin to the window behind me, and I turned my gaze and noticed a dark blue truck parked in front of the coffee shop. "But like I said, I help Dad and some of the others keep theirs up and running. An engine's an engine, for the most part."

It had been a few years since I'd seen the yachtsmen lined up on the lake dock with remote controls, captain's hats, and game faces. I'd always found it both ludicrous and sort of sweet at the same time. "Someone said they might do a memorial for Kat on Thursday."

"I'm sure they will. Her dad is a member of the club, and they did it for another person earlier this year. The whole town will probably turn out."

George was likely devastated at the loss of his daughter, and his friends would want to show their support. "How does the memorial work? I think I heard something about a tiny cannon?"

"Yeah. It needs to be seen to be believed."

I nodded as I decided to try to find out more about who Kat was . . . or had been . . . lately. "Was she liked around town? Kat?"

Jake seemed to choose his answer carefully. "George is. Kat and Cal . . . maybe not so much."

"Kat was always a bit of a strong dose," Deb offered, leaning her elbows on the counter. "She had a talent for rubbing people the wrong way."

"I think the guy who runs Windham's would put it a bit harsher than that," Jake added.

"Windham's? The big store out by the mall?" I asked.

"And Kat's mortal enemy," Deb noted with an unscientific touch of drama.

I felt something cold shoot down my spine. "Kat had an enemy?"

Jake shrugged. "If you ask me, Kat had lots of enemies."

So Kat had lots of enemies. Were any of them fierce enough to do her harm?

Jake, Deb, and I made small talk for about another thirty minutes, but I struggled to keep up with the conversation while my brain clanged, *Kat had lots of enemies.*

In fact, when I headed down to the shop an hour before

opening to install the new sales software on the shop's computer, my brain was still wrestling with this new information. If Kat had had enemies, was my theory about her non-accidental death so far-fetched, after all? Or was this just my imagination running away with my good sense?

While the hard drive whirred through the installation, I did what I'd been avoiding: scanning Kat's social media. Kat's Kutz had an app, and part of me thought to download it just to see what would happen. I resisted the urge and instead scrolled through her accounts on several platforms.

I was expecting a taste of her clever marketing in the posts, but what I got was a heavy dose of her opinions. And Kat had had *lots* of opinions. None of them very nice. Kat's talent for sharp edges had ventured far beyond cutlery.

"It's hard enough to make it as a solopreneur in this world," she said in a video that showed her standing in front of her van. "But places like Windham's are going out of their way to make it harder. Offering services for free or far below cost. Luring in customers with deals no small shop can hope to match." She leaned closer to the camera. "But will you get service? Does Windham's give anything back to the community? No, sir. Vote with your money, people. Support your local businesses and not these behemoths."

I was all in favor of supporting local businesses—the Needle was a huge part of our lives and had made lots of things possible for our family. But regarding a big outfit like Windham's, I took the view that there was room for both in the world.

Kat, on the other hand, had declared her view on the matter with all the swagger of a cowboy in a "This town ain't big enough for the both of us" high noon gunfight.

So, had someone brought a knife to that gunfight? A few minutes ago I'd remembered a detail Chief Tallen had mentioned to me at the crime scene that I'd been too shocked to notice then: the knife embedded in Kat was a Bour du Chef knife. Very expensive brand, serious cook stuff.

And the brand was sold by Windham's.

Intrigued by Kat's accusations of Windam's providing free services and below-cost deals to undercut the competition—which seemed more like a discount retailer tactic than something Windham's would do—I closed the installation screen on the shop computer and pulled up Windham's website and clicked over to the kitchen section.

There it was, the proverbial knife in Kat's ribs. *Buy your Bour du Chef knife at Windham's and you can bring it in for sharpening for life. No other store offers this service.*

Lifetime sharpening seemed like more than a Windham's store policy. It seemed like a jab directly at Kat. If I was looking for evidence of animosity, I'd found it.

"Hi, boss!" came JanLi's call from the shop's back door. "I'm declaring it to the world that we will have a better day today than yesterday."

There were days when JanLi's high-strung personality was a bit much. Today, however, I appreciated her determined optimism. It offered a nice balance to my muddled cloud of suspicion about the cause of Kat's death. Even if it was now a highly caffeinated cloud.

"I'm all for it," I replied. "A nice quiet Sunday is just what I need."

JanLi headed for the hot water kettle. "I brought my strongest tea. Should I put some on?"

I shook my head. "None for me. I stopped in at CHNO earlier."

Her dark eyes sparkled. "Ooh, good choice. What did you get?"

"I went all in and got the . . ." I struggled to remember the name. "Az something."

"You got an Azido?" Surprise widened her eyes.

"After yesterday I felt like I needed it. Although I think Jake was right—I do feel like I'll be awake for a week."

She pulled an exotic-looking tin from her bag. JanLi stocked the Needle with the most interesting collection of teas—even a dedicated coffee drinker like myself had to admire the various scents that filled the shop when she brewed her tea. "Jake London? From the garage? Nice guy." She winked. "And just about your age."

I'd had enough of Mom's friends kicking their matchmaking skills into gear on my behalf to have a highly sensitive radar for that sort of unwelcome attention. "We didn't discuss demographics."

One dark eyebrow waggled as JanLi chose a mug from the tray on the counter and dolloped a generous amount of honey into it before adding a tea bag. "What *did* you discuss?"

"Kat Katsaros's long list of enemies."

Her eyes narrowed. JanLi had some of the most expressive eyes I'd ever seen. The woman could say volumes without uttering a single syllable. And she could nail you with a glare when she chose to. "Why?" She drew the question out like a warning.

"Doesn't that seem important for a woman who was found yesterday with a knife impaled in her chest?" I felt defensive for no good reason.

JanLi left her tea and came to stand in front of me, completely undeterred by the foot I had over her in height. "Don't you be doing that. What happened to Kat was a terrible accident. An odd accident, I'll grant you, but nothing more than a reckless young woman falling victim to careless safety practices. This is not one of those television shows. There's no crime to solve here."

I'm not so sure, my brain shouted back, but I kept silent. Now was not the time to make waves and start turning over rocks in Gwen Lake.

JanLi gave a little *That's that* harrumph and returned to brewing her tea. "You need to pick a project."

She wasn't wrong. It was a good idea to dip myself back into the world of needlepoint and get started on something. Plus, it was a far better place to focus my energy than the whirl of scenarios currently occupying my imagination. The police were investigating, and Kat's long list of conflicts seemed to be public knowledge, so I had little to contribute to the investigation. Even if I did, the police department wasn't open for nonemergencies on Sunday, so I had no place to take any theories, anyway.

Not that I had theories. I had wild, unfounded speculations—and even I know those are not the same thing.

"If it will make you feel better," JanLi suggested, "you could work on one of Kat's designs. Some of them are really nice. You should do that."

"Well, it does seem like the least I can do." I let JanLi pull me over to the table where Kat's designs and scissors were still laid out from yesterday's canceled event. Most of the canvases had the same intricate designs as her scissors. Some were geometric and abstract; others were combinations of natural elements, like leaves; and some reminded me of mandalas with their undulating designs. Like her marketing and the woman herself, the designs were distinctlive and elaborate. You'd never confuse her work with anyone else's.

I touched one that boasted a mosaic of multicolored diamonds that moved in color waves from black to blue and back again. "She really was talented," I said as I picked it up.

"She had an artist's touch," JanLi remarked. "But she also had an artist's personality. I can't picture her handling a prickly customer the way your mother would."

I turned the canvas this way and that, trying to decide if it had a right side up. It seemed you could view it any way you wanted. "Or you would. I saw you with that woman yesterday." JanLi was full of energy, but she could put on that *You can trust me . . . I know what I'm doing* air that made a customer feel better.

"Oh, her? She was eyeing something way too hard for her." She waved her hand. "That pillow would have been doomed. She wanted to impress her friends, but that had no hope of turning out impressive. Would've been a mess. She'll love the one she chose."

"The one you chose for her," I corrected. According to Mom, JanLi had an uncanny knack for choosing the right canvas for a customer and still making them believe they'd chosen it for themselves.

JanLi winked again as the kettle boiled. "She doesn't know that. And that's the trick. Guide them to what they need instead of what they want."

I stared down at the canvas in my hands. "So what do *I* need?"

She pointed to the canvas. "Exactly the one you picked up. See? Your mother was right—it's in your blood." She turned toward her tea. "Go get your colors. And a set of Kat's scissors. And a project bag. I'll mount it to stretcher bars after you've picked everything out."

Stretcher bars are frame-like bars that fit together on the edges of your canvas to create a smooth and tight surface on which to stitch. You could just hold the canvas as you work, but putting it on stretcher bars helps preserve it, keeps your stitches smooth and even, and gives you a better sense of the piece as a whole. Mom frowned on even experts working without stretcher bars and practically insisted on them for beginners. "It's friendly tension," she'd declare. Maybe friendly tension was exactly my path out of this mess.

I walked over to the vast wall of colored fibers, feeling . . . well, launched. As if I'd somehow put the trauma of yesterday at least somewhat behind me and could step into my work here for the month ahead. Here, in JanLi's intuitive guidance, I felt back in the saddle. I could now hope to show Mom I was in control the next time she called. There was something about running my fingers across the cards and small twists of thread, flexing my graphic design muscles to find the right color for Kat's clever progression from blue to black and back again. The anticipation of getting it *just right* sank deep into all my unsettled places.

The exotic scent of JanLi's tea wafted up as she stood next to me. "Good eye," she said with a motherly pride. Then she frowned. "But you don't want that black."

I'd chosen a particularly dark, rich black, which she promptly plucked from my pile of thread cards. She chose a slightly more charcoal set of threads. "You want this one."

I hadn't thought that bold enough for the piece, but when JanLi laid it down next to the other colors, I saw it was perfect.

"You're right. I do." The smile that crept across my face eased the knots in my back.

Her head bobbed. "I'm always right."

This morning I couldn't argue with that.

Business stayed at the welcome speed of lazy all afternoon. A few regulars and almost all the NYAGs stopped by to check in on me. I had no doubt they were texting updates to Mom, so I made sure they found me calm, collected . . . and stitching. By the end of the day I'd managed several respectable rows on my new Kat-designed canvas. JanLi was right—it did make me feel better to be bringing some of Kat's art work to life. Every time I snipped a thread with my new pair of her beautiful scissors, it felt like I was keeping a bit of Kat in the world.

I owed her that much.

CHAPTER 8

Alone in my apartment later that night, all the peace of my afternoon at the shop seemed to evaporate. I tried to turn to the stitching to soothe me, the way Mom and JanLi said it would, but outside the company of the shop, I found the rhythm of the needle pricked at me instead. Nothing about the way Kat had died seemed to add up. There was no good reason for her to have been sharpening a knife—and perhaps the wrong way at that—in the park's parking lot yesterday morning.

I could ask Chief Tallen my questions, but he had no reason to share such information with me. How long did it take for someone to bleed out like that? How long had she been dead when I found her? What did it mean that the sharpening machine had sprayed all that water on the van wall? That didn't seem normal to me. I had no professional basis for such questions, and Tallen and whatever detectives had been assigned to the case surely knew what they were doing. They were surely following up on things, given that Kat's unpopularity was commonly known, right?

I kept saying "surely" to myself, but I found I couldn't quite swallow it. "What do you think?" I asked Nabbit when he came for his nightly visit. I looked forward to our "conversations," one sided though they were. Like every cat I'd ever known, he had a finely tuned talent for sitting on whatever I was working on—book, laptop, or needlework. Still, he was an excellent listener, and I'm the kind of person who needs to sort through problems out loud.

"I can't let go of this urge to do right by her," I admitted as Nabbit sat on my project bag as if it were his personal furniture. "I mean, I certainly didn't back then. I have to believe there's a reason I'm the one who found her. It can't be dumb luck—I don't believe in that."

Nabbit gazed at me with something as close to affection as a cat has. I confess it looked more like the *I suppose I don't mind sharing the room with you* attitude I had all too often given Kat.

I tossed the small stitched heart that had become his designated toy. "It'd be better if I knew more. All I know is the NYAGs and Mom didn't want her to take over the store. And now, of course, that's off the table."

On purpose? My brain added as Nabbit leapt from his perch on the bag to pounce on the heart. He rolled around with it, ignoring my monologue. "A needlepoint shop succession plan hardly seemed grounds for violence. And if lots of people didn't like her, the only other one I know about is whoever runs Windham's. That's hardly much to go on."

Or was it? Tomorrow was Monday, and the shop was closed.

I grabbed the heart after Nabbit swatted it back to me. Somehow I'd adopted the only cat I knew that played fetch—or at least across-the-floor swatting catch. "It may not be much, but it's all I've got, and I'm not going to sit here and do nothing. Tomorrow I'm going to go buy a knife at Windham's and see what happens."

Windham's was the kind of department store that somehow managed to feel like an enormous upscale boutique. Not your discount retailer by any stretch of the imagination. The clothes had that gorgeous, effortless Southern style that was second nature to Jessica. I saw a few things I wouldn't mind getting, but I wasn't here for retail therapy. Whether I'd admit it to Nabbit, myself, or the world, I was here to investigate.

The kitchen department looked like the kind of place that has never heard of ramen noodles or microwave popcorn. Stunning dishes, chef-level pots and pans, and gadgets I didn't even recognize lined the shelves.

As I wandered the aisles, a sophisticated man around my father's age, in a perfectly tailored jacket, asked me, "May I help you?" His tone achieved that unsettling balance between a desire to be of service, and a doubt I belonged in the store. It's why I rarely shop at places like Windham's.

"I've got a new apartment," I replied, "and I want to set the kitchen up just right." I embellished a bit. "My boyfriend's a serious cook, so I want to get the good stuff."

He smiled. "Always a smart investment. You're so much better off in the long run with quality items." He extended a hand. "I'm Leydon Windham. This is the store my father founded. Are we starting from scratch, or do you have some pieces now?"

I was surprised the owner took the time to lead me through the department as we picked out starter pieces for me in one of the high-end lines of cookware the store carried. The medium-sized frying pan alone cost more than the last really good dinner I ate. I had no hope of buying any of this anytime soon, unemployed as I was. Still, it set the right stage for when Mr. Windham and I got down to considering cutlery.

"My boyfriend said to get Bour du Chef," I offered as casually as I could.

"Your boyfriend has excellent taste," Windham complimented. "Knives are one place you definitely don't want to cut corners. Pun intended."

I'd worked out what to say next. "Do I need to buy a sharpener?"

"Oh, no. That's one of the best reasons to buy your Bour du

Chef knives at Windham's. Bring your knives back here, and we sharpen them for free. For life."

"I don't live close. I heard there's someone who comes to you . . ."

His face turned sour. "Absolutely not. I wouldn't recommend that dreadful woman at all."

So Windham knew exactly who I was talking about. And he was behaving as if he hadn't yet heard that Kat was dead. That seemed unlikely the way news traveled in this town.

"Really?"

"We've had tremendous trouble with her. I had to resort to banning her from the store. Not that she complies. I have no doubt she'd be assaulting you right this minute if she were here. Kat's Kutz is absolutely not anyone you want to be dealing with."

I didn't know too many businesspeople who'd be quite so quick to bad-mouth a competitor, even one they disliked as fiercely as Windham seemed to dislike Kat. I decided now was the time for a little investigative work. "Still, it's dreadful what's happened to her, don't you think?"

His face was unreadable. "Yes, of course it's a terrible accident." He did not sound like a man who meant that at all. "But I can hardly say I'm surprised. She isn't—wasn't—the sort to respect rules or good sense. I can't remember the last time I had to ban someone from the store."

"What did she do to get banned from the store?"

Leydon waved a hand. "What *didn't* she do? She parked her van right in front of the store. She talked customers out of sales. She wrote letters to the paper calling for people to boycott us." He fixed me with a glare. "We are a successful family company. We are large because we do what we do very well. Windham's is a Carolina institution. It can't be my fault that she can't make a go of her business."

He definitely looked like a man who would physically throw Kat out his door.

"Still, to be stabbed like that . . ." I used the word intentionally and watched the tiniest bit of something flash behind his eyes.

"It's my understanding she met with an accident."

"Well," I said, backpedaling, "an *accidental* stabbing by a knife she was sharpening. It was a Bour du Chef knife, in fact."

One of his bushy blond eyebrows lowered with suspicion. "And how do you know this?"

"I was the one that found her. I'm Shelby Phillips. My mother is Nina Phillips. She owns Nina's Nimble Needle, and Kat was supposed to have been at an event at our store when she went missing. I went looking for her and . . . well . . . found her."

Again, I felt as if I could see facts clicking together behind his eyes. Leydon rocked back on his heels. "That had to have been difficult. Yes, I can see the resemblance now. I do know your mother. And your sister, Jessica, is a regular customer."

That wasn't hard to believe. Jessica's kitchen could have been a showpiece in any of the department aisles. Any part of her life, actually, from housewares to furnishings to "better sportswear." Jessica's sportswear wasn't just better; it was "the best."

My personal connection to the incident softened his words. "I am sorry to hear that happened to you." I noticed he did not say he was sorry it had happened to *her*. "I would never wish harm on anyone, but I'm not lying when I say I'm relieved to know she won't be a problem for us anymore." He straightened his shoulders. "Well . . . ," Leydon said in a *Let's move on to better subjects* tone. "Let's just get that first set of knives wrapped up for you."

I had sprung for three Bour du Chef knives, but my "starter set" came with some very interesting information.

CHAPTER 9

A few hours into the shop's opening on Tuesday, Leona grinned at me from over the cash register. "You know, today almost feels normal."

I took it as the compliment Leona intended. After my tumultuous first days as manager of the Nimble Needle, Sunday afternoon and this morning did feel normal. A welcome sort of ordinary—and, I hoped, a better indication of how the rest of my month would go.

Faye Sanders looked up from her work at the table where she and fellow NYAG Livvy Swanson were stitching. I had quickly learned that it was a rare day at the Nimble Needle when there wasn't at least one—if not all four—of the NYAGs at the table.

"You're doing splendidly," Faye said, straightening the classic cardigan over her trim sheath dress. "I know you had a rocky start, but you've taken to it like you were born to run the Nimble Needle."

"Wasn't she?" Livvy chuckled as she peered over her round glasses. "She's Nina's daughter."

"Mom has two daughters," I felt compelled to add. It still stumped me why no one seemed to see Jessica as the Needle's heir apparent. In my view, she was the better choice, and everyone seemed to gloss right over the fact that I didn't want the job.

"Jessica's a lovely woman . . . ," Livvy replied, but she never finished the thought. She just raised an eyebrow in a gesture that could have meant a thousand things, from *But everyone wants you* to *She clearly doesn't need the tryout you've been given*.

Faye knotted her thread with an expert twist of her fingers. "I think it's nice that you're here. You made your mother so happy."

"And Nina has faith in you," Livvy said. She pulled a pencil from her gray-blond bun and made a mark on the notebook next to her project. "We all know she could have easily come running back when all this nasty business with Kat happened, but she trusted you to handle things."

"It took a lot of convincing to assure her I could handle things." Up until today, I confess I wasn't quite sure I could pull this off. This morning I had awoken with a settled sort of confidence. Nabbit had taken up permanent residence in the apartment, I was proud of the clever way I'd gained information at Windham's, and I'd sliced up a mean bell pepper stir-fry with my new cutlery for dinner last night. "But I think Mom's able to focus on her trip now, and that's what matters."

"It certainly is," Faye said with a smile.

A smile that disappeared when the bell over the door chimed, and a big, burly man carrying two duffel bags filled the door. It took me all of three seconds to recognize him: Cal Katsaros.

As opposed to his late sister, Cal hadn't changed much since his high school days. A big, lumbering sort of guy who had never looked comfortable in his own skin, he hadn't discovered Kat's bold confidence. Cal moved through the world as if he needed to apologize for all the space he took up.

Leona darted out from behind the counter. "Oh, hon. I'm so sorry for what's happened to your sister. You must be so shocked and sad."

Cal gave a grunt and a nod. Really, what proper response was there to the tragic death of your little sister? I felt a quick surge of pity for whoever had landed the job of finding Cal and delivering the horrible news. They had been closer when they were younger, but Kat's remarks had spoken of serious friction between them as they got older. It wasn't hard to see how her newfound success might have grated on him.

"We're all sorry for you and your dad," Livvy said. "Terrible loss."

"Dreadful," Faye chimed in.

Cal's eyes scanned the room, absorbing the collection of sympathy, until his gaze landed on me. The expression in his eyes was easy enough to read—sadness, anger, confusion, and that particular general bafflement that had always made Cal a blunt instrument of a guy.

"I'm very sorry for what's happened," I said. It didn't feel like enough, but I wasn't sure what else to say. "Is there anything I can do for you?"

"Well, yeah, actually." He shrugged and hoisted the bags he held in either hand. "Can we talk a minute?"

I wasn't quite sure a man of his size would fit in Mom's small office, but he clearly didn't want to have whatever conversation he had in mind out here on the shop floor. "Of course," I replied. "Let's talk in there." I pointed toward the back of the shop.

We walked to the small office, and I shut the door. After I sat down at the desk and Cal squeezed himself into Mom's guest chair, we made a few minutes of awkward-feeling small talk until I repeated, "Tell me how I can help."

Cal jutted his chin in the direction of the bags, which were now at his feet. "Kat's still got a lot of stuff."

I wasn't quite sure what Kat's possessions had to do with me until he elaborated.

"Canvases, scissors. All the stuff she sells." He reached for the nearest of the two bags and unzipped it. "I brought some of it. Can you still sell it?"

The idea of putting a dead woman's art up for sale in the Needle gave me pause, but then again, where else would her work go? It was beautiful, and it should be able to find its way into the hands of people who would appreciate it.

"I'm happy to help," I replied, "but is it legal? Do you have the . . . ?" I searched for the right word. "Legal status to do that? I mean, does she have a will saying where her stock should go if something happened to her?" Precious few people my age bothered with estate planning, and someone as reckless as Kat didn't strike me as the kind of woman to have all her affairs in that kind of order.

"I'm her family." His words held a hint of challenge, and I watched his big hand grip tighter on the handle of the bag.

"So's your dad," I pointed out, "is he okay with this?"

"He doesn't care about this stuff. She'd want me to have it. What I really want is the van, but I guess this'll have to do for now, until Dad comes around."

I had wondered if this was just a precursor to Cal's laying claim to the Kat's Kutz van and its business. The absurd image of Leydon Windham trying to escort someone of Cal's size out of the Windham's kitchen department invaded my mind. I didn't share those thoughts out loud, naturally.

"She was taking her stuff here to be sold, anyways, right? Even before the thing on Saturday?"

I had seen records indicating that Kat had consigned canvases and scissors here for a while. "Yes, I suppose that's true." Did I need to check this out with someone before I agreed to take the stock? This was the best place for it.

"I'll take it back if there's a reason you can't," he said. He lowered his voice before adding, "I could use the cash. Just, you know, until we get everything squared away." Here was the old, scrambling Cal I remembered. Not exactly the most dependable guy around. When I didn't reply, he pressed, "C'mon. You know the people who want it are here."

This was, in fact, one way I could do right by Kat. Cal was correct: Kat's customers were the Needle's customers. If I was genuine in my offer to help Cal and his sister's memory, then taking her final stock on consignment made sense. "I'll take it, but I'll get Mom's lawyer to okay the consignment fees going to you. Technically, this may be considered part of her estate. I don't want to cross any lines here."

"Yeah, okay."

I opened the laptop on the desk. "Do you want to wait while I write up a receipt for all this?"

"Um, no. I'm good."

That wasn't a smart business response, but I wasn't dealing with a savvy businessman. I was dealing with a cash-hungry Cal. Which meant if I didn't take the goods, he might take them to someone else, someone who would take advantage of him. I felt a greater sense of assurance that I was doing the right thing. The thing Mom would have done, certainly.

"Do you have an email address? Someplace where I can send the documentation?"

"Yeah."

I pushed a piece of paper and a pen across the desk to him. "Give me your email and phone. I'll get in touch when I've got everything set up."

"Thanks." He stood up after he'd written the information down. "There's more, by the way. At her apartment."

I stood up, as well. "Let's just start with this."

"Yeah." He paused for a minute. "So you're back."

"Just for a while."

"Only a while? Do you want to run the shop?" The edge of challenge had returned to his voice.

"I'm not really thinking about it now." It seemed the most conciliatory answer I could give.

"She did."

"I know."

"Not that it matters now, huh?"

I gave him the kindest look I could. "I'm really very sorry for what's happened."

"Yeah," he said as he turned to leave the office. "Everybody is."

I thought again about the impaled knife and the nasty remarks Leydon had made. Was everybody really sorry?

Jessica held her phone up after knocking on my apartment door that evening. "Did you see this?" she asked as she stepped inside.

I had been a bit preoccupied and hadn't checked my phone since lunch. That in itself was a minor phenomenon, but after weeks of unemployed inactivity, it felt nice to be busy. And not a frantic, meet-this-deadline or placate-that-client busy, but the happy, creative busy of people making art. I found it remarkably satisfying. I could almost understand why Mom had found it hard to leave.

I dug in my handbag for my phone. "What should I have seen?"

"Honestly, they're like teenagers on a road trip." I couldn't tell if my sister was amused or mortified. Not having seen the photos yet, I thought maybe she was both.

"They *are* on a road trip. And I'm glad they're having fun."

Jessica raised one blond eyebrow and pushed her phone in front of my face. It showed a shot of Mom and Dad in a pair of crazy matching T-shirts in front of some cheesy roadside souvenir stand.

I tried not to cringe. "I didn't peg them for the matching T-shirt type." Then again, I hadn't pegged them for the nomad-in-a-van type, so it just goes to show you never can tell. Four images had been texted to my own phone, all of them depicting some form of roadside diversion. "Good for them?" I secretly hoped they'd get all the tacky tourist stuff out of their system before they headed back. I secretly hoped they would head back eventually. Those broad smiles above the matching shirts did give me a moment's doubt.

Jessica headed into the kitchen. "We need to tell them we're going, so they won't feel like they need to."

I followed her, but didn't follow her sudden change of topic. "Going where?"

"The yacht club thing. For George. For Kat."

"And for Cal," I added.

Jessica deposited her trendy tote bag on the kitchen counter and then sat on one of the counter stools. But not before wiping it off, as if it might mar her crisp white pants. "He's back?"

"He came into the shop today with some of Kat's stock to consign."

Her lips pressed together. "Well, that sounds just like him."

I fetched a pitcher of lemon water out of the fridge, along with two glasses. "Well, I admit it took me back a bit at first. And he did admit to needing the cash. But I do actually think it's a good idea." I poured a glass for her and one for myself. "The Needle is the best place for her work if it's going to go anywhere. Cal's the type who might just foist it off on some thrift store if I said no." I sat down next to Jessica. "It's what Mom would have done, don't you think?" I surprised myself by honestly wanting her opinion.

Jessica nodded. "You're right. It is Are you going to ask her?"

"Like you said, I'm trying not to bug Mom with stuff. Leona and JanLi both agreed, and I'm going to get the lawyer to review whether Cal has the legal right to consign Kat's merchandise. There might be some legal technicalities involved. I'll get Mom's okay when I know exactly how I want to handle it."

"Good. But we should definitely plan on going to the Gwen

Lake Yacht Club memorial. I'll call Mom and Dad tonight and let them know. And I'll tell them you're doing just fine."

There it was—that gently cutting edge tone my sister wielded with such skill. As if she needed to report in on her little sister's performance minding the shop.

Nabbit chose that moment to come sauntering out of the bedroom, where I was sure he'd taken a long nap on one of my sweatshirts.

Jessica froze. "That's a cat."

Defensiveness prickled between my shoulder blades. "Yes, it is."

"You have a cat."

I couldn't tell you if she said it with an air of doubt or I just heard it that way. Still, I swear Jessica looked at me with the same expression that she'd viewed Mom and Dad's absurd matchy-matchy fashion choice.

Your standard adult female is entitled to a cat, however impulsively acquired. I felt very entitled to this particular cat—or perhaps this particular cat felt entitled to me. Either worked.

"I do now," I declared. How could she get my goat so easily with just two simple statements? "You can let them know that, too, if you think it's relevant." Snarky, perhaps, but I was having trouble shaking off the "I'm gonna tell Mom" vibe she was throwing off. Isn't it amazing how you can be a fully grown adult and still somehow revert to childhood dynamics for no good reason?

Jessica threw me a *Don't get like that* look, which I returned with a *Don't you get like that* look of my own.

"It's on Thursday, at four. Get JanLi to cover the shop, because Leona will want to be there, too."

I did not care for her telling me how to run the shop. Even if I hadn't thought of that detail yet, I would have. "I'll be there." I couldn't bring myself to thank her for the tip. And even though she still hadn't told me what all would happen at this odd event, I was no longer interested in asking her.

"Okay then." Task accomplished, Jessica stood, collected her trendy tote bag, and whooshed out the door to whatever accomplishment awaited her next.

Nabbit hopped up on the counter where Jessica's tote bag had been—something I'm sure my sister would have found unsanitary—and stared after the closed door.

"That's Jessica," I explained. "She can be a bit hard to swallow sometimes." I stroked Nabbit's soft striped fur. "She's going to announce you to Mom and Dad, by the way."

Should I care? Nabbit's expression seemed to say.

"No," I replied to his silent question. "You should not."

CHAPTER 10

I stared at myself in the mirror late Thursday morning. What does one wear to a model yacht memorial? I fought the urge to call Jessica and ask, knowing whatever the perfect outfit was, she'd be in it.

I'd chosen a navy blue print skirt with a cream top—not all somber, not all light. Was this considered the funeral? Or more like a wake? The nautical double meaning made me laugh, lifting Nabbit's head off my pillow.

It was a beautiful day, warm and green in the way only North Carolina pulls off spring. Sun and a collection of fluffy blue clouds adorned a turquoise sky. If nothing else, I'd spend an afternoon on the shores of Gwen Lake—not a bad place to be, even given the circumstances.

I walked over to the large boathouse on Gwen Lake's shoreline, next to a small beach. When I was younger, it was just the boathouse. Now somehow it had been "upgraded" to the Gwen Lake Yacht Club. It seemed as if they kept taking the odd concept farther and farther—members now wore matching navy jackets. While no one actually had an ascot, the commodore did have a very official, very nautical-looking hat. Everyone was very serious, and I found the gravitas they gave the situation touching. They were paying tribute to their friend's loss.

In a most unusual way, grant you, but it was a tribute nonetheless.

It had been years since I'd seen Kat's father, George Katsaros. Still, he was easy to spot. Standing next to each other, he and Cal hardly looked related. Kat had looked a lot like her father at one time, but she'd done so much to change her appearance that no member of that family bore any resemblance to another anymore.

Even from my distance across the dock, I could sense friction between the father and son. These were not two grieving family members consoling each other. These were two people trying not to blow up at each other under trying circumstances. They hardly spoke to each other, but the sideways glances they shot in between saying hello to people were hard to miss.

Deb came to stand by me in the crowd. "I hate to say it, but I'm kind of surprised how many people are here. Kat wasn't exactly everyone's favorite person."

"I suppose they're here for George," I replied. "And Cal."

"Well, George and Cal certainly aren't here for each other." Deb's low whisper was punctuated by a cocking of her head toward the pair.

"You see that, too?" I whispered back.

"Hard not to."

George shot a dark look toward his son. "Grief does things to people." I turned to Deb. "The only time I ever remember my parents really getting into it with each other was just before my grandmother's funeral, and it was over the stupidest thing."

"True, but I doubt you'll ever see George Katsaros on the cover of *Great Parents Monthly*." Deb shrugged. "It isn't hard to see where Kat got her hard edges from."

"Kat was his daughter. And she died in the most awful way. Mean or not, the man deserves pity." I was surprised to feel a small surge of pity for Cal, too. He looked lost. His face bore a bewildered, angry expression, as if he had more emotions than he knew what to do with. Understandable, given the circumstances.

I felt a tap on my shoulder and turned to see Jessica. Even before I got a full hello out, she looked my outfit up and down and said, "Where's your doubloon?"

I blinked. "My what?"

"Your doubloon. The gold-coin necklace Dad gave each of us three years ago. You're supposed to be wearing it to things like this." She gestured toward the gold coin on a chain around her neck.

Looking around, I answered, "I didn't know."

"Of course you didn't. Do you even know where it is? That's a special gift from a member of the yacht club."

Now not only was I incorrectly dressed, but I was also an ungrateful daughter. "In a box in Mom's attic, probably." I leaned in. "It would have been nice if you had told me."

"I didn't think I had to."

I wanted to say, "I thought it was just jewelry," but I bit my tongue. Jessica would take it as just another piece of evidence that I'd left home and left Gwen Lake behind. She wouldn't be entirely wrong, and that stung as much as her chiding.

Still, a doubloon? Like pirate-ship treasure? Weren't our yachtsmen taking things a bit far?

Scanning the crowd again, I noticed all the other people wearing the coins. I did remember a little speech Dad gave me when he presented me with the necklace. I just hadn't registered the meaning.

George had one around his neck. Cal did not. What did that mean?

I didn't have much time to ponder such details, as the small ceremony began and the boats were all lined up beside the dock in a pint-sized flotilla. I had to admit it was rather impressive. There were model versions of pleasure yachts and a few historical three-masted ships. One of the larger ones looked like a miniature Titanic steamship. Three sailboats had little black ribbons fluttering from the top of their masts, and there were a few military-looking ones, including the largest battleship with three tiny brass cannons on deck. A red boat had an odd-looking contraption on it and looked like a cross between a container ship and a dump truck. I'd never seen anything like it in all my life.

"May I have your daughter's doubloon?" the man in the commodore hat asked George.

"Kat has a doubloon?" Cal snapped. "You gave one to her and not to me?"

George scowled at his son. "I haven't given one to either of you. I was saving them for when I felt you deserved them. For whatever families you might have when you got yourselves together."

Ouch, I thought.

"So Kat deserves one *now*, does she?" Cal's hurt was palpable. As if her terrible death had been her fault. Then again, didn't people think that? Assume that her reckless disregard of safety measures had finally caught up with her?

"She's *dead*, Cal. Why don't you just shut your mouth for once?"

The commodore held up a hand. "Gentlemen," he said, "let's all try to settle down. George, may I have your daughter's doubloon?"

George turned to the small table behind him and proceeded to open something that looked—no joke—like a small treasure chest. He made an anguished growl and then whirled on Cal. "They're gone! I had two doubloons, and they're gone!"

"I didn't take them. I didn't even know you had them," Cal shot back.

"Stealing doubloons. That's low," Deb murmured.

"Who'd steal my doubloons? Who'd do that?" George asked the crowd the questions, but it wasn't hard to see who he felt was the culprit.

Cal threw his hands in the air. "I didn't take them. I don't want your silly coins, anyway."

The commodore and George both bristled at the put-down. There was a tense silence as people seemed to try to figure out what to do next.

The commodore cleared his throat. "What would you like to do, George?"

After a moment's thought, George removed the coin from around his neck and handed it to the commodore.

"She gets yours?" Cal protested.

"Will you *shut your mouth*?" George growled.

It was hard to say which struck me more—the ferocious tension between Cal and George or the absurd but sweet nature of the memorial. Still, I couldn't squelch the powerful sensation that Kat deserved better. She had seemed so starved for attention. Or maybe it was respect she had craved—she certainly didn't seem to have gotten any from anyone I talked to. And today's attempt at a memorial seemed to be quickly turning into a dramatic disaster.

"What happens now?" I asked Jessica. I found myself genuinely curious about how gold coins, miniature boats, and three tiny cannons combined to pay tribute to a life.

Jessica drew in a deep breath and, with the resigned tone of someone explaining physics to a five-year-old, said, "The fleet goes out into the center of the lake. They fire off the cannons, and then the red ship tips the doubloon overboard."

At least it wasn't a symbolic tiny miniature casket. I doubted Kat wanted to be buried at sea—even metaphorically.

I glanced at the coin hanging from the chain around Jessica's neck. "They dump—" The immediate flash in her eyes had me opting for more respectful language. "I mean, they *send* the coin to the bottom of the lake?"

"They do. Been doing it for years." Again, the "If you had stayed here, you'd know this" in her tone dug under my skin.

The whole thing struck me as heartfelt but just plain ridiculous. "And they stay there?" Wouldn't it be a more fitting tribute to donate the coin to a cause Kat had cared about? My mind envisioned a pile of gold coins glittering at the bottom of Gwen Lake. Sunken pirate treasure indeed. "No one's ever tried to . . . I don't know . . . steal them back?"

Jessica's eyes flashed. "Who would do such a thing?"

Cal with scuba gear? my brain countered, since I remembered Cal's admission of being short on cash. *Or perhaps someone with a model submarine and remote salvaging gear?* If those things were as valuable as people seemed to treat them—if they were valuable enough to steal—weren't they valuable enough to try to bring up from the bottom of the lake?

Jessica nearly tsked. "Honestly, Shelby, what kind of people did you spend time with in Georgia?"

"Shhh," chided a woman in front of me. "They're about to fire the cannons."

All the men in the crowd around me took off their hats, and the crowd fell silent. From the deck of the large battleship, a trio of small-scale cannon shots rang out. A few seconds later I could just make out the red boat and its mechanism slide the shiny coin into the water with a small splash.

A man behind me began singing a hymn, several people joined in, and then the ceremony was over.

Chief Tallen came up to me as Jessica left and Deb went to talk to some other people. "How are you, Shelby? Had kind of a rough welcome into town. Everything okay?"

For a moment I wondered if Mom had put him up to the inquiry. Then again, with Leona and JanLi watching me, Mom had no need to recruit law enforcement. "I just feel bad the whole thing happened."

"It was a terrible accident."

I couldn't resist. "So you're certain it was an accident? I keep hearing how many people didn't like her."

"This is a small town. Lots of people don't like each other. They fight. All the time. Sometimes they throw a few punches, but they don't murder each other. Your mother's enjoying her vacation, and that big feature in the travel magazine is coming up. Don't go inventing some sort of murder mystery adventure while Gwen Lake is getting a nice media boost. Rose really wants that to go well, and I want to have a nice spring." Chief Tallen's wife was Mayor Rose Tallen—they were Gwen Lake's version of a power couple if ever there was one. One of the advantages of a small town was that you could get away with things like the mayor being married to the police chief. "And I want George to have some peace about a terrible tragedy."

"But now George's doubloons have gone missing." It seemed very possible—plausible, even—to me that the two events were related.

Chief Tallen's glare gave Jessica's a run for the money. "How am I going to keep you from making trouble for the few weeks you're here?" My temporary resident status came through loud and clear in the near growl of his words.

"It won't be a problem," I replied. "I'll let you do your job."

He put a hand on my shoulder, half reassuring, half restraining. "You stick to pillows, and I'll take care of the perpetrators." He nodded toward his jacket lapel, where I had just noticed a doubloon affixed as a pin. Evidently these didn't all come in the form of necklaces. Somehow that just made the fact that I'd virtually ignored mine all the more regrettable. "Where's yours?" he asked. "If Jessica has one, surely you do."

Was the whole town going to call me out on my lapse in doubloon protocol? Protocol I didn't even know about until an hour ago?

"Somewhere in a box in Mom and Dad's closets. I didn't take everything with me to Savannah on account of a tiny apartment." The need to make excuses for myself pinched at my stomach. "I didn't know how all this stuff went. And I'd forgotten how seriously everyone seems to take it."

Tallen pulled in a deep breath. "Traditions are important. Even odd ones." He leaned in. "Like doubloons in a yacht club of tiny boats." He gave a small smile as he looked around the crowd, which was slowly dispersing. "This was around when you were here. It can't look that odd to you."

I didn't want to use that word. "Quaint, maybe? Quirky in a heartwarming kind of way?"

His chuckle was reassuring. "That's a good way to put it. If Gwen Lake is anything, it's quirky in a heartwarming kind of way. Go tell that to Rose. She'll probably tell them to put that in the article."

CHAPTER 11

"Do you have to get back to the shop?" Deb asked as she walked back up beside me. "Do you want to come have an early dinner at CHNO?" She leaned in. "I make a panini that can beat a yacht club memorial casserole by a nautical mile."

"Sure," I replied. "Just let me go say a word to George and Cal." It would be the polite thing to do, after all, and despite my doubloon faux pas, my mama did raise me right.

George looked weary and overwhelmed when I shook his hand. "I'm so very sorry for what happened to Kat."

"You were best friends in school," he said, a touch of melancholy softening his otherwise hard features.

And there it was again—the lopsided nature of my friendship with Kat. It stung my conscience that I'd been so much to her while she'd been so little to me. I'd never been mean to her, but I couldn't escape that I'd been unkind in thousands of small, thoughtless ways.

"I'm sure Mom would want to continue featuring Kat's work. Cal brought over some pieces yesterday."

The sharpness returned as George narrowed his eyes at Cal, who was across the dock, talking to some other people. "Did he now?"

That brought me up short. "I assume he has your permission? I mean, I'll check with Mom's lawyer and all, but I agree with Cal that they shouldn't disappear, and the Needle is the place where her work will be most appreciated."

"And paid good money for."

I didn't know what to say to that. He wasn't wrong—only needlepointers would recognize and pay for the quality of Kat's work. But George saw the move as capitalizing on the situation—and he wasn't wrong, either.

George let out a long-suffering sigh. "Well, at least he's taking the initiative on something. I suppose I ought to support it." He grunted. "He wants the van, you know."

"He said as much."

"Maybe how he handles this will show me if he's got any business sense at all. My daughter was difficult, frustrating, and downright odd, but she had a business head on her shoulders."

That was only half of what she was. "She was a talented artist, too. Her work really is lovely."

He waved the compliment off. "Not my thing. Never was."

I could point out that the world was filled with many talented male needlepointers and that some of the leading canvas designers were men, but I knew George didn't want to hear it.

"Watch him."

It was odd to hear a man dismiss his daughter's passions and warn me off his son, as if his own children were liabilities to be managed. Jessica and I were as different as night and day, but Mom and Dad loved us, celebrated us, and put up cheerfully (mostly) with what they didn't understand.

Kat's mother had died when she was in the seventh grade. Now all Cal and George had was each other. And based on what I'd seen today, they didn't really have that, either.

After a delicious panini at CHNO, which did, in fact, beat whatever had been served on the dock by "a nautical mile," I put in a few hours at the shop and made two important calls.

The first was to Mom, to check up on the Nimble Nomad's

adventures and get the okay to consign the pieces of Kat's work that Cal had brought over. As expected, Mom said she'd be delighted to offer Kat's designs and products to the customers, who she knew would appreciate them. She agreed with me that this was a concrete thing we could do to support the Katsaros family. "Unless there's a legal reason why we can't," she said, "I'd want to do it. It's the right thing to do. And I'm glad you're there to take care of it for me."

I then received a four-minute speech on the virtues of state fair corn dogs and why gas station espresso drinks are "so much better than you'd think." They were having fun—I could hear it in her voice. Mom added a gush of "Honey, I love yous," which made my throat tighten in comparison to the way I'd seen George talk about his children.

"Do you want to talk to your father?" Mom asked. "He's right here." She handed off the phone.

"Hi, Dad." I did want to talk to him, and I didn't. An overwhelming need to apologize for leaving the doubloon behind—and for never really recognizing its importance in the first place—caused me to choke up after my hello. "I . . . um . . . I didn't realize about the Gwen Lake Yacht Club doubloon." I meant more than just wearing it today, but I didn't know how to say it.

"I should have told you. I figured Jessica would."

"She did. Just after I got there. They are beautiful," I admitted. "I'd totally forgotten about mine." I owed him that much of an admission.

He caught my meaning. "You were focused on what was waiting for you in Georgia. And you don't need some silly old coin to tell you how much you mean to me."

My throat tightened again. "I want to go find it. Where is it? Do you know?"

Of course he knew. "In your mother's dresser drawer. Next to where she keeps hers." After a tender-feeling moment, he cleared his throat and asked, "Did you see how they send one into the lake in tribute now? Bet you've never seen anything like that before."

"No, sir, that was a first." I recalled my "quirky in a heart-warming way" description. "But Kat didn't have one."

"She didn't?"

"When George opened his little chest with the doubloons he said he was keeping, they were both gone." I recounted George's remarks about denying Kat and Cal their coins until they "deserved them," which brought a disapproving moan from my father. "He had two waiting," I went on, "but both have disappeared."

"Lost? Really?"

"He thinks they were stolen," I explained. "And by Cal, from the looks of it."

"So what did they do?"

"George gave the commodore his own coin from around his neck, and they sent that one into the lake. The whole thing was painful and sad."

"All the more reason we should make sure that girl's work finds its way into good hands," Mom called from nearby. "That family is a mess. Tell Warren we'll do whatever it takes to be able to consign the stock."

As it turned out, our family attorney, Warren Young, said as long as we had the family's permission—in this case Cal's and George's—we could consign any and all of Kat's work. But he had the same warning as George. "Watch him, that Cal. He's a piece of work, that boy."

Enormous Cal was hardly a boy, but it spoke volumes that people still thought of him as George's misfit son. Were people still as dismissive of Kat, and was that why she had striven so hard to gain people's attention?

Following Dad's directions, I found a small box marked SHELBY'S DOUBLOON in Mom's dresser drawer. A lump rose in my throat as I opened the box to find a coin exactly like Jessica's. After picking it up by the delicate gold chain, I twirled it in the stream of late afternoon sunlight coming through Mom and Dad's bedroom window.

I wasn't much of a jewelry person myself, and it was definitely never a style I'd wear. But this wasn't about style—this was about relationships. A gesture whose importance, thanks to my bold ambition to go prove myself to the world outside Gwen Lake, I'd overlooked.

I thought of Kat's coin—her father's, really—resting at the bottom of the lake. She didn't even get her own true memorial. She'd had to borrow her father's coin. And not even *borrow* it, as there would be no "returning" this particular gift. It seemed unfair that life had taken even this final swipe at everything she deserved. My future was in a bit of a jumble, but at least I had one.

What really happened to you, Kat? I wondered. For whatever reason, my brain just would not accept that her strange death was accidental. *What don't I know? What is everyone dismissing? And, most importantly, what can I find out?*

After snapping the box shut, I slipped it into my pocket and made my way back toward the apartment. I don't know when I'd decided to launch whatever this was. . . . Was it an investigation, some sort of penance for past behavior, or just nosy curiosity? I just knew I was had started some journey that would hopefully lead me to answers.

And that meant starting with the only lead I had: Kat's artwork.

I fished my shop keys from my pocket and opened the front door of the darkened shop. Switching on the lights, I headed back to the stockroom, where I had stashed the two duffel bags of items Cal had brought over.

Just because I couldn't think of anything else to do, I hauled the bags out onto the shop floor and spread the contents out.

It was like a window into Kat's mind. Bold designs—more angles than curves—filled most of the canvases, although a few were surprisingly delicate. It wasn't surprising that she favored darker colors. I had to laugh at the two canvases featuring defiant expletives, but my chest pinched a bit at one with a long-legged bird that somehow managed to look as lost and needy as the artist who had painted her.

I was staring at the collection for a good ten minutes before I noticed it. A tiny detail that showed up in many of the canvases. A set of crossed lines with leaves trailing through them, sometimes realistic, other times abstract. You had to look hard at some of the pieces before the design showed itself, but once you found it, it stood out.

It seems that like many artists, Kat had a signature motif. Given how fiercely the woman had branded herself, it made sense. What didn't make sense was how the crossed lines and leaves looked somehow familiar. I'd seen this design before, but I couldn't place where. It was similar to her business logo but still not identical.

What was I seeing, and where had I seen it before?

I literally gasped out loud when it came to me. I jammed my hand into my pocket, pulled out the box with the necklace inside, opened it, and gave another gasp.

The design was a stylized version of the image on the back of the doubloon.

I nearly jumped out of my skin when I heard someone rapping on the shop window.

"I'm sorry," Jake London said when I raced to the front door and pulled it open. "I didn't mean to scare you. I just saw you alone in the shop and thought I'd come say hello."

"It's okay. I just got a bit spooked by something I found."

Jake looked around. "Hard to believe there's anything scary in here." I watched him take in the shop and all its hues. "I've never been in here before. There's a lot of . . . color."

The color feast for the eyes was one of my favorite things

about Mom's shop. I can't ever remember a world not jam-packed with color and creativity. Graphic design was such a natural choice for me as an adult because of my lifelong saturation in hues. Every once in a while—like now—I am reminded how unusual that is. Foreign, perhaps, to a guy who spent his time in the monochromatic world of car engines.

"It's wonderful, isn't it?"

He raised an eyebrow. "Okay, but spooky?"

"Well, normally, I'd agree with you. And I wasn't really spooked by anything in the shop." I pointed to the spread of canvases and scissors on the floor beside me. "It's what's in there."

Understandable bafflement filled Jake's eyes. "What? Just looks like more of the same to me."

"These are Kat's. Cal brought them over earlier to consign."

Jake shot me a dubious look. "Is it legal to sell your dead sister's needlepoint?"

"We've gotten the okay from George and from Mom's lawyer. As long as everyone's in agreement . . ."

That brought a scowl from Jake. "George agreed to that? Cal selling Kat's work?"

"Surprisingly, yes."

"That family." Jake shook his head. "Did you see those two at the memorial? I thought it was going to get ugly there for a moment." He kneeled down and looked over the collection I'd spread out on the floor. "So what's scary about all this?" He picked up one of Kat's more ornate scissors. "Okay, these look sharp, but the rest just looks like crafty stuff to me." I was grateful he quickly added, "No offense."

"They are sharp. Kat's scissors are top-notch quality. The pair you're holding costs a hundred dollars. And I know of some that cost even more than that."

Jake stared at the implement in his hands. "You're kidding. They're *scissors*."

"They're very good, beautiful handmade scissors," I corrected. "And people who like 'crafty stuff,' as you called it, can be very particular about their tools." I gave him a direct look before I added, "Aren't you?"

He sat back on his haunches. "I make my living with my tools."

"I happen to think art is just as important as any professional pursuit." I had been thinking about graphic art, but I was surprised at how much I meant it in terms of the art around us, too. I had somehow forgotten how crafts and art had shaped my life, had molded me into the person I was now. Just because I'd gotten laid off on account of some corporate algorithm didn't change that.

Jake's smile offered an affirmation. "I'll give you that. I suppose anything that makes you happy is worth an investment. I mean, I don't even want to think about how much some of those model boats out there today cost."

I don't know what made me ask. "Do you have a hobby? Where do your happiness dollars go?"

He laughed. "Lots of them end up in Deborah's cash register at CHNO. I do like my coffee."

"Coffee's good, but it's not quite what I was asking."

Jake set the scissors down carefully. "Well, then, you're talking about Sheila." He said the name with obvious affection.

I pointed a chiding finger at him. "A girlfriend is not a hobby."

"No. But a Datsun 280ZX is."

I was no car aficionado, but I knew enough to know all those letters and numbers probably signified a sports car. "You drive a blue truck."

"I drive a blue Ford. I lavish affection—expensive affection—on a temperamental red and black coupe."

"So Sheila is a car." Mom and Dad weren't the only ones to name their cars. I like my white Honda, but I don't even think of it in terms of gender, and I have no intention of giving it a name."

He laughed again. I found myself liking how easily his laugh came. "Don't let her hear you say that." There was a glowing little moment of something between us before he returned his gaze to the items on the floor. "But we were talking about what's scary in all this."

I picked up the pair of scissors Jake had just put down. "See the markings here?" I pointed to the crisscross that decorated each handle as well as the small leather casing the scissors came in.

He peered at the scissors. "They're pretty, I guess. Ornate. Not the kind of thing you'd give your average kindergartner to cut up paper."

I gave him a look of mock shock. "Oh no. You don't ever cut paper with this kind of scissors. Ever." Anyone who works with needlework or fabric considers that a mortal sin, but I didn't expect a mechanic to know such a thing. Still, it was fun to tease him.

"Okay. I'll try to remember that. But what's so important about the markings?"

I picked up the small box with my doubloon from where it sat on the floor, and opened it again. I pulled out the doubloon turned it back-side up. "They match this," I explained, pointing to the stylized criscross. "I didn't see it at first, but this crisscross motif is all over Kat's work." I pointed to the several places it showed up in just the half a dozen canvases near us. "It's in almost every piece."

"Well . . ." Jake scratched his chin and narrowed his eyes in thought. "Those coins are supposed to be important gifts, right?"

Again, a pang of guilt struck me over how I hadn't treated my doubloon right. I loved my dad and hated the thought that I might have hurt him with my indifference. "But Kat never got one. Remember how George said he was withholding hers—and Cal's—until he felt they deserved them?"

"Again, one mess of a family. Who does that to their kids?"

Kat's neediness was starting to make sense. She had been looking for the affirmation she clearly hadn't got from her own father. I wondered if she had felt the only way to ever get a doubloon was to create one for herself inside her work. "It's sad when you think about it. When you see it."

Jake stood up and offered a hand to help me up as well. "You don't think it was Kat who stole the doubloons from George, do you?"

It had never occurred to me. "It'd be a heck of a way to get back at her father, but I suppose it's possible," I replied as I stood up. The thought made a sick sort of sense that landed heavily in my stomach. "In a way, she'd be stealing them from Cal, too."

It was a dramatic form of revenge, but when had Kat ever shied away from drama?

CHAPTER 12

"You're putting all this on sale?" Faye's face held the same *Is this legal?* expression I'd seen the night before on Jake's face. Leona and I had just opened the shop half an hour ago, and the NYAGs were gathering around the expanded display I'd made of Kat's work. I had filled the glass display case with all her scissors and had dedicated two full display boards to her canvases.

"You don't think we ought to sell them?" I asked.

Faye's mouth bowed down into a frown. "It's morbid."

"It's unconventional, but that's who she was." Dot picked up one of the two pairs of scissors I had lying on the counter, tethered on a purple velvet cord to prevent theft. She donned her reading glasses—held today on a chain of shiny purple beads—and inspected the scissors. "These are gorgeous." She threw me a sideways glance. "My birthday's coming up. Think I'll drop a few hints."

"Didn't everything she sold here go on consignment?" Faye asked. "Now who gets the money?"

"Cal." When everyone looked surprised, I explained, "He came in with the idea, George and Mom's lawyer okayed it, and I think he's right that this is the best place for her work to find people who want it."

Livvy, who usually went for more traditional patterns, cooed over a dark but beautifully detailed canvas of a crescent moon and stars. "I want this one," she declared. "It's not my usual thing, but I rather like it."

That was a perfect way to describe Kat's work—not most stitchers' "usual thing" but still compelling. Part of me wondered what kind of amazing artist Kat would have grown into given the chance. Of course, we'd never know.

"I sent out an email this morning that we have an exclusive collection of Kat's work." I'd crafted some language about "thanks to the generosity of her family," because that sounded better than "her brother needs the cash."

"It would be nicer to give the proceeds to charity. Or to the town scholarship fund," Tilly said.

"I hadn't thought to suggest it, and it's really not our call." I touched one of the scissors, and my finger found the crisscross motif, which I now seemed to see on everything she did. What did it mean? I turned to Tilly. "It's really no different now than it would have been at the trunk show. Just Cal instead of Kat."

"That makes a difference to me," Dot said. "He's even odder than she is. *Was.* And all that business at the memorial."

The NYAGs all murmured their mutual disapproval. That's a small town for you—sympathy comes and goes, but judgment lasts.

Leona stepped in. "Were you all planning to buy something from the trunk show? You all were here."

Each of them said yes in some form.

"Well, then, you shouldn't feel any reservations about buying something now. It's still beautiful work. And talented stitchers like you deserve beautiful things to work on."

Soothed by the compliment, each of the NYAGs eventually picked out a canvas, and two even purchased the less expensive editions of Kat's scissors. I made a mental note to ask Mom how to drop a hint to Dot's daughter about the scissors

Dot was hoping to receive as a birthday gift. Mom was famous for her canny ability to plant gift hints into just the right ears.

Faye, however, turned up her nose at the idea. "I just don't think it's right." She was a stickler for rules and protocol. She always displayed a keen sense for how things ought to be done.

Dot waived a dismissive hand in Faye's direction. "Lighten up, Faye. You know you want a pair of those really good scissors." While they were good friends, everyone knew Dot's disregard for such things drove Faye crazy.

Faye's chin rose. "I do not."

Dot was having none of it. "I heard you saying that you couldn't understand how anyone as strange as Kat Katsaros could make anything so beautiful."

"That doesn't mean I'd buy them."

"I don't know," Livvy said. "I think that's exactly why you should."

I needed to nip this argument in the bud. The NYAGs always settled everything in the end, but they could sure get into it when they disagreed on something—which they did often. The dustup over the tattoos was the stuff of Nimble Needle legend.

I held up my hands. "No one has to buy anything unless you want to. Mom and I both agree it's the right choice to carry Kat's work. It should be here. If you don't like the idea of supporting Cal, think of it as supporting the shop. Or a talented artist's memory."

"Or as a sympathy ploy from a man with no decorum." Faye may have said it under her breath, but she said it loud enough for all of us to hear it.

Dot practically snorted. "I'm getting this one." She pointed to a black and red square that proclaimed STITCHY & BITCHY in loud letters.

"Of course you are," Faye moaned.

"My grandchildren bicker less than you two," Livvy said.

"And they're in kindergarten."

"You found your doubloon," Leona said, trying to change the subject. "I was sure you had one. Where was it?"

"My mom kept it for me," I admitted. On impulse, I'd put the necklace on this morning. "No one told me you were supposed to wear it to things."

"You've been gone a while." Faye's tone made it impossible to tell if she considered my absence an excuse or a fault.

"Sad about Kat's, don't you think?" Tilly said. "I got a lump in my throat when George gave the commodore his own. Who do you think stole George's collection?"

Faye, Dot, and Livvy all said, "Cal," in startling unison.

I shook my head. "If Cal has those two gold coins, I don't think he'd be looking for quick cash."

"Oh, honey," Livvy said, "they're not gold. They're not worth much at all, actually."

I touched mine. It was heavy. I'd thought it was gold. "Really?"

"They're just replicas," Dot said. "Made for the yacht club, but they only look like treasure."

"Depends on how you see it," Faye replied. "They *are* valuable. Just not in the way you can take to the bank."

"Then why steal them?" I asked the group.

"Beats me," Dot commented. "But my money's still on Cal. Either he's too dim to know they're not worth much or he's sore his dad didn't think he was worth enough to own one."

I glanced again at the crisscross motif that showed up in so much of Kat's work. Whoever had taken those coins, it was looking to be a very personal crime.

Crime. That word seemed to clang in my head no matter where I was or what I was doing. I'm not saying the ghost of Kat Katsaros haunted me, but her presence and her memory weighed heavily on me.

Part of it was being surrounded by her brilliant—now halted—work, as it was displayed in the shop.

"All good artists are odd in their own way," JanLi said to me the next day, as she caught me staring at Kat's most exquisite pair of scissors as I held it in my hands. "Their art is like a peek into their soul, isn't it?"

I set the beautiful implement down, my eye catching the crisscross motif yet again. "I'm really grateful she didn't make knives. I don't think I could bring myself to sell them, no matter how much Cal asked. It'd be too gruesome, given how she died and all."

JanLi tsk-tsked and shook her head. "I know her father said she wasn't careful, but still. You don't think of a machine as being able to do something like that."

A customer looked up from her consideration of an eyeglass case canvas. "Clearly you don't read science fiction. Or spend much time around farm equipment."

"Nope, on both counts," JanLi said.

I shook my head. "I'm more of a sweeping historical romance reader. And I can't keep a houseplant alive."

"It is terrible to think about," the woman said, "but my husband works down at the plant, and he's told me stories of . . . Well . . . I'll spare the details, even if he doesn't."

I was glad she did. My brain was having trouble letting go of the image of Kat's bloody hand flopping to the van floor. I didn't even like looking at the dark burgundy thread on the shop wall.

Out of the corner of my eye, I noticed a young woman hovering near the front door of the shop. As if she wanted to come farther in but couldn't bring herself to do so. Mom sometimes spoke of people who were almost afraid to think of themselves as capable of creativity. As if all the beauty of the shop was meant for other, more special people. One of Mom's—and Leona's—gifts was encouraging "baby stitchers," as she called them, to try a small and simple project. If needlepoint had a gateway drug, my mom was a master dealer. Could I channel her skill?

"Hi," I said, waving her farther into the store. "Come look at everything."

"It is pretty," she admitted. "But I don't think I could do any of this."

She was considerably younger than most of the shop customers, but I took that as a good thing. Someone I could maybe relate to more easily. "I'd guess everyone who's ever come in here felt that way at some point. I did, and my mom owns the shop."

The young woman's face flushed. "I know who you are."

The tone of her words struck me as a bit off. "Well, then, what's your name? How can I help you?"

She lowered her voice. "You're Shelby Phillips. You found her."

That wasn't an answer to my question, and this wasn't a conversation about needlepoint. "Yes, I did. It was a terrible thing."

She had a tight grip on her backpack. "You were in Windham's the other day."

A small chill ran down the back of my neck at the notion of someone noticing me buying knives. Especially three of those knives. I merely nodded, not wanting to say too much.

She glanced toward the shop's office door. "Can we talk? Not out here?"

"I suppose so." I led her toward the office, ignoring the suspicious look JanLi gave me as we passed her.

After we stepped into Mom's office, I left the door slightly open until she stared at it and said, "Please. I can't say this in front of anyone except you."

"You look upset," I offered as I latched the door shut. "How can I help you . . . ?" I left a pause for her to fill in her name, but she merely shook her head and continued to clutch her backpack with white-knuckled fingers.

"I work at Windham's. They can't know I'm here." She

glanced around the small office, as if to assure herself there were no Windham spies hiding in the stock shelves. "I heard you and Mr. Windham talking. About her."

"I understand she was no friend of the store." That seemed the safest way to put it.

"She was an enemy of the store. Mr. Windham hated her. They got into fights anytime she came in—and she did, a lot, even though Mr. Windham had banished her." She gave the word *banished* a dramatic emphasis.

"Kat was talented, but she did seem to have a gift for irritating people."

The young woman leaned in. "He threatened her. I heard him."

The chilled place down the back of my neck now had hairs standing on end. "How?"

"The last time she came in, she didn't bother the customers. She went straight up the escalators to Mr. Windham's office. I just happened to be there doing my time sheet. I wasn't spying, honest."

"I believe you," I reassured her. "What did you hear?"

She swallowed. "He told her if she ever walked into our store, he'd make sure she never walked anywhere ever again. He told her she'd find out what knives could really do."

I paused a moment to take that in. "Are you telling me you heard Leydon Windham threaten Kat with physical harm? Harm with a knife?"

She pressed her lips together and nodded.

"Why haven't you talked to the police? They need to hear this."

"Are you kidding? If Mr. Windham ever found out that I heard what he said and told it to the police, I'd be gone within the hour." Her brows furrowed with worry. "I like my job. And nobody'd believe me, anyway. Not against him."

She had a point. I was sure Leydon would deny it or contend that she had misunderstood the conversation. "You're sure you heard him threaten Kat like that?"

"Why would I make it up?"

People make up things against their bosses for all kinds of reasons. Still, something in my gut told me she was telling the truth. And was scared to be doing so. "I'm not sure what you think I can do."

"You could tell them. Say someone told you they heard Mr. Windham say those terrible things to her." She had leaned in so far now that I was worried she'd tip over the chair. "He wouldn't even have needed to do it himself, probably. He could have hired someone."

I had my doubts about North Carolina's knife-wielding hit-man population. "That's a serious accusation. I can't take it to the police without more facts. Or at least you coming with me."

She shook her head. "Oh, no. I can't. I won't." She popped upright, backpack still clutched to her chest. "But somebody had to know."

Without another word, she pulled the office door open, headed for the front door, and dashed from the shop as if it was burning down behind her.

My mouth was still open from the "Wait! Stop!" I never got the chance to say.

Why did *I* have to be the somebody who had to know?

CHAPTER 13

"She really said that? And you don't know who she is?" Jessica looked at me as if I had failed some test by not getting the store employee's name. She'd shocked me by asking me over to the house for coffee Monday, and I'd spilled the whole story of my Friday encounter before she even handed me the sugar. What to do with what I'd learned had gnawed at me all Saturday and Sunday, and I needed someone to help me sort through it.

"She was afraid Windham would fire her if he knew."

Jessica scowled. "Well, she's right. Leydon would. Talk about throwing your boss under the bus."

I grabbed a piece of the sugar-free fig bar thing that filled the plate between us, hoping it would taste better than just "healthy." "I have to tell Chief Tallen. Even if I can't back it up. If someone made threats to Kat, he has to know."

Jessica broke an itty-bitty piece off one bar and ate it. "The Windham family is a big deal around here. Chief Tallen isn't going to do anything other than give you a speech about keeping your nose out of other people's business."

"I already got that speech," I replied. "And I didn't go looking for this clue. It came looking for me."

Jessica lowered an eyebrow at me. "It's not a clue. This isn't an investigation. It's one probably disgruntled employee taking advantage of a conversation you shouldn't have had with Leydon Windham, anyway. What did you think you were doing buying those knives? Sleuthing?"

I didn't care for the way she nailed me with a judgmental glare. Or for the fact that she was right. I was sleuthing. Because no one else seemed to be taking seriously the possibility of Kat's death not being an accident. Shouldn't someone—especially Tallen—be at least considering the possibility?

As I bit into the fig bar—which wasn't half bad, despite a regrettable absence of chocolate—I realized I'd completely monopolized the conversation since walking through the door. My mother had taught me better manners than that. "I didn't mean to bother you with all this."

Jessica looked tense. Strained, even. Why had I launched into my own problems when she seemed to have a reason to invite me over? Was it possible my perfect sister's life wasn't going so perfectly?

"Hey," I said, touching her hand and feeling a surprising surge of sympathy for her as I gazed at the dark circles under her eyes. "Is everything okay?"

I expected Jessica's usual "Everything's great." I didn't get it. Instead, she pressed her lips together before giving me a quiet "Well, not exactly."

This was a stunner coming from my sister. "What's wrong? Is it anything I can help with?"

She arched her back and rolled her shoulders as if they were sore. "Sort of. It's why I asked you over while the boys were gone."

Jessica and I did not do "girl talk." We weren't sisters who confided in each other. We each confided in Mom, I suppose, but we were both trying not to bother her while she was off rediscovering life with Dad. The chink in Jessica's facade of perfection tugged at me. "Of course I'll help. Whatever you need."

She took a sizable bite of the fig bar—indulgent by her standards. "I'm not sure what I need." After a pained moment, she added, "Honestly, I have no clue what to do about Taylor."

Taylor was an amazing kid. He and his brother seemed to master anything they tried, and the glittering display of trophies on the shelf in their living room proved it. "What about him?"

"He's refusing to try out for travel soccer." She delivered it like the gravest of news. "Hal is furious."

Hal, a baseball star in high school and college, wouldn't take kindly to one of his boys not following in his athletic footsteps. Hal was one of those dads for whom sports had stopped being a game you played for fun a long time ago. I went to one of their T-ball games a few years back and felt nearly ill at the yelling from the sidelines.

"Not every kid wants to play soccer, I suppose." Not exactly profound, but I wasn't quite sure what to say. I've never been a parent, and sports has never meant much to me, either. "I doubt I'm much help to you in this one."

"Actually, you can be. Help, I mean."

"How?"

"Taylor wants to join the art club instead."

Now, this made more sense. I lived in the professional art world. Or had, at least, until the dismantling of Batterson. "That seems good."

"No. It's not. No one gives art scholarships to college. I need you to talk him out of it."

All my sympathy for Jessica evaporated in a puff of smoke. "You're kidding."

"It's not the kind of thing you can make a living at. I mean, haven't you just proved that?"

So now I'm a cautionary tale for soccer-weary nine-year-olds? "Lots of very smart people make their living in arts fields. My boss drove a Mercedes."

"Ex-boss," Jessica corrected.

I tried to swallow my shock and be something close to nice. "Not every male of the species needs to be a jock. Never really been a fan of them, actually. Taylor liking art isn't some kind of character flaw. I can't believe you're asking me to talk him out of this. I was expecting you to ask me to encourage him."

"Encourage him? We can't encourage him in this. Hal would never stand for it."

There was something in the way her voice cracked during that last statement. "Hal would never stand for it," I repeated. "What about you?"

"We are an athletic family." Her declaration had a rehearsed ring to it.

I stared my sister straight in the eye. "Your son is telling you he wants to do something other than athletics. You're not going to listen to him?"

"He's nine. Hal says we can't let him quit just because it's not fun right now."

"Because he's nine and it's not fun is a very good reason to quit. And he's not quitting. He's telling you he'd rather do the art club. You're acting like that's some kind of mistake. The mistake would be not to listen to him, Jessica. I won't help you do that."

"What do you know about parenting?" she shot back.

"Absolutely nothing," I returned, unashamed at my lack of qualifications to back up what I absolutely knew to be true.

Her eyes narrowed. "You won't help me talk Taylor out of this."

"I won't. And if he comes to me, I'll support him." I wanted to go scoop the kid up right now and tell him art was a wonderful place to put his energies. I could just hear the "sissy" terms Hal might use for such an idea.

Jessica snatched back the plate of fig bars and reached her hand out for my coffee mug. I'd clearly lost my welcome here. "Well, don't expect any help from me when Chief Tallen chews you out for bringing him gossip."

I made up my mind right then. "I'm heading over to the police department right now, actually."

"You shouldn't do that." Jessica's eyes flashed. "Don't mess
this up for Mom, Shelby."

So now refusing to ignore what might be important crime
facts was "messing things up for Mom"? Jessica may aspire to
some version of a perfect, glossy life, but I never have. Nor has
Mom. I wasn't going to call Mom and ask her advice on this.
Mostly because I already knew what she'd say.

"Are you kidding me?" I shot back, now sorry I'd come
and any sympathy I'd had for Jessica gone. I don't know why
the mean streak rose up in me with such force, but I never
could stand Jessica telling me what to do, especially when I
thought she was wrong. And she was wrong. Not about everything, but definitely about this. "Maybe because I would go to
Tallen is the reason why Mom asked me to watch the shop and
not you."

It was a low blow. I regretted it the minute I said it, even if
some part of me did feel that way. My big sister was used to
coming out on top in everything she ever did, and I couldn't
escape the sense that parts of her perfect, glossy life were unraveling at the edges. Unbidden, a picture of frayed needlework—with the kind of unraveling that happens when you
don't weave in the ends or tie your waste knots correctly—
came to mind. The front of the canvas would usually look
good, but when you turned it over, you saw all the mess.

Right now, I was seeing mess everywhere.

"You've already signed your statement, Shelby," Tallen said
when I walked into his office half an hour later. "We've got all
we need from you."

"Actually, you don't." I sat down in the chief's guest chair.
His office was surprisingly homey for a police chief. Then
again, when your wife is the town mayor, I suppose some dec-

orating privileges come with the pairing. Was it a conflict of interest or a smart alliance to have a husband-wife mayor–police chief combo? I hoped neither of them would give me Jessica's level of grief for what I was about to share. "Someone came into the shop Friday and told me something I think you need to hear."

"Today's hottest needlepoint tips?"

His wife, Rose, was, in fact, quite a skilled stitcher. A needlepoint version of the town seal graced the wall over the chief's shoulder. "Well, a hot tip of a kind."

"What?"

I told him the story of the mysterious young woman who had refused to give her name and the threats she claimed to have overheard.

He listened politely but shook his head when I finished. "Shelby, I thought we went over this. And I can't treat third-party hearsay—especially from someone who won't even come forward herself—as credible evidence. My daughter works there and tells me employees gossip all the time, especially about Leydon and his son. I'm sorry you've been dragged into this, but you need to tamp down your imagination here."

I didn't care for the way his words echoed Jessica's. "I didn't imagine what she said to me. She came to me. Why lie about something like that? And doesn't the fact that she's afraid for her job tell you Windham might be the kind of person to do something drastic?"

Tallen pinched the bridge of his nose. "Leydon is a lot of things—like a pain in my wife's side for any number of reasons—but he didn't murder Kat Katsaros."

"How do you know?"

"Because *no one* murdered Kat Katsaros. Not that I should be discussing the details with you, but the coroner's been all over this, and there's almost no sign of foul play."

I caught that one word. "Almost?"

"Well, she's never seen someone impaled by a knife thrown from a poorly used sharpener before, so we're short on precedent, but she knows what she's doing. Believe me when I tell you *there's nothing here.*" His exasperated tone softened. "It's sad, and I know you two were friends. Have you ever thought that maybe the trauma of finding her is twisting your judgment here?"

How do you respond to something like that? If I say, "It's possible," then Tallen can dismiss anything I've just said. If I say, "Absolutely not," then I come off as someone in denial of their emotional state. I hesitated for a moment, trying not to grind my teeth together. When I spoke, I kept my words as calm and level as my rising frustration would allow. "Of course I understand that what's happened affects me and how I view things. But I can't figure out why no one is even willing to entertain the possibility that this bizarre accident wasn't an accident. She had plenty of enemies, and I've not been able to uncover a single incident of a knife impaling someone this way."

That may not have been the wisest admission. Tallen's eyebrows furrowed down. "Been conducting your own investigation, have you?"

"Wouldn't you?"

"Yes, because it's *my job.*" He gave the last two words an edge worthy of Kat's Kutz. He steepled his hands on his desk. "So that's how this woman knew you were in Windham's? Because you were in asking questions of Leydon?"

"I went in to see what it was about the place that had bothered Kat so much. Why she was so vocal about her dislike of the store."

"And what did you find out?"

He was humoring me, I knew that. But at least I'd get a chance to tell him what I'd learned, so I was willing to swallow the condescension—for now. "Windham's sells the kind of knife that . . ." I still stumbled on the word. "Impaled her."

Tallen gave a slight nod. "Makes sense. High-end stuff."

"Did you know that if you buy a Bour du Chef knife from Windham's, you can bring it back to get it sharpened for free? For life? In fact, you can bring any knife you buy there back for sharpening for free. Seems rather deliberately aimed to squash Kat's business, don't you think? I went in and bought three Bour du Chef knives just to see if it really was true, and it is."

Tallen's sigh dripped with annoyance. "That's not an attempt to squash Kat's business. It seems a perfectly reasonable service for a high-end department store housewares department to offer."

"Ah, but it's the *only* service like that they offer," I went on. "Not luggage or watch repair or even jewelry cleaning. That's awfully specific, don't you think? And banning Kat from the store? Permanently? What went on between those two?"

"Kat was very disruptive. She harassed customers. And staged protests from her van in the store parking lot. I'd been called there on her account. More than once."

I pointed at the chief. "So there. They were enemies. That's motive, isn't it?"

His eyes grew narrow. "Being angry—justifiably angry, I might add—with someone does not mean you murdered them. Or that they were murdered."

"But it could," I countered. I had no idea whether Leydon had sunk that knife into Kat's chest. I wasn't even sure I wanted to know if something so disturbing had happened. I just needed someone to be at least considering the possibility. It was making me crazy to think I was the only one seeing these connections.

Tallen pulled out a piece of paper. "If I promise to put a note in the file about this supposed threat you've been told about, will you stop playing junior detective and let the professionals handle the situation?"

As long as the chief was in the mood to make deals, the idea for a counteroffer popped into my head. "Would you allow the coroner to talk to me and explain how she knows—or why she thinks—the sharpener could have thrown the knife at Kat and killed her?" If the chief wanted me to "drop it," knowing the answer to that question would go a long way toward my doing so.

"You're serious."

A hefty dose of facts might shut down the storm in my imagination. I needed to be getting a better quality of sleep, that's for sure. "It's what's been bugging me. If I can just get that settled in my mind, I'll be out of your hair."

Given that Chief Tallen was bald, that may not have been the best choice of phrase. He registered the poor metaphor the same moment I did. This meeting wasn't going to end on a high note, but I was in no mood to have Jessica proven right. I held my ground as he considered what I was sure was the strangest request of his day. Maybe even his month.

He pressed his lips together, then pushed out a breath. "You have your father's stubborn spirit."

I wasn't expecting that remark. "I guess I do."

Tallen pulled open a desk drawer. "This is highly unusual—*highly*—but on account of how much I like your mom and dad, and that Dr. Masters is a friend, I'll ask her if she'll talk to you. But this needs to be where this ends, Shelby." He handed me a tattered business card for Dr. Anna Masters, county coroner. "If Anna says no, it stops there. Don't make me regret this."

"I won't."

CHAPTER 14

I didn't need to be at the store until noon on Tuesday, so I spent the morning buying cat supplies and one of those carpeted "cat condos" for Nabbit to be able to look out the window from a high perch. I did a bit of stitching on my canvas and spent an hour polishing my résumé. I had lunch at CHNO. Anything to spend at least a few hours not pondering Kat Katsaros and her untimely death.

When I finally showed up at the shop, JanLi met me with a look of pleasant surprise. "We sold it all," she declared. "Someone bought the last one of Kat's canvases thirty minutes ago. And there's only one pair of scissors left."

I cast my glance over to where the display sat empty, with only a single pair of scissors lying inside the glass display case. "It's only been ten days since the trunk show. Well, what would have been the trunk show. That was fast." Mom usually said it took a month, sometimes more, to sell out trunk show merchandise.

JanLi's gaze softened. "It's sad that a deceased Kat sells better than a live one, don't you think?"

"Human nature," Tilly said from behind us. She was at the table where the NYAGs were yet again gathered. A short, round woman with bright eyes and gray hair that still hung on to a hint of its former red hue, she was the history buff of the bunch. "How many famous artists were poor as church mice in their lifetimes? Like Bach. Or van Gogh."

"That woman was no van Gogh," Faye muttered.

"I think we should just try and be happy we were able to get her work into the hands of people who appreciate it," I said.

"And maybe help Cal out, too." Tilly shook her head. "He seems like such a lost soul."

"George seems to think of him as a lost cause," Faye added, cutting off a thread with a decisive snip. "Did you hear him at the yacht club memorial?"

Hard not to. We'd all heard how they snapped at each other.

"All the more reason to lend the boy a hand." Tilly looked at me. "Does he have more? We shouldn't let any of it go to waste."

"I suppose it's worth asking." It was. Even with the consignment fees paid to Cal, the postmortem version of this trunk show had put the month into a very successful column for the store. I still wasn't sure how I felt about that. I didn't want anyone to think the Needle was profiting off of someone's misery.

"You don't have to ask," JanLi said, holding up a note. "He called this morning and asked if you wanted to come over to Kat's apartment and pick out more things to sell. He asked for your cell number, but I wasn't sure I should give it to him. So I just took the message."

"Didn't your mother tell me Cal was sweet on you in school?" Tilly asked.

I hadn't heard anyone put it quite that way outside of an old-fashioned movie. "Sort of," I admitted.

"Well, then, make sure you call him back from the shop phone," JanLi advised.

"And maybe take someone with you when you go over there," Faye added. "Maybe Jake London."

I'd forgotten how you can barely blink in a town like Gwen

Lake without someone seeing you. And talking about it. One of the reasons I had fled to Savannah was how gossip spread like a wildfire here.

"I'll be fine," I assured them. "But yes, I'll use the shop phone. In fact, I need to make a few other calls, so I'll be in the office for a bit." I wanted to follow up with Anna Masters before Chief Tallen had a chance to change his mind.

I sat down at the office computer and fired up the inventory software I'd had a chance to break in with Kat's merchandise. Mom did most things on sheer retail instinct, but I liked having hard data to back up decisions. After a few minutes of analysis, I learned the shop had made more on Kat's canvases than on the high-priced scissors. Still, the scissors were exclusive. They were also the kind of thing a stitcher's friend could buy as a gift without needing to know a lot about a needle pointer's taste or skill. It's always a smart move to have those kinds of items in any craft shop. "Husband-ware" Mom used to call it, although she boasted several skilled male customers. She could just have easily called it "Daughter-ware" or "Sister-ware" or "Friend-ware" and been accurate.

I calculated the store could easily bring in thirty more canvases and half a dozen pairs of scissors, offer Cal a consignment 5 percent higher than that on his first batch of items, and still come out admirably. A glow kindled in my chest at being able to apply my business skills to Mom's shop. The smart, capable feeling I got staring at that report was a gift. A potent antidote to the paltry unemployment check and Jessica's barbs the other day.

Riding off my data high, I dialed the county coroner's office. I expected a receptionist or at least a bureaucratic phone tree, but a friendly woman picked up the line. "Coroner's office. Masters here."

I don't know why the thought *She sounds so nice for someone who works with dead people* came to me. After all, the woman who made the most beautiful graphics at Batterson was the meanest employee we had.

"Hello, Dr. Masters. I'm Shelby Phillips. Chief Tallen told me I could call you about Gina Katsaros."

Her tone sharpened. "Are you a reporter?"

"No. I'm the person who found her. We were friends in high school." This seemed like an okay time to use that term, despite the way it still poked me in the gut.

"I'm sorry you had to go through that. Nasty business. How can I help?"

"I have some questions I'm hoping you can answer. Some things are bugging me, Dr. Masters."

She gave a small laugh. It was a compassionate laugh, not a mocking one. "You can call me Anna. And I think a lot of things would bug me if I found my high school friend with a knife in her chest. I'm limited as to some things, but I'll answer what I can. People tend to need answers when something like this happens. Sometimes I've got them. Other times I don't."

I realized I hadn't thought through exactly what questions I wanted to ask. I didn't think "Could she have been murdered?" was a good starter, so I opted for "I can't quite see how it happened. I mean, how could the machine have thrown the knife with enough force to . . ." *Stab* didn't want to come out of my mouth.

"Cause a lethal wound like that?" she said, finishing for me.

"Yes."

I heard the squeak of an office chair, as if she was leaning back. "Well, I admit, this is a first for me. Knife sharpener is an uncommon profession, and Ms. Katsaros used . . . shall we say . . . vintage equipment. There is a safety shield that usually goes on one of those, but hers had been removed. Mr. Katsaros tells me his daughter wasn't much for safety precautions."

I tried to think of a way to press the issue. "Wouldn't the knife have had to be going really fast? With lots of force?"

"Not necessarily. The knife was extraordinarily sharp, and it hit at just the right angle. An inch or two to either side and it would have struck bone and not been able to penetrate so deeply."

I recalled the terrible detail of the knife having sunk to its hilt in Kat's chest. "So just the right place—or, in this case, just the wrong place."

"You could say that. That very sharp knife severed a large artery, which is why there was so much blood."

"There was a lot of blood." I looked down at my hand, as if I expected the smear would somehow reappear.

"Look, Shelby, I'm not sure all these details are going to be helpful to you."

"No, no, they are," I replied. "It all seems like such a freakish, near-impossible thing."

"I agree. This ranks up there with my most unusual cases. And she was young and quite talented, as I understand it."

"She was. It's so sad. I can't stop thinking about it." My morning of diversions hadn't been very successful—I had kept thinking about Kat as I'd done all the things that were supposed to keep my mind off her.

"Has Chief Tallen suggested you see a trauma counselor? It might be a good idea if you are having trouble processing what's happened."

"I think I'm okay," I replied. "Getting my questions answered is helping."

"If it's any comfort," Anna went on, "she died relatively quickly. The body goes numb with wounds like this, so she probably didn't suffer much. I don't see any signs of struggle. Does that help?"

No signs of struggle didn't point to an attack. But if Kat didn't see it coming . . .

"Anna, I really feel like I need to ask this. Is there any possibility that this wasn't . . . accidental?"

There was a long pause on the other end of the line. "Are you asking me if it's possible Ms. Katsaros was murdered?" The words were slow and careful.

"I guess I am."

Another pause. "That's not a question you ought to be asking."

"Chief Tallen says that. But I can't help it." I almost spilled the beans about my mystery woman from Windham's but held back.

"I'm not treating this as a murder case."

That seemed like a slightly evasive answer to me. "So you're ruling it out?"

"I wouldn't be much of a coroner if I ruled things out without clear evidence to back it up. Is there something I should know?"

Tallen's warning blared from the back of my mind. "People didn't like her. She had a lot of enemies."

"I know that. And I'm telling you, I'm not treating this as a murder case."

"Would you tell me if you were?"

She paused again—something I found rather telling. "No, I wouldn't." Her sigh sounded too much like Tallen's. "Let the police do their job. Television lets everyone think they're an evidence tech or a rogue cop—and there isn't anything to chase here. You sound like a nice person, Shelby. A caring person. So take my advice and do what you need to in order to move past this. It's best for everyone, including you."

I did not take Anna's advice.

I also did not invite Jake to serve as my unnecessary bodyguard when I met Cal in front of Kat's apartment the next day.

I did, however, phone Deb and let her know where I was and tell her that if I did not call her within a few hours, she should worry. This felt like the right balance between sensible and paranoid. Besides, Cal needed me to continue our business deal—kidnapping me would only cut off his cash supply.

"Hey," he said when he met me in the apartment's small parking lot. His sheepish tone seemed odd from a man of his size.

"Hello, Cal. How are you doing?"

His chin jutted out. "My sister's dead, and my dad's being a jerk about it. How do you think I'm doing?"

Despite the fact that Cal could have behaved better at the memorial, I could only imagine how a public dismissal like his father had given him stung. Cal had to sense how everybody had been talking about it since then—and not kindly.

He lumbered ahead of me up the driveway, then stopped to glare at the Kat's Kutz van. "That should be mine," he grumbled.

I could only shrug. "Maybe they can't release it for police reasons." That felt safer than asserting my stubborn belief that it might be a crime scene.

"No," he said, "I mean it should have been mine *all along*. It was my idea, you know. I thought it up years ago. She jumped on it before I had the chance. I was gonna do it. Really."

The Cal I remembered was "gonna do" a lot of things but never could get around to actually *doing* any of them.

I offered a pleasant smile. "Let's go in and see what we can do with the pieces your sister left behind. They're selling incredibly well. Thank you for giving the store the opportunity." I hoped a little compliment would prevent this from dissolving into an emotional purging. Cal seemed to teeter between grief and anger each moment. Perhaps that wasn't unusual for someone in his position. I certainly waffled between wanting to know more and itching to put it all behind me. Kat's ghost, it seemed, cast a long shadow.

For all of Kat's edgy style, her apartment was tidy and downright cozy. I shouldn't have been surprised at the stunning collection of knives in her kitchen, but I did notice that none of them bore the bright blue Bour du Chef logo on their hilts.

The one nod to her Gothic tendencies was the full-sized suit of armor in one corner of her living room. The pair of long-handled axes he bore hinted at her logo and looked eerily sharp.

Cal noticed me staring. "That's Edgar. She bought him at the Renaissance Festival with the first cash she made from selling her scissors. Come on. The stuff's in here."

The way he said "stuff" had none of the respect I heard stitchers display when referring to canvases or tools. It's not stuff. Cal seemed to view Kat's work not as art but just as a means to quick cash. Again, all the more reason to seize the chance to put this "stuff" into the hands of those who would appreciate it. Puffed up as it sounds, I really did feel a sort of noble obligation to her memory. Fate had handed me a chance to make up for how I'd treated her in our earlier days, and I wanted to make sure I took it. I kept trying to keep my focus on Kat's art and her talent rather than obsessing over the thought she might have been murdered. It wasn't really working.

Cal led me through a hallway to a pair of back rooms that served as Kat's studio. In the first room a vibrant but darker version of the rainbow that was on the Needle shop floor met my eyes. It was like a film noir rainbow: blacks and purples and burgundies filled the canvases, with pops of white and silver. Her style, her personality, fairly leapt off all the canvases in this room. You would be able to pick out her work in a sea of other canvases immediately.

"Wow," I exclaimed, at a loss for a better comment. "This is all hers?"

Of course it was, but it was still shocking to see the sheer volume of Kat's artistic output. It was easy to see why she had hoped to take over the Needle—she had needed an outlet for all this.

"Told you there was a lot more. And we haven't even gotten to the scissors."

The second room was a workshop, complete with metals, soldering irons, and a bunch of other implements I couldn't name. On the wall hung easily two dozen sets of scissors, including several pairs that topped two hundred dollars.

"Lotta cash in here, huh?" Cal said at my wide-eyed expression.

Could he really not see the beauty in what his sister did? How could anyone look at all this and not be impressed at Kat's talent? I certainly was. *I like this Kat*, I thought, now finding my initial awkwardness at the shop silly and judgmental. I wished I'd known this Kat. Why hadn't I seen her or known her in high school?

"How much of it can you sell?"

"All of it, I'm sure," I replied. "Just not all at once. We're going to have to spread it out a bit. This much stock could last us six months, to be honest."

Cal's face fell. "That long?"

My business sense kicked in with an explanation. "These kinds of things need to be paced right. High-end products need to feel exclusive, special." I removed one of the top-end scissors from its hook on the wall, marveling at its beauty. The crisscross design was visible in the engraving on one handle. Given the sore spot the doubloons were for Cal, I chose not to say anything. "I know you want maximum dollars for these, so it'll take a bit of strategizing."

It wasn't the answer he was hoping for. Cal Katsaros was not a strategy guy. He was more the "whack it into submission" type. "If you say so . . . Could we just put the whole lot up on the Internet or something?"

That was exactly what I hoped to avoid by coming here. That type of fire sale did no good for Kat, Cal, or the Needle. "I hope you know you can trust me to do this right. You don't want to just throw everything up on the Net. Kat deserves better." I gestured at the collection of amazing tools around us. "All this deserves better."

He shrugged. "If you say so," he repeated.

"Why don't we pick out another twenty pieces for me to bring back to the shop tonight. I'll have a consignment agreement ready for you to sign, with prices, by lunchtime tomorrow."

He wasn't a fan of that idea. "Why don't you just take it all now. It's not like I want it." He picked up a box on her desk that looked like a treasure chest. "Take all her stuff."

I furrowed a brow. "I'm not sure that's legal, Cal."

He set the box back down and then flailed one of his big hands in the air. "Dad told me I could do whatever I wanted with any of it. Except the van." His voice grew sharp. "He wants to keep that from me." He looked out the window at the Kat's Kutz van in the driveway and muttered a string of curses.

This family really was a mess. I wasn't sure I wanted to get in the middle of it, either.

"How about I just take some things now and we come back later?" I offered.

Cal tossed the apartment keys to me. "Whatever. Just call me when you've got some money. And make it fast."

With that, he turned and headed for the door and banged it shut behind him.

I stood in the middle of Kat's workshop, a bit stumped as to what I ought to do next. How had I gotten to be so enmeshed in Kat's life? In her death? It felt spooky—and then a bit fateful—that I was here in her home, among her art. The nagging sense that I'd somehow been chosen to handle this, to be the one to find her, refused to leave me no matter how illogical it was. Kat's death felt like something that had been *placed in my path*.

I began by selecting the twenty items I thought would sell well and at the high price points Cal was seeking. After an hour, I had a box of her top-end scissors and a selection of canvases in several sizes and with various themes.

All the while I was choosing, my eye kept wandering back to the treasure chest Cal had picked up. All this pirate/treasure/maritime stuff was so very odd. If we were on the coastal side of North Carolina, I could see it. But here, near the mountains? It seemed out of place. Still, the doubloon tradition had clearly meant something to Kat if she used a stylized version of the back of the coin in so much of her work.

I let my curiosity get the better of my shame over snooping and lifted the lid of the treasure chest. It held a collection of odd mementos: dried flowers and threads and such. Some photos of a much younger Kat with her mother made my heart pinch—how hard it must have been to grow up with a dad like that and no mother.

A beautifully stitched buttoned pouch sat at the bottom of the chest, and it crackled and jingled as I picked it up. I unbuttoned to open it up and found a dozen folded pieces of paper.

And two doubloons.

CHAPTER 15

Kat had doubloons? Not one, but two?

Two doubloons her father didn't know about? Ones her father hadn't given her?

Clearly, Cal didn't know these were here, either, or I suspect he'd have snatched them up. Or maybe not. They weren't worth much to anyone outside Gwen Lake.

So who had given these two to her? And why?

Despite the small itch of conscience on the back of my neck, I fanned out the papers on the desk and picked up the top one.

> *My dear Gina,*
>
> *I miss you. I miss what we could be together, what it would be like to walk over the lake bridge with my arm around you for everyone to see. We both know that day won't come, but I'm content with what we have. I know I'm keeping you from someone who could be everything you should have. Everything you deserve. But I'm too selfish. I like to think I make you happy. You're so dark and sad for someone who makes all that beauty. I guess we both know how life can cut to the bone, huh?*
>
> *It's too long until we spend time together again. Soon, I promise.*
>
> *Love,*
>
> *B*

Reading a dead woman's love letters was spooky enough that I jumped when the wind knocked a branch against the window. I gazed around the room, unsure what to do with what I'd just learned.

Kat had been in a relationship. Actually, from the details in two more of the letters, it was easy to speculate that Kat had been having an affair. I couldn't be certain, of course, but B's words spoke of having to keep their love a secret. And it was a pretty good guess that B was from Gwen Lake. I didn't think there were any nonlocal members of the yacht club, and I didn't think anyone else had doubloons to give away. Then again, I had one now, didn't I?

Ah, but *did* the doubloons come from B? Given that they were in the same box as the letters, it made sense that they had, but I couldn't be sure. Who was B? Why the need for such secrecy? Were they his doubloons? Was I even sure B was male? And why two coins? Suddenly I had dozens more questions than I'd had an hour ago.

I didn't feel right leaving this treasure chest and its contents in the open, where Cal or George could find it. And to be honest, my curiosity was raging about Kat and B, whoever B was. In a wild thought, I wished the world still used telephone books, so I could pore through the Gwen Lake or other local editions for every person with a first name beginning with the letter *B*. Then again, did I have a right to know B's identity?

Given that I seemed to be the only person in Gwen Lake willing to consider Kat hadn't met her end by accident, maybe I did. "Lots of people have been murdered for love," I pronounced to the empty room, then nearly laughed at the absurdity of it.

Before I could talk myself out of it, I put the treasure chest in the box with Kat's other items, turned out the lights, left the apartment, and double-checked to be sure the apartment door was locked behind me. A chill raced down my back as I passed the van, the sharp lines of Kat's logo jabbing at my composure. I wished I'd done this during the daytime. It was only early evening and the sun was just setting, but I swear it felt like midnight.

My brain was running in too many circles for me to go back to my little apartment above the shop. I always did my best thinking and problem solving aloud, but Nabbit wasn't enough of a companion for something as stupefying as this.

Still, I had to be careful. Kat's possible affair with someone in Gwen Lake was explosive stuff. People might get hurt depending on how and where the suspicion got out. I wasn't sure I had the right to defile her memory like that. What was the old saying about letting sleeping dogs lie? And if George and Cal heard even a whiff of such a scandal, they did not seem like the kind of people to be calm about any of it.

Unless . . . One thought occurred to me. What if George had secretly given both the doubloons to Kat, withholding one of them from Cal? Cruel, yes, but George Katsaros seemed the kind of man to show that kind of blatant favoritism. Still, that didn't make sense given the way George had acted at the memorial. I also couldn't assume the coins and the letters were connected—they could both be treasured items she had kept in that box.

Now what?

I'd been gone too long from Gwen Lake to make any sense of what I'd just learned. I couldn't call Mom or Dad. I didn't dare drop a bomb like this on Jessica. Chief Tallen would give me a long lecture about snooping and jumping to conclusions. Where was I supposed to turn?

I got my answer when I drove past CHNO and saw the lights on.

Deb's warm smile as she opened the door was welcome after the chilling events of the evening.

"Sorry. I know you're closed."

"Only just. I'm taking care of some tedious stock stuff, so the company's good." She eyed me as she ushered me into the shop. "Besides, you look like you've just seen a ghost."

I managed a weak laugh. "Sort of accurate, actually." I looked around the shop, glad to see a collection of teas amid Deb's high-voltage brews. "Got anything calming?"

"Ever heard of the big coffee chain's 'horse tranquilizer' drink?"

"Yeah," I replied. "Several of the insomniac IT guys at Batterson swore by it."

She grinned. "Mine's better." She reached for three of the canisters behind the counter. "What's happened?"

As she brewed a tea for me and a coffee for herself, I told her what I'd found at Kat's apartment. I dialed down my description of Cal's cash-hungry bitterness, figuring I owed him the benefit of the doubt and wanting to steer clear of blame casting just yet.

"Plus," I added, taking a deep breath, "you should probably know something."

She set the pair of steaming mugs down in the booth opposite the counter and we sat down. This shop was certainly Deb's calling—she had a gift for making people feel at ease and welcome. I surely needed the welcome of a trustworthy friend at the moment. "What should I know?"

"I . . . There's a big part of me that thinks it's possible Kat's death wasn't an accident."

That got her attention. "You mean like . . . sabotage?"

I made myself say it. "I mean like murder. I can't shake the notion that the knife that . . . did her in . . . didn't get there by that machine. I think she could have been stabbed."

Her eyes widened. "Seriously? Why? How? Have you told Tallen?"

"He laughed me off. And I don't have any real evidence . . . yet. Just that a lot of people didn't like her. I did a little bit of research, and I can't see how the sharpening machine could have thrown the knife that way. And the knife? A Bour du Chef, which might have come from Windham's. Someone came into the shop and told me they had heard Leydon Windham threaten Shelby. That's an awful lot of weird coincidences, don't you think?"

She looked understandably skeptical. "Coincidences aren't evidence, Shelby."

Suddenly I felt slightly ridiculous. "I just wish Tallen was even considering it."

"Maybe he is, and he just can't tell you about it. Or there just isn't enough to go on." I could see her scientific brain pondering the facts. "I'm not sure there is."

I decided to tell Deb everything. "There's more, actually. I found letters. Love letters. To her from someone who signed themselves B. *I'm sorry, Kat*, I lamented in my mind. *I'm trying to help. I'll be as careful as I can.*

"*B?*"

"Yes. And they were being very secretive about it. There was someone—I don't know who—who could cause a lot of trouble if they knew. So I'm thinking it may have been that Kat was having an affair with a married man."

"But who?" Deb asked.

"Well, that's the big question, isn't it? I can't exactly go around asking everyone with a *B* at the beginning of their name if they are . . . were . . . having a secret affair with Kat. And even if I could figure out who, that doesn't mean they were the murderer." The words were sour and serious when I spoke them. What had been a far-fetched notion was starting to solidify into an unsettling possibility: Kat was murdered.

"Unless it does." Deb's face formed an expression I had come to recognize as her "analyzing face." Not an expression of disbelief, but one of serious pondering. I realized the untightening sensation in my chest was relief at the notion that I wasn't alone in my thinking. Someone else now considered it possible that Kat hadn't met an accidental death.

She pointed at me. "What about the doubloons? Are they connected? You found them together."

I sank my chin in one hand. "I have no idea," I replied. "George?"

"Can I see them?" Deb asked.

I ducked out to the car, grabbed the chest from the box of Kat's work, and returned to the shop to set it on the booth table between us. My stomach did a small, nervous flip as I sat down, opened the little treasure chest, and showed her the coins.

"Well," she said as she peered at the doubloons, "I can tell you these didn't come from George."

"How do you know?" The coins looked just like the one my father had given me.

"They're silver. Commodores get gold ones. Well, not actual gold, just gold colored."

I hadn't noticed the distinction until Deb pointed it out. "So they could be from *B*. I mean, they're supposed to be special gifts, so you don't hand them out to just anyone, right?"

I recalled the casual way I'd dismissed the one my father gave me. If he'd been hurt by the way I probably rolled my eyes at the odd tradition, he'd hid it. I made a mental note to apologize again in person when he returned.

"*B*'s a good guess. People don't hand these out casually. Guess it means they are . . . were serious."

Something in her face made me ask, "Has anyone ever given you one?" I immediately regretted the blunder. "I'm sorry. That was a thoughtless thing to ask." After all, in Gwen Lake it was tantamount to asking, "Does anyone care that much about you?"

Deb didn't seem bothered. "My parents weren't from here. And while I appreciate the sentiment, I do find the whole thing a bit silly. Maritime traditions four hundred miles from the Atlantic Ocean? Who would have thought?"

I pointed to the crisscross design on the coins. "This shows up all over Kat's work. I don't think she found it silly at all. I think she was really hurt by how her dad withheld the coin from her, so she put the design in her work to make up for it. Cal says she didn't care, but this box says otherwise to me."

"I know creative people can be sensitive, but I admire them. I can formulate a theory or a process, but art? I'm not sure I've got it in me."

I thought about my nephew Taylor and how his own artistic yearnings were getting soundly squashed. "I think everybody has art in them. Just different kinds. You have to discover it." An idea came to me. "I think you'd like needlepoint. It's specific, can be simple or complex, and working a canvas is like following a formula. I'd forgotten how relaxing it can be until I picked it up again recently."

Deb cast her eyes out the coffee-shop window in the direction of the Needle. Mom always talked about what it was like to introduce someone to the idea that they could create and how she lived for those moments. Watching the small glimmer of *Really?* that played in Deb's eyes, I began to see where Mom's passion for new stitchers came from. It wasn't just new sales—it was new possibilities.

"Why don't you come over to the shop tomorrow and pick out one of Kat's designs? Or any design you like? We've got a bunch of small coffee cup pieces, and I know JanLi would help you work *CHNO* onto one of them."

Deb pressed her lips together for a moment. "I'll need your help. I don't have any idea what I'm doing."

Gratitude for being able to return Deb's hospitality filled me. "Come on over tomorrow night. We can get together. We'll be a younger, cooler version of the NYAGs."

"The NYAGs?"

"Those ladies—Mom's friends—who hang out at the shop. They call themselves the NYAGs."

Deb raised one eyebrow. "Which stands for . . . ?"

"Not Your Average Grannies. And believe me, they aren't. Anyone who thinks needlepoint is some stuffy, old-fashioned hobby should spend ten minutes with the NYAGs. Dot was stitching up a pillow yesterday with a phrase I wouldn't utter around my nephews."

Deb laughed, and I felt more of the earlier darkness slough off my shoulders. "I guess I need to rethink my position on needlepoint." After a pause, she added, "And maybe on Kat's death."

I had an ally. It wasn't Tallen—and I wasn't sure it would ever be Tallen—but at least I wasn't alone. "I believe she was murdered, Deb. I don't know how I'm going to prove it, or how I'm going to convince Tallen, but I have to. Even though it'll be an uphill battle."

"With the big feature in that magazine coming up, it will be. This is the worst time ever for Gwen Lake's first murder." Deb pushed out a breath. "Rose would give him no end of grief, especially if the press got any wind of it."

"That can't matter. Justice needs to count for something. Even if it's inconvenient . . . or poor publicity. Kat deserves it."

She sat back in the booth. "I agree. But you've got no proof."

"I have lots of things," I muttered into my tea, "but none of them are proof. Not yet, anyway." I kept waiting for the fragrant brew to soothe my nerves, but it wasn't happening.

"So then, keep looking," Deb declared. "Find something to bring to Tallen that you know he'll take seriously."

I eyed her. "In other words, go amateur sleuth on this."

"Yes."

I managed to crack a small smile. "And here I thought needlepoint was my new hobby."

"Well, in this case—literally *in this case*—they go together."

And so it was that I became the unofficial champion of justice for a murdered Kat Katsaros. Where does that go on a résumé?

CHAPTER 16

Jessica walked into the shop the next morning and pushed her phone into my face. "Did you see this?"

"Oh, I saw it."

I had. Mom had sent the slightly mortifying photo to Jessica and me at the same time. I had nearly spit out my coffee on my kitchen counter when I saw it. Mom and Dad had renewed their wedding vows last night. At an Elvis chapel in Las Vegas. I'd wanted to shout, "Who are you people, and what have you done to my parents?" at the phone image.

Still, they were grown adults, and I didn't see where I had any say in the matter, despite the recoil that still sat in the pit of my stomach. "I guess they're having fun," I offered weakly.

"You're not embarrassed by this?" Jessica snapped the leather cover on her phone shut with a huff. "Dad's wearing a white leather jacket. And that veil looks like it came from the chapel gift shop."

"It probably did," I replied. "Look, it's a bit"—I searched for a positive term—"whimsical, but wasn't that the whole point of this trip? For Mom and Dad to do whatever they wanted?"

Jessica sat down in one of the chairs ringing the shop gathering table. "I was thinking more along the lines of the Grand Canyon. A couple of state parks. Some charming bed-and-breakfasts. That sort of thing."

I sat down opposite my sister just as Leona came through the shop door. We were due to open in fifteen minutes. "Look, I have enough friends whose parents' marriages have dissolved into nasty divorces. Maybe we should just be thankful ours still want to double down on theirs."

"Like *that*?" Jessica nodded toward her phone.

"Like what?" Leona asked.

Despite the *Don't* look Jessica gave me, I swiped to the screen on my own phone that held the photo in question and showed it to Leona.

"Oh my." Leona giggled at the image. "Guess you've got the shot for this year's Christmas card."

Jessica sank her forehead into her hands. "They wouldn't."

"No," I assured her, "I don't think they will. They're just having fun. I bet half the reason Dad agreed to it was because he knew it would make us moan."

Jessica moaned, as if to prove my point. She's never been the lighthearted one in the family. If you ask me, my sister cares way too much about what other people think. "I've never been more grateful neither of them does social media."

I couldn't resist. "The shop's got a page . . ."

The look she shot me could have frozen Gwen Lake.

"That reminds me," Leona said as she began opening the register system. "Rose is stopping in this morning. It's the Needle's turn to offer up the monthly Shop Gwen Lake Prize, and she wants to know what we're doing."

I blinked at Leona. "Should I know this?"

Jessica looked slightly alarmed. "Mom didn't set that up before she left?"

Leona turned the CLOSED sign on the shop door to OPEN. "It's promotion. Maybe she thought you'd be good at handling it. You've got to come up with some kind of game or deal. Every month a different shop pulls together some sort of giveaway or discount."

I turned to my sister. "What did Mom do last time?"

Jessica answered, "She designed a little Christmas ornament kit with the lake bridge on it. Rose will expect something exclusive."

"We don't have time to design anything special like that." I scanned the shop. "Can we just do a giveaway?"

Jessica stood up. "You might get away with that, as long as it's something special. Rose will have high expectations."

Aren't you the high expectations expert in this family? I thought. Still, if I was supposed to be running the shop, it fell on me to come up with a prize idea. And I was sure I could figure out something—just not in the next ten minutes.

Even though the speed with which Jessica stuffed her phone into her handbag told me otherwise, I asked, "Wanna stay and help?"

"I have spin class."

She wasn't dressed for an exercise class, but this wasn't an argument worth having. "Well, okay. I'll handle the mayor and whatever she wants." As I followed Jessica to the door, I ventured, "How's the Taylor thing going?"

A momentary lost look filled her eyes before the standard-issue Jessica perfection face slid back over her features. "Later."

The answer told me things were not going well for my nephew. Maybe I should invent some reason why he should come spend the afternoon at the shop or my apartment. I could just imagine the kind of pressure Hal was putting on him. Hal was the only person who exceeded Jessica in the high expectations department. Those boys weren't even ten. How would he handle the teen years? College applications? I felt a sympathetic tug on my Aunt Shelby heart.

"Okay, later," I said, risking a quick touch to Jessica's arm just as she was heading out the door. "I want to help." I really did. I just wasn't sure Hal would appreciate the kind of help I'd give.

I followed her for a few steps until we both spied Mayor

Tallen coming down the block. Jessica turned in the opposite direction and took off as if she really *was late* for spin class.

"Shelby!" Rose Tallen barked. It was more of a command than a greeting.

Rose Tallen had been the phys ed teacher back when I was in grade school, and she had never needed a whistle with that voice. I nearly jumped at the sound from sheer muscle memory. She held out a hand when she reached me. "Well. Here you are. Nina's daughter running the shop." Her tone cut such an edge between admiration and doubt that I didn't know how she felt about it.

"Only for a while," I amended as we walked into the shop together. After all, it didn't really matter how Mayor Tallen felt about my stint as interim manager. "Just until they get back."

"Well." I quickly remembered how Mrs. Tallen—as I knew her back then—started nearly every sentence with the word *well*. "No one really knows if they're coming back, now, do we? I mean that photo. Elvis?"

Oh no. Mom hadn't really shared that shot outside Jessica and me, had she? Feeling like a life-size facepalm emoji, I replied, "They sure look like they're having fun. But of course they're coming back." I didn't feel the certainty of that statement. The remote possibility that Mom and Dad would decide to adopt the nomad lifestyle permanently squeezed my chest tight.

I opted to move the conversation forward. "How can I help you today, Mrs. Tallen?"

She huffed and waved her hand. "I think we're past the Mrs. Tallen stage of things, aren't we? You must be past thirty by now." She said it as if my age was a surprising outcome.

"Thirty-one, actually." She'd been a master of intimidation in school, and she hadn't lost her touch.

"Well, you should call me Rose. Adult to adult and all. Or Mayor Rose works, too." Her forced grin seemed designed to make me feel affirmed. I think. Mom said she and Rose didn't always see eye to eye, so maybe the mayor thought my tenure was a chance to get the Needle on her good side.

"Okay, then, Mayor Rose." It felt too weird to address her just as Rose. "What can I do for you?"

"Well, of course you know about the monthly Shop Gwen Lake promotion."

I do now. "Of course."

"It's the shop's turn to offer the prize. And with the upcoming tourism press . . ."

She gave those last words so much emphasis I wondered if she wasn't putting unrealistic weight on one magazine article.

"I haven't heard what the shop is doing to contribute." She pinned me with a gaze worthy of *You didn't turn in your homework.*

"I'm sorry. Mom didn't leave any instructions for me. But I'm sure we can pull something together. When do you need to know?"

Rose's eyes pinched at the corners. "Last Friday."

"Things have been a little hectic since Mom left. I'm sure time just got away from her before the trip." And then there was the little complication of Kat's death. Realizing I had no parameters to go on, I asked, "What kinds of things do businesses usually offer?"

"Unique value. Something exclusive. Something to generate excitement. It's an opportunity for Nina's Nimble Needle to affirm its commitment to Gwen Lake." Translation: *Don't mess this up.*

Wanting to see how she'd react, I asked, "Would you consider some of the pieces we have from Kat Katsaros? They're quite beautiful and in high demand."

The pinch that had started near her eyes now took over her whole face. "Well, of course not. I mean . . . she's . . . deceased. It's macabre, don't you think?"

I wasn't too surprised at the reaction. "Perhaps something else, then."

"Yes. Definitely something else."

"Can I get back to you next Wednesday?"

Rose frowned, as if this were a monumental inconvenience. "I suppose if you think you need to take that long."

"It is Easter weekend, so we've got things going on that I need to take care of. And, of course, I want to make sure whatever we offer is special." Both of those things were true, but I also just needed to buy myself some time. Maybe talk to Mom. In fact, I had an idea forming in my brain. A set of prizes that might give me a chance to do some very casual, innocent-looking investigating.

"Write up a page about your prize and have it in my office by Wednesday. And remember, special. Unique. Let's make sure Gwen Lake knows how much this shop values its hometown customers."

I wasn't in the mood to let Mayor Rose have the last word. "The shop values all its customers, but of course our Gwen Lake stitchers are extra special. You'll have the info by Wednesday, I promise."

I was proud of how I had handled all this, until Rose turned back just before going out the door. "Look at you. Little Shelby Phillips, all grown up and running Nina's Nimble Needle."

Her grandmotherly tone set my teeth on edge, but I just smiled and nodded.

It wasn't long before the NYAGs were gathered around the large table, discussing "the photo," as I now had come to think of it. I mentally catalogued all the crazy, regrettable things I'd done as their child, and wondered if this was me getting what my grandmother would have called "my comeuppance."

"Your folks sure look like they're having fun," Livvy joked with a wink.

"Nina has always loved Elvis," Tilly said with a sigh. "I always wished Ed and I had done something wild like that."

"Your sister's mortified," Faye said as she settled herself in the chair at the head of the table, the one she always took. It was funny how each of the NYAGs had "her seat." I was always afraid that if anyone new took us up on the COME ON IN AND STITCH A BIT sign in our window, they wouldn't have a place to sit.

"It is a bit . . . out of character . . . for them," I admitted as I brought in a chair from the stockroom and set it against the wall. I wanted us to be able to squeeze in a newcomer should one arrive. "I'm trying to think of it as a nice thing that they're still so committed to each other."

Faye's mouth drew down in a pinched frown. "Rare thing with the way marriages don't last these days," Faye said. "People used to know how to commit to each other."

I leaned against the wall. "Out of my friends from college, I'm the only one whose mom and dad are still together. Maybe if it takes a cheesy Elvis chapel photo to keep that going, I shouldn't complain."

"I'm all for whatever floats your boat," Dot chimed in. "I'm just not sure *everyone* needs to share *everything* with *everyone* else. I sure don't need to see what my grandkids ate for breakfast." She took off her reading glasses and let them fall on their chain—black-and-white beads today, which matched her bracelets and earrings. "My grandson sent me a photo of a snakebite he got camping. Honestly, did I really need to see that?"

The other NYAGs began a litany of all the grisly, shocking, or just plain ridiculous photos their children and grandchildren had sent them. Sure, finding my parents' antics embarrassing was a bit of a turnabout, but in the end, everyone was able to laugh it off. Mom used to call the NYAGs her "best source of perspective," and I began to see why.

After that catalogue of accident shots and other regrettable photos, I decided to wade into some risky waters. I walked over to stand by the NYAGs' table. "I know all kinds of accidents happen, but do you really think what happened to Kat is one?"

The lighthearted conversation ground to a halt. Clearly, I had misread the room.

"Whatever do you mean?" Livvy asked.

I told myself to stay the course, albeit delicately. "It's such a freak accident. I can't even figure out how it happened."

Faye recoiled slightly. "Gracious. Why would you even want to?"

I chose my words carefully. "Don't any of you worry that . . . well . . . that it wasn't an accident?"

Every woman around the table had the same fast reaction. "No!"

"Shelby, how could you think such a thing?" Faye asked.

Livvy shook her head. "Y'all been watching too much of those television crime shows."

Tilly put her hand over mine. "Bless your heart, child. Don't twist yourself into knots trying to make sense of something like that. Accidents happen." She patted the back of my palm. "You heard it yourself. Kat wasn't careful. I tell my kids that recklessness catches up with you. Always does."

Dot leaned in, eyes wide. "I don't know. I heard Tallen brought in George, Cal, and Leydon Windham for questioning. Seems to me you don't do that for an accident."

Fay sneered. "Stop that ridiculous gossip, Dot. You don't know that for a fact, do you?"

"Well, no," Dot replied. "But it certainly is more interesting that way."

The chorus of chastisements Dot received showed me I wouldn't find any support for the idea that Kat had been murdered among these four. I was not even sure Dot had entertained the possibility. Perhaps she just enjoyed the fun of a juicy rumor. After all, that kind of thing just didn't happen in Gwen Lake. Or if it did, it was kept very quiet. The good, upstanding people of Gwen Lake may have kept their knives sharp, but they didn't embed them in others.

You can "bless my heart" all you want and tell me not to tie myself into knots by trying to make sense of what had happened to Kat, but none of that altered my constant conviction that someone, not something, had sunk that knife into Kat. It stumped me how no one else in Gwen Lake could imagine that. Or, at least, no one who seemed ready to do anything about it.

I stared into Nabbit's yellow eyes later that night as I weighed my options. "Near as I can tell, there are two things I can pursue. First, I can figure out if Kat's sharpening stone really could have sent that knife flying into her." I dished out Nabbit's evening meal as he played feline sounding board. "Second, I can dream up some way to figure out who B is."

I set the dish down in front of Nabbit. I'd never had a cat before, and it turns out I rather liked it. Nabbit was a good listener, excellent company, and just plain cute. "Look at me talking about leads. How did babysitting a needlepoint shop turn into this?"

The shop. I still had to run the shop. And on a more personal side, I was pretty sure I needed to do something about Taylor. "It's okay—in fact, it's great—for Taylor to like art. And we've got to convince Hal that it's not some sort of character flaw that he's more into soccer jerseys than soccer itself. That's gonna be an uphill climb."

Seems there was a lot on my plate. How had I thought this would be a boring month minding the store? "I need help. And more than you can provide, mister."

Nabbit narrowed his eyes at my insult to his capacities. "Sorry, but unless you can whip up a Gwen Lake census, I'm going to have to look somewhere more human."

Census.

Wasn't that exactly what I needed? A list of Gwen Lake residents with first names beginning with *B*? And even more than that, I needed handwriting samples. Or at least some innocent-looking way to gather them so I could compare them to the handwriting on the love letters Kat had stashed away.

"That's it!" I declared to Nabbit. "I need a giveaway that focuses on initials. Monograms. And if I use raffle tickets that require people to fill out their names by hand, I'll have handwriting samples. It's the perfect solution."

Within ten minutes, I had a plan.

CHAPTER 17

The shop closed early on Good Friday, so that gave me the perfect opportunity to share my plan with Deb as we sat around the shop gathering table after closing. She'd just chosen her first project, a small canvas of a coffee cup with a swirl of steam rising out of it.

"If you like, JanLi can help you stitch *CHNO* onto the cup after the basic stitches are done."

She held up the square, which I'd just tacked to stretcher bars for her. "I'm not really the crafty type. You really think I'll like this?"

"Absolutely. It's specific, soothing, and satisfying. You can always see your progress—even if you only get to spend a little bit of time on it each day. Perfect for someone like you." Again, the surge of pleasure that comes with sharing art pulsed through me. I had always thought Mom was exaggerating about how good it felt to introduce someone to the possibility of creativity in their life, but she wasn't. I could get used to this. It doubled my resolve to gather some younger versions of the NYAGs—so that it would not be just Deb and me. If the NYAGs could be such a support group to each other, why couldn't people my age have the same thing?

I reached for one of the two decadent coffee drinks Deb had brought over. The thought of spending the next hour sharing coffee, stitching, and my new plan practically hummed under my skin.

I showed Deb how to tie a knot far outside her design—what we call a waste knot—which would anchor her first thread until she had worked it into the back of her design. I knew her scientific brain would appreciate the structure of needlepoint.

"What are you working on?" she asked as she worked her first careful stitches. "One of Kat's designs?"

"Yes, this one." I showed her the design I'd been stitching. I'd begun to incorporate a variety of stitches, enjoying how the piece became my own as I worked it. "That's the thing I like most about needlepoint. You start with the canvas and work it in different stitches the way you like. You can get as complex or as simple as you like."

She peered at the bold graphics on my canvas. "So you could work that all in that basic stitch you just showed me?"

"I could. But since I know several stitches, I can use them, too. It's as if Kat and I are partners in making whatever this will turn out to be." I turned the conversation toward the project I had in mind. "I could use your partnership with something, if you're game."

Deb smiled as she finished a perfect row. Neat, even stitches. She had taken to it like a natural. "Sure."

"I have an idea to let the Nimble Needle's shopping prize help out with uncovering who B is."

She halted her stitching for a moment. "That sounds clever. What?"

"A giveaway where people have to fill out raffle tickets. That way, I have a perfectly innocent reason to get handwriting samples from people, which I can then compare to Kat's letters."

Deb nodded. "That is clever."

"Only that's a lot of entries," I added. "And how do we get everyone in Gwen Lake to enter? I don't know that I've got a prize exciting enough to attract that kind of attention."

Deb thought for a moment. "We have to narrow it down, then. Have a way to sort through the entries for the Bs."

"I know. That's why we should use something needlepoint is full of—monograms. If we give away something monogrammed with a B, we get mostly B entrants. It even gives us an excuse to go looking for B entrants."

Deb pulled her thread up through the canvas. "It's a smart idea, but Rose will never go for it. She wants something everyone will get excited about."

I finished a row of stitches and began to work a new row back across my canvas. "You're right. She'll want the whole alphabet, even if I just want the Bs."

"So why not do a whole alphabet of something?" Deb asked as she took a sip of coffee. "Twenty-six prizes should keep Rose happy and distract everyone else while you concentrate your efforts on the B entries."

"Coasters," I declared as the idea began forming in my head. "Sets of monogrammed coasters in each letter of the alphabet. They're easy, small, and tailor-made for a monogram."

Deb nodded her agreement with my new plan. "Coasters sound perfect. You can never have too many of those. But . . . are you sure there's a connection between B and what happened to Kat?"

"Well, no," I admitted. "But it might explain a lot if there is. It's the only thing close to a lead that I have right now. And I seem to be the only one even looking for leads. Shouldn't I follow it and see where it takes me?"

Deb leaned in. "You should. And you're not the only one. I'm with you on this. And I'll help however I can."

"Well, then, there's two things we have to do next."

She grinned. "Stitch and drink coffee?"

I laughed, enjoying the tiny bit lighter the joke made me feel. "That too. But I was thinking along the lines of talking the NYAGs into making our sets of monogrammed coasters."

"What if we do it?" Deb offered. "What if we pull together the next generation of NYAGs—or whatever we call ourselves—to tackle this? We could meet up here or at CHNO."

I grinned right back. "I always knew you were brilliant." I had a solid plan, and now I had help. But I was going to need more help than just Deb's if I was going to pull this off. And I had a pretty good idea where I was going to find it.

Jake gave me a dubious look as we sat at the small desk in his cluttered garage office Saturday morning. "You want me to needlepoint. Me. A guy."

"Don't be so sexist," I countered. "Lots of men stitch. Did you know Harrison Ford said he does cross-stitch?"

"I did not." He did not look as if that fact went a long way toward enticing his cooperation. "Still not convinced."

"I don't want to depend on the NYAGs for this. And Deb and I need the help. Well, I need the help, and Deb's giving part of it." I gave him my best persuasive smile. "Please."

"Is it hard?"

I was pretty sure I had him. "Are you in possession of fine motor skills?"

A tiny surge of pride sparked in his eyes. "I can dismantle a transmission in under an hour. What do you think?"

"I think you're just the guy for the job. Deb will bring the coffee, and I'll supply the pizza." I frowned. "But you can't eat pizza and do needlepoint at the same time," I warned. "No sauce on the fibers."

"Do I get the pizza first?"

Now I knew I had him. "Help me out with this, and you can get the pizza anytime you want. If you can manage to bring a friend, I'll buy you both pizza."

I could see him calculating the ding to his manhood card if he invited a friend to needlepoint. It bothered me a little—Mom had several very talented and very masculine customers—but I wasn't in a position to get picky at the moment.

"Okay, maybe. But explain to me why we're doing this again?"

I gave him a shortened version of my theory, my investigation, and my plan to use these prizes to gather the writing samples I needed.

"That's pretty clever." After a pause, he added, "You really think Kat's death wasn't an accident?"

"I don't know," I replied. "But I'm annoyed that no one seems to be taking the possibility seriously. I mean, a knife sharpener flinging that blade into her? If you ask me, murder is a less outlandish theory than that."

"I wouldn't say that to the Tallens—chief or mayor." Jake furrowed his eyebrows. "Deb's right. You're going to have to tread carefully. And I see why it might be risky to involve those shop ladies of yours. They're first-class gossips. You don't want to be seen as stirring up trouble. That won't go well for you or your mom when she returns."

I sighed, glad that Jake understood the fine line I was walking here. "I know that. And the last thing I want to do is make trouble for Mom when I'm supposed to be helping her. But I just can't let this go. It's like Kat's memory is nagging at me."

"Haunting you?" he teased.

"Nothing like that. I just . . . Well, I wasn't very nice to her in school, and this sort of feels like a chance to make up for that. People were so quick to write her off. She deserves to get justice if someone really did murder her."

Jake leaned in. "Do you have theories? Suspects?"

"The list is growing all the time. Not that I'm used to playing investigator, but I think Cal, George, Leydon Windham, or whoever B is could have done it. Or someone totally different, someone we don't even know about yet. You said it yourself. She was pretty good at making enemies."

Jake sat back. "This would be a lot easier with Tallen on board."

I nodded. "He told me off last time I tried to raise the subject. If I come to him with any theories, I'd better have some solid evidence to back it up. And I know he's not going to let me into that van to have a look around." I felt my stomach do a lurch from just thinking about the last time I was in Kat's mobile sharpening shop. "I don't want to go back there, anyway."

He tapped his fingers on the edge of his cluttered desk. "I think I may have a way around that."

Those words were music to my ears. "What?"

"Well, seems to me the first thing you need to do is disprove the idea that the knife sharpener could have done it. Or at least poke a few holes in the theory."

"That would help Tallen get his head around other possibilities."

"I got a guy who might help with that."

"You do?" I liked that idea very much.

"Mark is a machinist I use for special projects. Like when I need a new part fabricated that I can't buy. I think he's got one of those sharpening machines in his shop. He might be able to tell us if it really could throw a knife like that, and maybe even run a test of some kind."

I recoiled. "I do not want to launch a knife into anyone."

"I was thinking more along the lines of a sack of potatoes. Or whatever Mark thinks is good. Plus, he owes me a favor. Two, actually. So I can rope him into needlework, too." Jake rolled his eyes. "I can't believe I just uttered that sentence."

I had my second ally—one with some really clever ideas, too. "You might really like it."

"Gwen Lake might have an undiscovered sea monster, too. Neither is very probable."

Given all the coins and strange secrets I was uncovering in this town, I wasn't so sure there weren't a lot of things lurking at the bottom of Gwen Lake.

I ventured to put a hand on top of Jake's. "Thanks. I really mean it. I know this is odd—"

"It is."

"But I appreciate it."

He had broad, strong hands, warm but calloused. I liked his authenticity. So many of the men at Batterson had walked around with a long list of things to prove. The kind of opportunists who only half listened to you because they had one eye on who else was in the room. Jake paid attention. Combine that with a really charming smile, and the man had a lot going for him.

But right now, his number one feature was a willingness to help with my investigation, and a willingness—begrudging as it was—to pick up a needle.

"Monday night, at my apartment above the shop. I don't want to do this at the Needle, because someone will see."

"If I have to tell Mark the reason behind our little sewing circle, can I?"

After a brief sideways look to let him know what I thought of his terminology, I pondered the idea. "Maybe not. I think you're right that we need to step carefully until we've got more facts. It really could have just been a freak accident, and I'm letting my imagination run away with me."

"Could be, but could not. I'll just tell Mark he's helping me help out a friend."

Jake considered me a friend. That was some of the most welcome news I'd had all week.

CHAPTER 18

On the pretense that I was looking for a nice dress for Easter and that I'd offered to get Jessica's knives sharpened for holiday ham carving, I went to Windham's on Saturday. I brought two of Jessica's Bour du Chef knives into the housewares department and asked as casually as I could to watch while they sharpened my knives.

I got a curt "That's not allowed," along with a dark look, which let me know I couldn't press the topic. How the sharpening of cutlery had become such a major issue in my life was beyond me. But this gave me a convenient excuse to ask the staff there to show me up to the offices so I could complain to the managers about their lack of transparency.

Leydon was, predictably, not thrilled to see me. He stood up to his full height and pinned me with a glare. "Do we have a problem brewing here, Miss Phillips?"

"I just wanted to see how you sharpen knives," I replied with an innocent smile.

"Forgive me if I doubt it's just that. If you have knives you wish to have serviced, we will happily take care of that. But if you insist on stirring up trouble, I'll have to insist you take yourself off the store property." A flash of emotion glinted behind that well-heeled demeanor. Only momentarily, but it was there just the same.

"So you won't show me?" What did he have to hide?

"I'm going to ask you once again to leave, and I won't hesitate to call security if you don't."

I clearly wasn't going to get any farther here. I was walking toward the sales floor when a "Psst!" came from the hallway by the elevators. I looked around but found no one.

"Psst! Shelby!"

I turned toward the women's restroom to find my mystery young woman poking her head out of the door and waving me toward her. "You!" I called, glad to get the chance to talk to her again. "I need to talk to you."

She ducked back into the restroom, pulled me inside, and yanked the door shut behind us. She actually checked to make sure the stalls were empty. *What, are we in high school?* After all, she couldn't have been more than twenty-five, if that. She grabbed my hand. "I heard Mr. Windham yelling at you. Did you confront him about threatening Kat?"

I gave her a direct look. "You really need to tell me your name. And why it is you do so much eavesdropping on the job." That might have been a bit confrontatioal, but part of me was starting not to trust her.

She backed up against the sinks. "Why do you need to know?"

"I've got to be able to tell Tallen who you are."

She rolled her eyes. "It won't help."

"Of course it will. If you come forward with what you know, he'll need to take the information seriously. He'll need to investigate it further."

She shook her head. "Knowing it came from me won't help."

I was exasperated. "Why not?"

Her chin rose. "Because my name is Cherie Tallen."

The whack of the fact falling into place in my mind was nearly a physical sensation. "You're . . . ?"

"Yep, Chief Tallen's daughter," she said, finishing for me.

"And if you ask him, his hyperactive, overimaginative daughter who draws conclusions where there aren't any. Trust me, my name will not help your case. Not with Dad."

The second I recognized her mother's and father's features in her face, another thought burst into my brain. She could still help me. "Two questions. How do you feel about needlepoint? And are you free Monday night?"

I gave Nabbit my best owner glare Monday night. "Okay, mister, be a gracious host. We need these people, and we can't do this at the shop."

Cherie showed up first, and she looked downright shocked when I told her the rest of the guest list. "Guys? You got *guys* to help you with this?"

I smiled. Mom would be so proud of my craft evangelism skills. "I did."

"They all know how to needlepoint?"

"Actually, none of them do. You are all learning to help me out. And I really appreciate it." Spying Jake and Mark at the door, I pulled it open and let them in. "Hi there. I was just telling Cherie how much I appreciate you all helping out."

Jake held up a six-pack of a local IPA. "I promised Mark beer."

I looked at Cherie. "Are you legal?" She looked rather young, and I'd never asked her age.

She glared back. "I know I look young, but I swear I'm twenty-two. Want to check my ID?"

"No. And I did promise pizza, so it'll be here in an hour. It's best if we leave the food and adult beverages for after the lesson, but then we can socialize." I extended a hand to the tall, slim younger man next to Jake. "You must be Mark."

"Mark the machinist, that's me." He had a friendly smile, even if he did look like he was wondering exactly what Jake had roped him into doing.

"I'm Cherie," chimed in Cherie. As short as she was, she

had to tilt her chin way up to meet Mark's eyes. But she was very intent on meeting Mark's eyes. She seemed quite taken with him.

"Hi there, Cherie," Mark said. He seemed just as charmed by Cherie as Cherie was by him. Good. It should be far easier to get everyone on board if they liked each other. I certainly was in favor of a project that let me spend more time with Jake. Two birds with one stone—or is that one needle in this case?

"Is it just us?" Jake asked.

"And Deb. The five of us should be able to do it. The monogrammed coasters I have in mind are small, easy canvases. After the first thirty minutes, you all will be off and running. I'm sure of it."

On cue, Deb knocked on my door and waved through the window. I had gathered my team.

And we had a mascot, too. Once Deb had come inside, I announced, "Everyone, this is Nabbit. He's new but very clever." After all, it was playing fetch with Nabbit that had given rise to the idea of Kat's non-accidental death.

"He's a cutie," Cherie said. "I like cats."

"Dog man myself," Jake said. "But he seems nice."

"I was thinking," Deb said as I settled everyone around the kitchen table with the kits I had made up for them. "We need a name."

Jake balked. "Huh? Do we?"

"Well, the group from the shop is called the NYAGs," Deb explained.

"The nags?" Mark gave a doubtful look.

"NYAGs," I explained. "It stands for Not Your Average Grannies."

"Well, I'm pretty sure Mark and I are not your average needle pointers, but I sure don't want to be a NYANP. Do I have to be anything?"

Mark bumped Jake's shoulder. "Maybe by the third beer, we'll come up with something you can live with."

"Which reminds me," Jake said to me. "Does anyone know we're doing this?"

"That's up to you all. It'd be fun to promote the craft as okay for everyone, but at the moment, you're really helping me out, so I'll opt for whatever you want," I responded.

Jake gave an embarrassed shrug. "I'd prefer to keep it quiet for now, if that's okay. I mean, I'm fine helping you out on this, but I'm not ready to join the needlework ambassador corps." With a sheepish look, he added, "Yet."

I made a mental note to work on Jake's concept of crafts as not cool enough for the average guy. I get the unfortunate pressure on men to be "guy enough"—whatever that is. It was playing out right in front of my eyes with Hal's pressure on Taylor. Needlepoint was fine and admirable for Jessica, but it was off limits for Taylor. Wouldn't it be an amazing world if we all just stopped deciding what other people should and shouldn't do?

"Hey," Cherie chimed in. "That's it. We could be the Surprising Needlepoint Ambassador Corp. The SNACs."

Mark laughed, Deb smirked, and Jake groaned. "Much as I love snacks, I'm gonna say no on that for now."

Deb pulled the canvas square closer to her. "How about we just learn what we need to, to help out with Shelby's project? We can make plans for world needlepoint domination later."

"World needlepoint domination. I could get behind that . . . maybe," Mark joked.

I wrestled back control of the conversation and steered it to the task at hand. "Okay, everyone, pick up your needle and some of the white thread, and we'll start with the basics."

CHAPTER 19

Cal stared me down Wednesday, as we stood in Kat's workshop to gather more of her work to consign at the Nimble Needle. "I don't get it," he challenged. "This stuff is selling. You said so yourself. So put it all up for sale now."

I'd just written and handed him a healthy consignment check. Was this about financial need, greed, or just plain revenge? Greed is a top motive for murder, after all. Carefully, I asked, "Do you have another source of income, Cal?"

He jabbed his big hand toward the parking lot. "It's sitting out there. It's mine. Like I said, it should have been mine all along. She stole the idea from me."

So he kept insisting. "I'm not a lawyer, but I'm pretty sure the van is still Kat's until the police and the lawyers get through with it. Did she have a will? Leave it to you?"

"Of course not. Dad's in charge of all that crap. And what do the police need with it, anyway?"

I thought that was obvious. "It is the scene of a . . ." I started to say, "Crime," but only I thought that was true. "An incident."

"She's gone, and it's *mine*," he repeated. He stared out the window at the driveway. "I know where she keeps her extra keys. I could just take it and leave. Head out to Montana or someplace and get out of this petty little town."

"I'm not sure that's a smart idea, Cal." I opened the plastic crate I'd brought to gather more stock. "Let's settle down and pick the next items for sale in the shop. We can take thirty, I think, maybe even forty. The scissors are going fastest at the highest price, so let's take all of those first."

"Yeah, those. All of 'em." He began pulling the scissors off the wall pegboard on which they hung and slipping them into the small leather pouches they were sold in.

They really did look like art or jewelry the way she had packaged them. I had splurged on one of her most expensive pairs—half out of guilt, half out of admiration. I admit, it bothered me how he manhandled them, as if they were bricks instead of the treasures they were.

If Cal really was looking to hightail it out of town, I needed to get any evidence he could provide. "Do you know how to work the sharpening machine?" I asked as casually as I could.

"Who do you think taught Kat?"

"I guess I just assumed your father did. He used to do it in the hardware store, right?"

Cal thrust a pair of scissors into its pouch with extra force. "*I* used to do it in the hardware store. Before Dad gave the whole operation to her." He narrowed his eyes at me. "It was my idea, by the way. The van. I thought of it first."

He'd told me that three times already. Cal certainly wasn't striking me as the bright idea, entrepreneurial type. In fact, he was fast looking more like the homicidal type—ugly as that was. Kat, on the other hand, was highly entrepreneurial. I simply replied, "It's a clever idea." After a moment I added, "Is it hard? Sharpening?"

He huffed. "Well, you shouldn't screw up, if that's what you're asking." He grabbed more scissors off the wall. "Of all my ideas, I never did get why she jumped on that one."

I asked the obvious. "So you fought about it?"

"We had it out all over again just before you got here. I was sure your mom would pick her to run the store, and then I'd just take the sharpening business off her hands." He tossed the scissors into the crate. "Actually, she was, too. Sort of. And we all know how that turned out."

A small chill ran down my back at the thought that Cal might blame my arrival for his being denied the van business. *This is a man who might have killed his sister. I don't want him mad at me.*

I picked up a *Kat's Kutz Spring Sharp Special* flyer off her desk. "She seemed to be good at it."

He gave a sour laugh. "She was good at *selling* it. When she wasn't running around annoying people."

I skipped over that remark. "Well, sales is part of any good small business. You'll have to learn the sales part of it if you take over the van."

His chin rose. "I can do it. I'll be even better than she was."

Given what I'd seen of Cal's business skills, I wasn't convinced of that. George had given the business to the right child—not that I'd say that to my present companion. Certainly not with the number of sharp objects in the room with us.

Just find out what you can while we're packing up and cut this as short as possible, I told myself. "Had Kat ever hurt herself before? With the sharpening machine, that is."

"All the time. That big chunk out of the finger on her right hand? A meat cleaver from Swanson's did that."

I hadn't paid close attention to Kat's hands. "What happened?"

"What do you think? Meat cleaver, finger. Do the math." He wiggled the ring finger of his right hand for emphasis. "She wasn't careful. About anything."

"So they tell me. That machine looks powerful." I wasn't convinced it was powerful enough to launch a knife and plunge it deep into someone's chest.

He glared at me. "You want me to give you some speech about how sorry I am she got herself killed? You won't get it from me. Ha. I'm not even sure you'd get one from Dad."

His lack of remorse made my skin prickle. Sure, I have a lot of tension with Jessica, and my parents can drive me nuts, but I'd never ever say I was glad harm had come to any member of my family. "Won't you miss her? At all?"

Cal shook his head. "We weren't some shiny, happy family like yours, Shelby." He tossed the last of the scissors into the crate. "We weren't much of a family at all. I'm gonna grab the van the minute I can and put a lot of distance between me and Gwen Lake."

He really did sound like he might grab the spare car keys and disappear with the van. Should Chief Tallen be keeping it down at the police station or something?

He glared at me. "Did you know how much she wanted to run your mom's shop? She could have. You said yourself she was a good businessperson. Kat was really hurt that your mom turned her down."

I wasn't even aware she'd actually asked. Hinted broadly, yes, but asked enough that Mom felt she had to refuse? I fumbled for an honest but kind answer. "Mom just didn't feel Kat was the right person to take over the Needle."

"But you are?" It was more of a sour jab than a question. It was time to wrap this up.

"I'm watching the store only while they're gone."

He laughed. "Yeah, you keep telling yourself that."

I tried to think of what Mom would say if she were here. I've calmed down my share of agitated artists, but this was a whole other level. "Look, Cal, no one is happy about how this all turned out. I'm sorry you feel slighted. I'm sorry Kat felt slighted." Even though it felt risky to say, I added, "And I'm sorry Kat is dead."

"I'm sure you are." With one final dark look at me, Cal pulled open the desk drawer, fished out a set of keys on a K key chain, and stuffed them in his pocket. "Enjoy your family business, Shelby. I sure as hell ain't having a field day with mine." With that, he left the workshop, and thirty seconds later I heard the front door slam.

I stood there for a moment, asking myself what I would do if I heard the van engine start up and saw the van pull out of the driveway. Tell Cal not to do it? Call Chief Tallen? Let him go?

I raced over to the window and breathed a sigh of relief as Cal walked past the van. I sucked my breath back in again, however, when he doubled back and gave the side of the van a startling punch, which I was sure left a dent. He stood there for a moment, as if at a standoff with the vehicle. Then he put one hand on the van and leaned up against it in a gesture that could have either been anger or frustration—or both—but was likely not grief. Cal Katsaros was a storm of emotions right now, and perhaps a dangerous one. He seemed capable of anything, and that wasn't a comforting thought.

I waited until he was long gone before I put everything I could fit into the crate. I lugged the crate to my car, then went back and locked the apartment door and pulled it closed. The thunk of the shut door felt solid and final.

I can count the number of times Jessica has been impressed with anything I have done on the fingers of . . . one finger. I won an art show my senior year in high school, which placed my winning watercolor on display in the town hall for a year. The painting hangs in my parents' living room to this day. Jessica felt this a worthy achievement, and back then I treasured every little compliment. I suppose the reason Kat's clinging and pleas for affirmation had bothered me so much was that they had touched on what I wouldn't admit I felt about my older sister.

That's probably a little more armchair therapy than anyone needs to hear, but I will confess to deep satisfaction with the compliment Jessica delivered as we sat together on the couch at the shop on Thursday.

"Mom thinks your monogrammed alphabet coasters are fabulous. Rose feels like you've gone overboard, and Rose loves it when people go all in on her ideas. Good job."

The "good job" may have smacked a little of childhood parenting, but I took it, anyway. "Thank you."

"And you got some people helping you? Not the NYAGs?"

"Why?" I asked. "Are they mad I didn't ask them?" It wouldn't do to alienate Mom's most loyal customers.

Jessica spread one hand in the direction of the large table, which served as the NYAGs usual hangout. "Are you kidding? They're thrilled you got someone else on board. Everyone always assumes they'll do everything. Getting in some new blood scored big points with the NYAG crowd. Again, good job. I was in picking up my grass-fed beef at Sanders's this morning, and Faye was going on and on about you."

My heart glowed a bit at the praise. This alphabet coaster project was not only serving my investigation into the identity of B but making the Needle look good, as well. That went a long way in the plus column of my life, which had been feeling rather empty of late.

"Who's helping you?" Jessica asked. With a jolt, I realized the tone of her voice didn't quite hide the question "Why didn't you ask me?"

"Deb, Cherie Tallen and, if you can believe it, Jake London and his friend Mark."

Her eyes grew wide with surprise. "Guys? Seriously?"

A grin slipped onto my face as my shoulders straightened a bit. "Yep. It's rather a fun night, and the men surprised themselves by being quick learners." I could barely believe myself as I heard my own mouth say, "Do you want to come?"

She did. Very much. I could see it in her eyes long before Jessica said, "Sure. Only if you need the help, that is." It wasn't nearly as small as she tried to make it sound. My sister, my super-busy, ultra-talented sister, wanted in on my little project. My as yet unnamed circle of twentysomething and thirtysomething needle pointers.

It might be a bit tricky to navigate the dual purpose of this project in front of Jessica, but I wanted to try. While I wasn't ready to share my theories with her about Kat being murdered, that might eventually change. There was still some insistent, hopeful part of me that wanted my time in Gwen Lake to improve my relationship with my sister. Bringing her into the coaster project felt like a solid step in that direction.

"I could really use your help, Jess." I hadn't called her Jess in years, as she'd opted for the more elegant Jessica since college. "You've got more skills than all of us. That hanging you made for Mom and Dad's van? As fast as you did? That was amazing."

She glowed at the compliment. "I did go a little . . . overboard . . . on that. It was a good place to channel all my anxiety. Better than lying there wide awake at all hours."

It wasn't like Jessica to admit to anxiety about anything. "What's keeping you up?"

I was able to watch her decide how much to tell me. See the debate behind her eyes as to how much of that Jessica perfection to let fall. It struck a surprising chord of compassion where all that envy normally lived. "Jess?" I asked, pressing.

She put her hand to her mouth and sucked in a small, tight breath. The threat of tears gathered in those flawlessly mascaraed hazel eyes. She was wrestling with how much to reveal, and I could tell it was big. And painful.

I moved a bit closer to her on the couch, grateful no one was due into the shop for another thirty minutes. "Jess, what is it? You look really upset. Can I do anything to help?"

She blinked and delicately swiped one eye. "It's nothing. Well, nothing you can help with."

"I don't know. Try me. At least let yourself talk about it. I've got outstanding listening skills."

She gave me the oddest look. "You're not married."

My hackles rose for a moment, until I connected the dots. Jessica prided herself on her exemplary family, and she'd already admitted to tension over Taylor and soccer. "True, but

I've had a bit of experience with dumpster-fire relationships. Maybe I can offer an ear to whatever's bugging you about your amazing family." While I wasn't sure the professional-personal drama with Dave Batterson qualified as a dumpster fire, my compliment on her family was surprisingly sincere. I ventured to ask, "Is it something with Hal?"

The flash of pain across her face let me know I'd struck home. She pulled in another breath—the kind of stuttering inhale every woman recognizes as a "Do not cry" tactic—before she nearly whispered, "We're fighting."

I didn't need the details to know what a huge admission this was for my sister. "I'm sorry," I offered, taking her hand. "You guys seem like you've got a really strong thing going on. I bet you'll get through it."

She used her thumb to twist the large, shiny diamond on her left hand, as if it had begun to pinch. "We've fought before. Over the kitchen cabinets and the granite countertops . . . and occasionally my credit card bill. But over Taylor?" She held my gaze. "He's noticing. It's hurting him. He's so different from Hal or Chaz. It's like he's a little turtle, and I'm watching him pull into his shell all the time."

Taylor had all the markings of an artistic personality. He was a true introvert but could put on his family's outgoing personality when he knew it was required. Still, what kid doesn't want to be seen for who he really is? "The soccer thing, huh?"

Jessica shook her head. "It's just getting worse. We were in the store the other day, and there was a section of art stuff— colored pencils, kits, that sort of thing—right next to the sports equipment. Hal kept tugging him toward the baseball gloves. Physically, he had his hand on Taylor's arm and was yanking him." She cast her gaze over my shoulder, as if the whole thing were replaying just behind me. "But all I could see was the way his eyes were locked on the art stuff. He wanted to get that big set of colored pencils. I wanted to get him that big set." She looked back at me. "Hal just shot me one of his looks and muttered, 'Don't you encourage him.'"

I bit back the unkind words I wanted to say, making a sound somewhere between a grunt and a grumble instead.

"Taylor heard him." Jessica's voice cracked the smallest bit. "I know he did. I hate that Taylor heard his father say that. And at practice that night, Hal was harder on him than ever. He's too young for that. He's supposed to be having fun."

"Doesn't sound like anyone's having fun."

"Chaz is. He's doing great. But it just makes everything worse, you know?"

Sibling rivalry was taking dark turns all over Gwen Lake it seemed. I squeezed Jessica's hand tight. "Would it be okay if I came up with something, something mildly artistic, that I needed Taylor's help with? I don't know what yet, and I get that Hal won't stand for it if it's needlepoint, even if Jake and Mark are on board, but let me think of something?"

"You'd do that?"

I pulled her into a hug. When was the last time I'd pulled my sister into a genuine, nonobligatory hug? "Of course I'd do that."

"We'll have to pick just the right thing. It can't look like I set this up."

"I get it. Maybe we can add on to the shopping prize. After all, we should have kids involved, too. What's he good at drawing? He must have your eye for color, and surely, you've seen some of the things he's drawn."

She smiled. "I put some of them up on the fridge. They're all over his bedroom walls. In between the sports posters."

A plan started coming together in my head. "Aunt Shelby's on the case." *In more ways than one*, I thought.

Jessica held me right back. Tight. "I'm glad you're here."

I didn't realize until just this moment that I hadn't been sure she was glad. It felt nice to know she was.

CHAPTER 20

That afternoon I stood in Chief Tallen's office doorway. "I need to talk to you." I was determined to make him listen—if not about the murder, at least about Cal.

He looked up from his stack of forms. "Fancy that. I need to talk to you, too. I was going to stop over at the shop this afternoon, and you saved me the trouble." He waved his hand in the direction of his guest chair. "Sit down."

I put my hand on the knob of his office door. "I'd like to close the door, if it's okay with you."

He pushed the forms to the side of his desk blotter. "Sounds serious."

I sat down. "Well, I'm not sure what it is. But you ought to know in any case."

The chief rolled his hand in a silent *Go on* gesture.

"I think Cal is planning on stealing Kat's van and skipping town." It sounded so dramatic when I said it out loud. But less dramatic than *Because he may have been the one who murdered Kat.*

"What makes you think that?" His words had the practiced tone of someone used to carefully pulling facts from people. Which, given the fact that he was the police chief, made a lot of sense.

"Pretty straightforward," I replied. "He waved the keys at me, pocketed them, and told me that's what he wanted to do."

Tallen's eyes narrowed in thought. "And when did this happen?"

"Last night. We were picking out more of Kat's pieces to put on sale. He's acting like he really needs cash, pressing me to put everything on sale right away. He thinks George should have given the van to him and not to Kat."

"George didn't give that van to anyone. Kat took out a loan and bought it herself. The only thing George gave her was the right to pull the sharpening business from the shop."

That surely didn't jive with the bitter words Cal had had for his sister and how the business was handed down. I began to wonder if his declaration that the business was his idea in the first place was really true. Cal struck me as all ideas and very little action, whereas Kat had acted on her ideas with bold initiative. "Cal sure didn't talk like that. Does Cal know what you just told me?"

"I'd sure like to ask him."

That seemed like Investigation 101 to me. The whole motive-opportunity-weapon thing they cover in every crime show I've ever seen. From where I sat, Cal seemed to be steeped in motive. "So why don't you?"

The chief set his jaw with an exasperated grunt. "Because Kat's van was gone from her parking lot this morning and Cal is nowhere to be found."

"He went through with it? The van is gone?" Maybe Cal was more of an action guy than I gave him credit for.

"And Cal."

"Can he do that? I mean, isn't it a crime scene or something?"

"No, he can't. Well, he *can*, because he did. But he's not legally entitled to it. The van is not his property, and he took it. Pretty much my definition of *stealing*. And it's the location of a death, not technically a crime scene."

I was glad to see he gave the word *technically* a new emphasis. "Technically?"

I watched him choose to ignore that. "Did Cal give you any indication where he was going?"

"He mentioned Montana. But it sounded more like his definition of *anywhere but here* than an actual destination. He told me he felt Kat had stolen the idea—and, by association, the van—from him. He got pretty worked up. Punched the van, by the way. Hard. That man has the strength to hurt someone."

Again, the chief didn't walk through the door I had opened for him. I supposed it was not his job to jump to conclusions, like I was doing. "The good news is that van is easy to spot. We shouldn't have much trouble tracking him down. And now I can probably nail him for felony theft or grand theft auto."

"Or for harming Kat?" I asked, getting annoyed at how we weren't talking about what I saw as the real issue. "If Cal didn't harm Kat, I sure got the impression he was intending to."

"I can't run a police department on impressions, Shelby. There's no room for gut calls in what I do."

I knew what my gut was telling me. Yelling at me, actually. "You never listen to your gut on cases?"

"I listen to my gut all the time . . . but I follow the evidence most of all. Making assumptions is a dangerous thing in this business." He leaned in. "Look. Whether you believe it or not, I am, and have always been, open to the possibility that Kat's death might not have been an accident. I've brought in Cal and George for questioning. I've talked to Windham and a few of Kat's other known enemies."

So Dot was right. It wasn't just gossip. "Why didn't you tell me that?"

"Shelby," the chief began in a low, serious voice, "I'm not obligated to discuss any of this with you. I'm trying to be nice here, given how you found her and all, but don't press me on this."

I had about six dozen things I wanted to say. "Well, I'm glad to know you *are* looking into it."

"George came to me before the weekend and said he had concerns Cal may have done something. He had a whopper of an argument with Cal, and Cal made threats. Sabotaging the van, giving some damaging information to Windham's, general meanness."

Tallen was acting so calm, while I felt like a bomb had gone off in my chest. "Were you going to arrest Cal? Is that why he ran?"

Exasperation returned to the chief's face. "I can't arrest someone for an argument. Siblings have been hurling accusations or threats at each other for a thousand years. And Cal talks a big game, which he rarely backs up, if you hadn't noticed. Of course, he's in more trouble now by taking the van."

"So you're going to do something about that?"

"I'm glad to hear you ask it like that."

"Like what?"

"That *I'm* going to do something about that. Me, not you. I don't want you mucking around in this. I want you to promise me you'll let me handle this. Leydon Windham called me Monday to complain about the questions you were asking. I've got to walk a delicate balance here, and the last thing we need is you playing junior detective." He fixed me with a serious glare. "If you have anything *reasonable* you want to share, do so. Otherwise leave it to me." His last four words were practically a warning.

I thought about the letters. Were they related? Did I have the right to out Kat's possible affair? Withholding what I knew felt wrong, but I didn't feel right about turning over those letters. Not until I had an idea who they were from. So I chose a middle ground. "I'm pretty sure Kat was seeing someone. Possibly a married someone."

The chief furrowed his brows. "As in an affair?"

I was trying not to use that word. "I think so, yes. Or at least someone she had to keep secret." *Like B, for instance.*

"Are you certain of this?"

"Um . . . no." I wasn't certain. Well, maybe I was, but not in a way I was ready to back up with the evidence I had. Was I technically withholding evidence if the letters weren't related to her death? Kat had been so hungry for love in her life. Did I have the right to tear that down now? After all, there were no threats anywhere in those letters, and here Cal was hurling threats all over the place.

"Do you have any idea who she was in this so-called affair with?"

The way he asked it made me feel sorry I'd ever brought it up. "No." At least that was true. I still had no idea who B was or if this person had anything to do with Kat's murder.

But I was determined to find out.

"Okay then. So here's how this goes from here, Shelby, and I mean it. If you find anything that seems to be connected to Kat, you'll come to me. And you'll let me decide how to deal with it. You won't go running off on some crazy tangent. I have enough of that with Cherie." His expression shifted gears. "I heard you got her pulled into the Needle's shopping prize project, by the way. She's excited about it. Rose is, too. Nicely done."

Our conversation about Kat-related crimes and clues was clearly over. "Thank you. It's been fun to pull some new people into it."

Somehow, out of the corner of my eye, I caught a glimpse of a paperweight on the chief's desk. It was a big, old-fashioned silver whistle, but not in the usual shape. It was long and tubular, with an engraving of a British police helmet on it.

Tallen noticed my gaze. "Gift from some friends when I joined the force. I've always wanted to be a police officer, so it earned me the nickname Bobby in school."

My pulse made a momentary jump. "I've never heard any-one call you that."

"'Cause it's a terrible joke. I let only a few close folks call me by that nickname. And never in public."

Bobby. A B name only close friends are allowed to use. I'd been racking my brain, trying to figure out why Chief Tallen seemed to be dragging his feet, putting up unreasonable re-sistance to the idea that Kat hadn't died by accident. Was I staring at the reason? An wave of nausea rose up as I consid-ered the awful thought that Kat's B was sitting in front of me. He had to be around fifty if he was Cherie's dad, but Kat wouldn't be the first woman my age who'd taken up with a much older man.

"Yeah, sure," I said just to respond, despite the crazy swirl of thoughts in my head. It couldn't be, could it? It made so lit-tle sense, but then again, what about this whole thing made any sense at all?

Tallen went on, unaware of my shock. "You know your mom would be proud of you. Try to move past all this drama and enjoy your time in town, okay? This conversation will stay be-tween you and me. Don't let what happened take you down a rabbit hole that will just churn up a lot of unnecessary hurt. Everybody has secrets in a town as small as this. Take care what rocks you turn over. The consequences may be way dif-ferent than what you thought you were getting."

Was that a warning? Had he caught on to my reaction? He had no way of knowing what I knew, did he? I sputtered out some sort of reply, thanked him for his advice and his time, and left the station as quickly as I could.

I walked down Gwen Lake's main street, lost in confused thoughts. This was supposed to be a boring month minding Mom's shop. Instead, I seemed to be stepping further and fur-ther into a weird web of circumstances with connections I couldn't quite see.

Tallen? Odd as it seemed, I couldn't dismiss the possibility. Which meant I was going to have to be really careful about what I said in front of Cherie. My friendly group of stitchers now felt like a minefield, where I had to tread lightly. Still, it made sense to keep Cherie involved. I could learn things from her I wouldn't learn anywhere else.

I stopped on the corner in front of CHNO, halted by a new thought: Did I really *want* to know who might have killed Kat? Wasn't it easier—and far more pleasant—to join in with everyone else and consider her death a freak accident?

In truth, I wasn't eager to know. I didn't like the idea of someone I knew, anyone I could happen to talk to here on any given day, being a killer. Especially one who killed in such a brutal way.

But the deeper truth was that I no longer had a choice. For whatever reason, I'd been launched into this situation. Certain clues had found their way onto my path. Just like you can't *unsee* something, I couldn't *unknow* what I'd learned. My reluctance, while strong, wasn't as strong as the odd sense of obligation I felt to Kat. No matter if you called it fate or providence or bad luck or whatever name you wanted to assign to it, I was here. I knew what I knew. I had a collection of facts and clues no one else did, and I couldn't just stand by without acting on it. There were rocks in front of me I'd have to turn over, whether or not I ended up with the unexpected consequences Tallen had warned me about.

"Shelby? Shelby Phillips?"

I pulled myself out of my stupor to see a large man staring down at me.

He offered a genuine smile. "You *are* Shelby, right?"

"Um, yeah."

"Faye said you were in town, minding the shop for Nina. I haven't seen you in years." The man held out a big hand. "You sure do look like your mama."

"Mr. Sanders," I stammered out, trying to yank my attention back to the present moment. "Nice to see you."

He gestured around the town. "Look the same as you remember?"

That felt like a loaded question, given the past weeks. I shrugged. "I haven't been gone that long."

"Faye says you're doing a bang-up job with the shop."

"That's nice to hear." Faye was the NYAG I was most worried about winning over, actually. She could be the picky sort and was quick to offer an opinion—and not always a positive one. Mom would be glad to know Faye felt the shop was in good hands. "It was kind of a rough start, you know?"

His burly face softened. "So sad. Faye made no secret about how she wasn't fond of Kat, but she was a sweet thing. Always struck me as the sort of brilliant misfit that doesn't easily fit in anywhere. She did the knives at the shop, you know. Really well."

"She was very good at what she did." It still felt odd and uncomfortable to speak of Kat in the past tense. The words seemed only to emphasize how she no longer had a future. Especially when she ought to have so much of a future ahead of her.

Mr. Sanders shook his head. "It's a shock and a loss. Are you okay? Everyone treating you well?"

"I'm fine." That didn't feel quite true at the moment, but this wasn't the time to get into it—especially with the town butcher.

He nudged my shoulder. "Can I interest you in a good pork chop? On the house?"

It seemed wrong to decline, even though I had better skills with a chicken breast and Nabbit might enjoy something from the fish counter. "Sure, Mr. Sanders. That'd be nice."

"Come on by the shop, then." He looked at me again. "Sure you're okay? Your folks are far away, so Faye and I would be glad to help if you need anything."

"That's very kind, but I've got Jessica if I need anything. And really, it's all going fine, despite . . . what's happened. Everyone's been great. Really." I hoped my babbling didn't reveal my chaotic inner state. "Besides, I'm due back at the shop."

Sanders checked his watch. "Faye never misses it when the NYAGs get together. She rolls her eyes at Dot's crazy antics, but she'd never miss a NYAG day." He leaned in. "Although I think we've reached our quota of pillows and wall hangings, if you know what I mean."

Faye admitted to me the other day that she averages three hours of stitching daily. That's a lot of stitches. Who has that kind of free time these days? I shouldn't complain, however. Faye and enthusiasts like her keep Mom's shop in the black.

"Faye's a marvelous customer," I replied. "And a good friend to Mom."

"That she is. You take care now. Stop by for that chop, or I can send it with Faye next time the NYAGs do their thing."

As I walked back toward the Needle, I couldn't help but think that Gwen Lake had always been such a friendly town. When had it become dark enough to do harm to Kat Katsaros? Someone, not some malfunctioning machine, had ended her life. I was sure of it. And it seemed up to me to uncover who.

CHAPTER 21

The NYAGs were in fine form Friday morning. I couldn't remember a time when I had groaned so much and laughed so hard. Sure, they were a handful, but it was easy to see why my mom counted them not only among her best customers but also among her dearest friends.

"Nina's having a lot of fun out there." Dot leveled a cheeky grin my way as she stitched a shiny gold earring onto what she had dubbed her "potty-mouthed pirate." She got an endless kick out of shocking people. I had to admire her blatant, gleeful disregard for what other people thought. When I reached her age, I hoped to have a brazen quality like hers—but maybe only half as much. "You're sure she's coming back?" she teased.

I would never admit to having the same doubts. Mom's texts and photos—the latest were of her eating some enormous dessert called Frozen Hot Chocolate at Serendipity on the Vegas Strip—were as amusing as they were cringeworthy. She was having a lot of fun. The woman in these photos looked like my mom but acted more like my nephews. In fact, I'd wager my nephews were a bit more serious.

"She hasn't told me otherwise." Would she? Or would I wake up to a text a few weeks from now with the message *We've decided we're not coming back*?

"I don't know," said Livvy, with a maternal pat on my arm. "You're doing a top-notch job here. I'd miss the dickens out of her, but she would have earned it. She's worked hard for a long time. And the shop is in good hands."

It bothered me how much I needed to keep reminding people I was a temporary fill-in. The Needle was who Mom was. Her place in the world. I couldn't see her abandoning it forever—even to me.

But I also couldn't ignore how it was starting to feel like my place in the world, too. When I'd left, I had sworn to myself I'd never get sucked back into the world of the Needle. Convinced myself I was too trendy for fiber arts. Wow, was I wrong. Knitting, needlepoint, embroidery, weaving, all the fiber arts had become very trendy with the advent of "maker culture." Despite the fact that my mother did them—which ordinarily made most things uncool—crafts were cool. My appreciation and fascination had doubled in a few weeks. I found I didn't mind being pulled back into this world. Too much.

"What are you going to call the other set of us?" Faye asked.

I poured on the charm. "There is no other set of you. You all are irreplaceable."

"I mean the younger ones," Faye explained. "Your friends. The ones you gathered to do the store's shopping prize."

"And points to you for that," Tilly said, playfully jabbing an elbow into my side. "I was worried we were all going to have to bail you out at the last minute. Nice to have someone else do the heavy lifting around here."

I wasn't sure that stitching coasters qualified as "heavy lifting," but I knew what she meant. A satisfaction at being able to put my own spin on the project—as well as hopefully garner some intel on B's identity—still glowed inside.

"And men!" Faye said, raising her eyebrows in impressed surprise. "Two of them."

Funny how I'd never listed the members of my little task force, but still every member of the NYAGs knew who they were. Chief Tallen could say what he liked, but there seemed to be few secrets in Gwen Lake.

Dot gave a snicker. "Both handsome fellas. No chance you're stitching up more than coasters around the table?"

I ordered my face not to flush even as I felt my cheeks heat. Mark was a nice guy, but there was no escaping the rugged charm I saw in Jake. You'd think watching someone with traces of grease under their fingernails execute a perfect basket-weave stitch wouldn't have quite that strong an effect on a woman. Jake was straightforward. Uncomplicated. That felt refreshing after the swirl of complexity surrounding my old boss, Dave Batterson.

"They're new *friends*," I replied, emphasizing the final word.

"Is *that* what the kids are calling it these days?" Dot teased.

"Standard definition friends," I reiterated. "You four just call off your matchmaking impulses, okay?"

"When have we ever meddled?" Livvy asked, the sparkle in her eyes showing she knew just how much the NYAGs had meddled in countless Gwen Lake lives.

"I could cite the long list, Livvy, but I don't think I need to." It made me think, *Wouldn't it have been nice if they showed even half that affection toward Kat?* Was she lonely when she died? Or was she in the throes of a dramatic, secret relationship with B? There were no dates on the letters, even though they felt recent to me. Who was he, and how did he figure in her death?

Leona came up behind me and tapped me on the shoulder. "Mr. Windham is here. He's asking to talk to you."

Leydon Windham? Here? He certainly couldn't be a customer. What had I done now to earn an on-site dressing-down from the man?

I turned to find a man close to my age standing at the sales counter. He was tall and poised, despite his clear discomfort. This wasn't Leydon Windham, but his sleek hair and strong jawline bore a striking resemblance to Leydon's. It took me a moment or two to remember Leydon had a son who was a few years before me in school.

"Shelby. I remember you," he said before I had a chance to get out any kind of greeting. "One or two years behind me. Didn't you go off to art school or some such thing?" He tossed out the question in a frivolous tone worthy of the Windham family name.

"I did, Burton." My pulse jumped as I remembered his name—his *B* name. "I graduated from Savannah College of Art and Design and ran the business office of a sizable graphics arts company there." There might have been a bit of an edge to my reply.

"But you're back. And here." He gave a small gesture to the shop around us.

"I'm running it for Mom while she and Dad are on vacation."

"And doing a pretty darned good job of it, too," Tilly chimed in. I turned back to see that every one of the NYAGs was watching us and listening to our conversation with great interest.

Burton put his hands in the pockets of his very nicely tailored suit and rocked back on his polished heels. "I have some business I'd like to discuss." With a glance toward our audience, he added, "In your office, if you don't mind."

It was the office or Mom's office, not my office, but now wasn't the time to argue semantics. "Of course."

"Chamber of commerce business," he explained, loudly enough to make me instantly doubt it.

"Certainly," I replied as I gestured toward the office. We had no chamber of commerce business to discuss—I hadn't talked to the man in over a decade by my count—but I decided to play along. He was another B to add to my list, after all. Curiosity tickled down the back of my neck. It seemed threads and canvases were becoming only a small part of my job description lately.

I took a seat at Mom's desk while Burton settled himself

quickly in the guest chair. His tall frame looked a bit gangly in the small space. Like that of a fashionable scarecrow instead of Cal's cowardly lion. "I'll get right to the point. I understand you were connected with the . . . incident . . . involving Kat."

Not "Miss Katsaros," but "Kat." And there was something about the way he said her name. Things were definitely getting interesting.

"I'm the one who found her, yes."

He shifted in the chair. "I'd like to ask you . . . I was hoping to . . . I'd like to buy some things of Kat's. A pair of scissors and a particular canvas. Discreetly."

Kat? And Burton? It was hard to imagine two more different personalities, but I suppose opposites attract. She had clearly meant something to him, unlikely as it was. And maybe still did. Had those letters come from Burton?

If they had, it'd be hard to pick a relationship that would have irritated Leydon Windham more than his son being involved with the store's highly vocal nemesis. Still, it was possible. Since Romeo and Juliet, family feuds have doomed star-crossed lovers.

And let's not forget the sizable body count at the end of *that* story.

"I can imagine how . . . awkward . . . your relationship would have been, given her feelings about the store. And your father's feelings about her."

How he stiffened at the word *relationship* was as much of an admission as anything he had said or hadn't said. "I don't see how that's any of your business."

"I think it's a great shame," I offered in an empathetic tone. "She had a lot of talent."

He didn't manage to hide the glow of remembrance that lit his eyes. "And a talent for ticking people off."

I had to laugh. "That too. She did extraordinary work. I'd

be happy to help you." If nothing else, the relationship had to have been deep for him to brave coming here with his request. Then again, love had been at the heart of as many murders as greed.

Still, he didn't seem like the kind of man ready to join Jake and Mark among the Needle's ranks of male stitchers. "I don't have any of her canvases completed. We could find someone to stitch it up for you—"

"No," he cut in. "I don't need it . . . stitched up. I just want to . . . have it." Burton fished his phone from his pocket and swiped on the screen until he could turn it toward me with an image. Kat was standing, smiling, in front of a large canvas I recognized.

"I remember that one. Stunning."

"It's not been sold?"

"Not yet." I had noticed it tucked away underneath some of her other canvases. A large canvas like that can run upwards of four hundred dollars, so I was saving it until we knew how well the other big pieces sold.

"I want it," he demanded. "I don't want anyone else to have it. I can pay whatever you need to ask for it." It was an unusually realistic canvas for Kat, a dark sweeping landscape, with two figures standing on a rocky shore. The waves and clouds were stylized, but the figures were clearly a man and a woman. He and Kat, perhaps? Had they been there together? Planned to go there together? So much of the life Kat had yearned for showed up in her work. And yet, so much of it had never shown up in her own real life. It's part of the power of art, I suppose.

"I do have permission from her family to sell all her work here at the store. It's still back at her place, but I can arrange for you to have that piece." It would mean going back into Kat's apartment without Cal, but seeing as how he had left town, I'd have to do that for any restocking of her pieces.

"Do it," he ordered. For just a moment I saw a flash of pain, of loss—or of anger?—behind his demand. Could he have killed her? Would Leydon, if he knew about them, have been willing to do whatever it took to take Kat Katsaros out of the picture? A dozen possibilities popped into my head alongside the thought *Get a sample of his handwriting*.

"As I said, I don't have the canvas here." I slid a blank piece of paper and a pen across the desk to him. "Why don't you write down your address and I can drop it off? Do you know which pair of scissors you'd like?"

"Don't drop it off," he said quickly. He wrote only his phone number down on the paper—not really enough for what I was hoping to do. "Just let me know when you've got it, and I'll arrange to come by with the cash."

He really didn't want anyone to know about this. I quickly calculated 550 dollars for the canvas, based on how we'd priced Kat's other works. Cal would be thrilled—if I could find him to pay him.

"Depending on which scissors, that could be quite a sum."

"Her best scissors. I want the best." He demanded this in a way that let me know the Windhams were used to having the best of everything.

"I have one last pair of her finest. That and the canvas will run you nine hundred."

"I'll have it whenever you call. But no one knows about this, understand? No one. Especially not Cal. Or George." Reluctantly, he added, "Or my father."

"You have my word. This was a meeting about chamber of commerce business. And you can come by after hours to pick up the canvas and scissors if you like. I should be able to have it here next week." I wanted to add, "Are there any documents—letters, perhaps—that you might want me to retrieve while I'm there?"

Genuine relief slacked his shoulders for a minute, and I

could spot a flash of grief—or regret—in his eyes. Then, as quickly as it came, the emotion was gone, replaced by the standard-issue Windham "look down your nose" command.

He stood up, pocketed his phone with the extraordinary canvas still pictured on the screen, and put his hand on the office doorknob. "Well, then."

I likely had just made the largest sale of the day. Maybe of the week. Before I could make any reply, Burton was out the office door and making a beeline out of the shop.

I could have called, "Nice doing business with you," after him, but that hardly applied.

"Baffling doing business with you," was more like it, so I said nothing at all.

Mark's machine shop looked just as I had imagined it would—only neater. While Jake's shop was a barely organized clutter of parts, cars, grimy paperwork, and tools, Mark's looked more like an operating room. If an operating room was loud and smelled of motor oil.

A dozen different machines sat against each of the four walls as we stood there Saturday morning. Some of them I recognized as drills and saws; others I'd never seen before, nor could I guess what they did. Mark caught my bafflement and spread his hands wide, gesturing to the room with pride. "This is where I make stuff."

Jake turned to me. "This is where Mark fabricates amazing, intricate parts and anything else I need. I wouldn't be surprised if he fabricates his fiancée's wedding ring."

Mark grinned. "How'd ya know?"

Jake's response was half laugh, half scowl. "You're not really . . . ?"

"No," Mark responded. "Vicky's an understanding woman, but even she has her limits." He turned his gaze to me. "She's super impressed that I took up needlepoint, by the way. She's on a work trip at the moment. I think we can pull her in when she gets back, if you need extra hands."

More stitchers my age. We really were going to give those NYAGs a run for their money. "Thanks. I'll keep that in mind."

"Now," said Mark, "the reason you're here. I set up the grinding stone over here." He led us to a machine that looked more updated than Kat's, as far as I remembered, but essentially it has the same set of discs mounted vertically on an engine, which turned them.

It was a basic piece of machinery. The logical part of me knew that. I still could not embrace the theory that such a machine had killed Kat by accident. Even so, some irrational part of me looked at the thing like a predator. I could be wrong in my suspicions. The thing could be a knife-throwing beast of death.

Jake caught my hesitation. "Yeah, I know."

It felt good to know I wasn't the only person feeling a little . . . unnerved by the thing. And Mark hadn't even turned it on yet. I turned to our host and dared to ask, "Do you really think it could do . . . what people think it did?" A small part of me wanted Mark to prove me wrong, to demonstrate that Kat's death was an accident. But a stronger voice wanted me to see for myself that this "accident" could not have been an accident at all.

Mark pressed his lips together in thought. "The circumstances would have to be freakishly exact. But I hear about freak machinery accidents all the time. You have to be careful."

"And everyone says Kat wasn't. But still . . ."

He picked up three pairs of safety goggles from the table, handed a pair to both Jake and me, and donned a pair himself. "But I think I can show you what you're looking for. Do you know if Kat used clamps to hold the knives or held them by hand?"

I didn't, but I could make a guess. "She seemed to be a hands-on kind of person."

"Well, that would increase the chances of an injury if the knife slipped out of her grip. Ready?"

He flipped a switch on the machine, and it began to hum. I was expecting a louder sound, but it was just a low-grade mechanical sound.

Mark adjusted a knob. "The tube over here regulates how much water goes onto the grinding mechanism. You don't want to do this dry, whether it's an everyday kitchen knife or a really fancy chef's one."

"It was a fancy one that . . ." Despite my certainty, it was still a struggle to say it out loud. I still wasn't comfortable with finding the right words for what had happened to her. "They found in her."

Mark picked up a knife that looked like one you'd find in any kitchen. "Well, that only means it was probably very sharp. But the process is essentially the same." He tilted the knife against a stone that was spinning vertically on the machine, and it made the bone-chilling grating, scraping sound I'd been dreading. If something could sound dangerous, that did. I felt it in my teeth and bit my cheeks involuntarily.

"Which way is it rotating?" I asked. It was surprisingly hard to tell.

"Away from me. That's how you normally use it."

"That's what bugs me," I replied. "I don't see how the knife could have been thrust toward her if the thing was rotating the other way. At least not with the kind of force there would have to have been."

"You'd think," Mark replied, clamping a handle-like object onto the knife he'd selected. "But if you catch the stone just the wrong way, it could send the knife flipping into the air. And you can adjust the machine to rotate the other way, although I'm not sure what kind of sharpening you'd do that for. Like I said, it's unlikely, but I have scars from lots of 'unlikely' accidents."

"What about the water? Could you tell the direction from

the water?" There was a small well of water under the stone, into which it dipped on its way around.

Mark raised an eyebrow. "What do you mean?"

"The wall of the van behind the machine was wet. I remember seeing it."

"There shouldn't be much water anywhere if she had the shield in place."

Jake looked at me. "Only she never used any of the safety shields, right?"

Mark thought for a minute. "That could tell you which way the disc was rotating. Without the shield, a disc rotating away from her would kick up water toward her as it came out of the well. If it was rotating toward her, whatever was behind the machine would get water sprayed on it. Were her arms or chest wet?"

I swallowed at the image that came to mind. An image I'd probably never forget. "Only with blood. The water was on the wall."

Despite the whir of the machine, the room fell eerily quiet for a moment. If what we had just learned was true, the machine's grindstone had been rotating toward Kat. To me, that was further evidence that someone might have tampered with the machine. Unless Kat had set it that way, which seemed increasingly unlikely.

Mark motioned for us to back away to a safe distance and carefully positioned the knife against the grinding stone. The sound was like a metallic screech, shrill and rattling, with sparks flying. I couldn't imagine having a job where you'd have to listen to that all day. The sound's pitch changed—becoming almost like an animal's cry—as he slid the knife across the grindstone blade from hilt to tip. Mark flipped the knife over and repeated the process on the other side. Then he did both sides over again at a faster rate. By the end of the process, my ears hurt and I was gritting my teeth in a constant cringe.

"You do get used to it," he assured me. "Although I don't do this nearly as often as Kat does. Did."

"You said you rigged up an experiment of sorts for Shelby?" Jake asked.

"Well, the water tells us the disc was rotating toward her. But I know you wanted to see if the machine could have launched the knife the way they said it did."

In truth, I wanted Mark to prove it wasn't the machine that had killed her, even if the stone was rotating the wrong way. It just sounded too sinister to say that out loud.

Mark said it for me. He turned off the machine and stuffed his hands into his pockets. "Yeah, well, the short answer is that I couldn't get the machine to hurl the knife the way they claim."

Something shifted in my gut. "You couldn't?"

"Not really." He reached into a box on the counter and pulled out a short thin piece of metal the size of a domino. He pushed a tall tool chest over to a spot a few feet from the machine, then leaned a taller piece of plywood up against the tool chest. I thought instantly of those dangerous acts where some daredevil throws knives at a scantily clad woman in front of a bull's-eye. It wasn't a comforting association.

Jake—who clearly had the same thoughts—and I moved eagerly out of the way when Mark said, "Stand over there."

"It's not as if you would never switch the rotation of the grinding stone," Mark explained as he made some adjustments to the machine. "I have, for machine parts and that kind of thing. But hardly ever." He turned the machine back on and held the small metal piece with a pair of long-handled pliers, then stood off to the side before he angled the metal up against the moving disc. It skittered a bit at first and produced the same ear-splitting grinding sound and an array of sparks.

"You can definitely get nicked . . . ," he shouted over the noise, twisting the pliers a fraction of an inch. The metal piece flew out of the pliers' grip, sailed through the shop, and hit the plywood with a sickening thud before bouncing off it to clatter on the floor. I noticed there was a host of dings and gashes in the plywood from when he'd made earlier attempts. "But get a knife to sink in very far? I couldn't come close to making that happen. Just kept hitting against the board without embedding."

Jake pointed to the piece of metal on the floor. "You're sure?"

Mark walked over and picked it up. "Well, I wasn't about to stand in front of the sharpener with a knife and test the theory, but I say it can't be done."

Jake and I thanked Mark and left the shop. I wasn't sure I had anything I could take to Tallen . . . yet. He'd likely lecture me on "playing junior detective" by staging an experiment like this. I had to go to him with something he couldn't ignore, and I didn't have that yet. Still, I felt one step closer to proving my theory that Kat wasn't murdered by her sharpening machine.

So now the real question was how? And by whom?

CHAPTER 22

"Look at us, up to the Ls and all," Deb crowed as she lined up the coaster trios in neat little piles as my needlepoint friends gathered around my kitchen table for another session Monday evening. "Rose thought she was getting only one prize, but you are giving her a whole alphabet."

"Overachiever," Jake muttered in a mock jab.

"Admit it," I jabbed right back, "you like making these." In fact, Jake was already faster than I was. That might have had something to do with the fact that I kept being drawn back to work on Kat's artistic canvas. I kept thinking if I stitched up all those crisscross motifs, some hidden clue would surface and explain why she had replicated a feature of the doubloons in so much of her work. So far it hadn't.

"I do, actually. It's . . ." He squinted in thought, reaching for a word.

"Artistically precise," Mark offered. "At least that's what I like about it. At the machine shop, I can be as creative as I like in formulating parts to solve someone's problem, but if the fabrication isn't precise enough to get the job done, it's wasted time. This is like that." He blinked at me. "Does that make any sense?"

"A lot," Jake replied before I could. "I like that the back

matters as much as the front. You've got to look under the hood to see how good the work really is."

"You guys do realize you're talking about needlepoint, don't you?" Cherie teased.

Mark clutched his current canvas—an *M*—to his chest. "Yikes." He peered around in a theatrical panic. "Tell no one."

"I'm not sure anyone would believe me if I did," Deb offered.

"I admit, I didn't believe you at first," Jake said. "I mostly just did it to help you out."

I liked hearing that. The beginning of something was simmering between Jake and me, even though neither of us was ready to admit it. He knew I was coming off the wreckage of Dave Batterson, and although he had never offered the details, I got the feeling he'd had his own heart trampled on recently. I was just glad to have a friend in town, even if it never went beyond that. For now.

Cherie started in on a new row of her current *O* coaster. "When are you going to start asking people to put in for the drawing?"

I'd asked Mark, Jake, and Deb to say nothing about my real agenda for the coaster giveaway in front of Cherie. The chief's reluctance to consider a murder theory bugged me, and I didn't want Cherie reporting my theories back to her father before I went to him myself. It made for tricky conversation with Cherie in the room.

A knock on my door revealed Jessica, holding the three letter coaster sets, now completed, I'd given her just on Thursday—*P*, *Q*, and *R*—and a charcuterie board. In a single move, she'd put both my two sets of completed letter coasters and my measly bowl of popcorn to shame. Classic Jessica. "I figured since I was late, I'd better show up with some snacks."

And here I'd thought popcorn *was* a snack. The artisanal cheese and meat spread was a mini gourmet buffet.

"Real food," Mark said with carnivorous glee. "I'm starved."

I tried not to glare as the man attempted to pounce on the tray the minute Jessica set it down. Jessica swatted his hand away until she produced lovely little china plates. With tiny matching forks. "Don't get your hands messy, or you might stain the needlepoint," she chided.

The woman had table service for everything.

"How can you be starving?" I grumbled at Mark. "You just ate most of the popcorn."

"That's not real food," he countered.

Maybe I should have taken Mr. Sanders up on his offer of a pork chop—or six.

"Thanks," I said to Jessica, trying hard to mean it. She had really wanted to come, had done an amazing amount of work to help, and had just upped my hostess game, after all.

She settled into the chair next to me as the men filled their tiny plates without making fun of the tiny forks—which looked even tinier in their hands. "Which letters are left?"

I counted off the remaining alphabet letters on my fingers. "Thanks to your quick work, there are only six letters left." Again, I tried hard to make my gratitude sound sincere.

"In here?" She pointed to the shoebox on the counter, which held the three canvases for each of the remaining letters. She stood up, walked over to the box, and pulled out *S* and *T*. "I can take these," she pronounced as she sat down again "I'll probably polish one of them off just sitting here."

"It's not a competition," I wanted to say. "We're all at different skill levels. It's fine to do them at your own speed."

"I'm the slowest," Cherie admitted.

I regretted the tone of apology in her voice. "You're the newest. And I'm glad you're here. If we weren't so close to the end, I'd ask you if you want to bring a friend next time." I was really proud that we'd managed to bring someone her age into the craft, even if her presence did make for my having to carefully monitor what I said.

Cherie smiled. "You know what I like about needlepoint?"

I genuinely wanted to know. "What?"

"It's like coloring, but more complicated." She pulled her thread through the canvas with a careful touch. "You're filling things in according to what's on the canvas, but it's not mindless. I know lots of people think coloring is cool now, but I think it's boring. This takes just the right amount of attention to be relaxing."

"I like the way you put that." I did. She was imaginative and a bit distracted, but definitely articulate.

"I can post it on a Yelp review for the shop if you like," she offered.

I made a mental note to check the shop's online reviews. I doubt anyone from the Needle ever had.

"I'd like that, Cherie. We should do more on social media." For as visual as needlepoint was, Mom hadn't taken advantage of the social media that could bring new people to the shop.

"We could make a web page where people could sign up to win the coasters," she went on. "We'd reach more people that way."

Someone typing in their name on a keyboard would not accomplish what I needed. Thinking quickly, I replied, "I think that's a bit too much just yet. Besides, I've got the entry slips all printed up." I had actually only designed them and hadn't printed them. Still, it was the best evasion I could come up with on the fly.

"Ah." She nodded. "Old school."

I forced a laugh. "Yep, entry slips in a fishbowl for the drawing and all that."

"After all," Deb noted, backing me up, "Gwen Lake is nothing if not quaint. Can't ruin our reputation by going too high tech."

"This from the chemist turned barista," Jake teased.

"That's right," Jessica said. "I'd forgotten you have a PhD in chemistry. I've been telling the boys biochemistry will be an amazing field to choose in college."

They're not even in middle school, I shouted in my brain. *Do they have to be selecting college majors now?* And if Taylor chose art history or something else that did not ensure an immediate six-figure income, would they let him pursue it?

We passed the rest of the evening in pleasant stitching and conversation. Jessica settled down, abandoning her must-impress mode, and even complimented Jake and Mark on their stitching. It actually felt nice to have a group of people I could consider friends sitting around my kitchen table. I hadn't felt that way about Jessica in a long time. I hadn't felt that way in a long time, period. It was easy to see why most of the NYAGs went out of their way never to miss one of their gatherings.

When Jessica lingered after everyone else had left, looking more serious than she would if she was just staying to rinse off her forks and plates, I began to worry that some sort of lecture was coming my way.

"The real reason I was late is that I ran into Chief Tallen outside the school when I was dropping the boys off. I should have pulled you aside earlier, but I just couldn't figure out a way to do it."

"Why? Did he say something?"

"They found Cal."

"Where?"

"Sleeping in the van in a store parking lot outside of Chattanooga." She shook her head. "Very drunk, according to Tallen."

I dried off one of the dishes she'd just washed. "I'm surprised it took this long. That van would stand out anywhere." Cal wasn't exactly a brilliant fugitive, either, but he seemed to be acting on pure emotion these days rather than following any plan.

"They arrested him. For stealing the van and probably DUI, I suppose."

I stack the dried dish on top of the others. "That makes sense."

Jessica turned off the water. "There's something else Tallen wanted you to know."

"Okay."

"Well, it seems Cal was mouthing off quite a bit when they took him in."

"Again, not surprised." I couldn't read her serious expression. "Jess, what is it?"

"Cal was evidently going on about how Kat didn't die by accident. About how she was murdered."

CHAPTER 23

So, finally, I wasn't the only person who thought Kat had been murdered. The other person holding that opinion, however, had shouted it in a drunken, larcenous rage. And had previously insisted Kat's own carelessness had led to her death. Not exactly a trustworthy corroborator.

Jessica stared hard at me. "You're not surprised."

"No," I admitted. The small word felt enormous.

My sister's mouth fell open. "You've been thinking Kat was murdered? For how long?"

"It isn't the kind of thing you just blurt out in polite conversation."

Jessica parked one hand on her hip. "You clearly blurted it out to Chief Tallen."

"He didn't believe me. Kind of warned me off investigating it, actually."

"You've been *investigating*?" Shock pitched her voice so high that Nabbit looked up from his perch on top of the refrigerator, where he'd been hiding from all the company. She didn't say, "And you didn't tell me?" out loud, but her arched eyebrows shouted it.

"Not really."

Jessica is a ninja-level mom. Her doubtful *Don't you give me that* look practically pinned me up against the counter.

"I just don't believe the machine could have sent the knife into her like that. Mark even tried to re-create it and couldn't. It's too freak an accident, even for Kat."

Jessica flung her hand in the direction of my kitchen table, where we'd just been gathered. "You've been running *reenactments* with people?"

"How else am I going to get anyone to believe me? Not Tallen, that's for sure."

Jessica leaned back against the counter and crossed her arms over her chest. "All right, Shelby. Out with it. All of it. From the beginning."

We sat back down at the kitchen table, and I ran through everything. I hesitated a bit before talking about the letters, the doubloons, and Burton, but if I'd come this far, I might as well be all in. And for once, Jessica didn't seem to be judging me or my actions.

Smart as she is, she picked up on my plan right away. "So that's why you're doing the coasters? So you can collect Gwen Lake's Bs?" I thought she'd find the plan far-fetched, but she nodded. "Clever. And that's why you shot down Cherie's idea of the website raffle sign-up. You need handwriting samples."

"It's a stretch, I know, but it's the only thing I can think of. Those letters were passionate. There's a good chance that if B isn't our killer, he or she might know who is."

"Who else knows what you're up to here?"

"Everyone who was here tonight except Cherie knows we're using the coaster giveaway to try to find B. I haven't outlined my theory that B could be involved in Kat's murder, but I think most of them are picking up on my line of thought. Well, except Cherie. Though I think she already suspects something, because she's the one who put me on to the Windham's threats. She works there."

"She's also Tallen's daughter. That complicates things."

I sat back in my chair. "More than you know, actually."

"Why?"

This one felt risky to admit. "He's another B. Sort of."

Jessica pressed her lips together in thought. "Chief Tallen's first name is Evan. And he's too old for her."

"I know that. But he admitted to me that Bobby—the word for a British policeman—is an old nickname of his. He had one of those police whistles on his desk when I met with him the other day." When Jessica gave me another doubtful look, I went on. "There was just something in the way he said it, the way he looked after it slipped out. And it would explain why he has kept insisting Kat's death was accidental, even though I think anyone with any common sense would realize that knife didn't end up embedded in her chest by accident."

"But it doesn't explain why he wanted me to tell you that Cal thinks Kat was murdered. If he did it, he'd want to promote the idea that it was an accident." She rolled her eyes. "He couldn't have. I mean, he's much older than her, and he's the police chief."

"Maybe now that we have the van back, he's afraid someone will figure it out. What better way to look innocent than by steering suspicion in some other direction?"

Jessica's analytical face returned. "Cal must know something."

"Unless Cal did it and just can't live with himself. His life is pretty much a wreck right now. Maybe he just hit rock bottom. Maybe Tallen is just B, and Cal's our murderer. There're still too many possibilities. I have to be careful what I say in front of Cherie."

Jessica nodded. "This has to stay between us. Well, you, me, Jake, Deb, and Mark. Tallen can't know what we know about the coins and the letters."

What was it Tallen had said? *Everybody has secrets in a town as small as this. Take care what rocks you turn over. The consequences may be way different than what you thought you were getting.* I got the weird, prickly feeling that I was sitting in a minefield. One wrong step and people could get hurt—including me.

I noticed, at that moment, Jessica's surprising choice of words. "Between us?"

She looked almost embarrassed. "Well, yeah. We are together in this, aren't we?"

Had I listed all the possible outcomes of my time here in Gwen Falls, I doubt discovering a new partnership with my sister would have been one of them. Still, her expression was genuine. And she'd shared with me how things weren't quite as perfect at home as she led people to believe. Isn't that what a sister should be for?

I had never seen my sister look even the closest thing to needy. And yet through some sisterly bond, I'd picked up on her need to be here, on her need to be in this strange, unwelcome circumstance with me. For the first time in a long time— maybe even forever—I felt as if we were on equal ground.

The smile I felt cross my face was as warm as it was surprising. "Yeah," I said. "We are." And just because the moment felt too close and awkward, I added, "Whatever it is this is."

She grinned. "This is an investigation. A secret hunt for clues." She grabbed my hand, as if both of us weren't quite sure if a hug was the proper response to our new dark quest. "It's obvious where to start, isn't it?"

"Um, no."

"Of course it is. Cal gave you the keys to Kat's apartment, right? So you could go get more of her stuff to sell when you needed it?"

"I do." I did indeed have the keys to her apartment. And while that felt like first-class snooping, wasn't that exactly what was called for here?

"We'd better get back there before Tallen does."

* * *

Jessica and I drove over there immediately. Despite the fact that I had perfectly innocent reasons to be at Kat's apartment, guilt still chilled my spine as I turned the corner onto her street.

I expected to find her parking space empty, with the van wherever Cal had taken it, but I wasn't expecting to see a fancy sports car sitting in front of Kat's building.

I turned to Jessica. "Who do you think is there?"

"George drives a sedan. It's not him. Pull over and let's see if someone comes out." Jessica slumped down in her seat and put on her sunglasses, which struck me as a bit dramatic given the sun was setting. This wasn't a cop show stakeout.

After five minutes of nothing happening, Jessica opened the car door. "You have a valid reason to be here. I don't know who else would. Let's go find out."

"Jess, you can't just . . ."

Evidently, she could. She grabbed one of the Nimble Needle crates I'd brought along to transfer new stock to the store—something I felt I at least ought to do while I was here—and began to walk up the sidewalk as if she owned the place.

I grumbled something about who was really in charge here, grabbed the second crate, and dashed to get to the door first.

I didn't need my key. The door was pulled open just as I reached the top step to reveal a very startled Burton Windham.

"What are you doing here?" he demanded with a very Windham-worthy sneer.

"I could ask you the same thing," I shot back. "I'm here to get the last of Kat's work to sell at the store, just like I told you. How did you get in here, anyway?"

Jessica stepped forward. "Did Kat give you a key on account of your relationship?"

I would have liked her to have been a bit more subtle. Turns out I have a keener gift for sneaky than my big sister. I met Burton's angry glare with the simple admission "She knows."

"I asked for your discretion," he growled.

"Relax," Jessica replied with an oversized sigh. "Neither one of us is going to fill Daddy in on your clandestine affair with Kat."

I threw a *Take it down a notch* glare of my own to Jessica.

"Yes, I do have a key. I was looking for something." He had a package in his hand. Something wrapped up.

Letters? I demanded in my head. *Doubloons?* If he had a key, why did he come to me, looking for the canvas he wanted? "What?" In a matter of seconds, I figured out what he was doing. He was taking the canvas and scissors we'd discussed. All his "Money is no object" comments rang hollow. He'd come to me only to confirm they were still here. Maybe he planned on blaming Cal for their sudden disappearance.

Burton's chin lifted in uppity defiance. "I don't need to explain myself to you."

I nodded at the package. "Taking something that doesn't belong to you is my definition of *stealing*. Probably Chief Tallen's, too."

"Where's Kat's van?" Burton demanded, ignoring my accusation. "Did you take that to sell, too?"

"No," I replied, reining in my growing annoyance. All the pity I felt for Burton's wounded heart evaporated. "Cal took it. Cal stole it, actually. They just found it—and him—sleeping off a bender in Tennessee." For a moment I wondered if I was at liberty to share that.

Burton snorted. "Sounds like Cal."

"Too many people seem to be taking things from Kat." I glared at him. "Including her life."

"Her death was a terrible accident," he countered. It struck me that Burton's father had used the same wording. Coincidence?

"I don't think so."

"What?" He looked genuinely shocked. Or he was a very good actor. Tough to know which.

Jessica crossed her arms over her chest, meeting Burton posture for posture. She could get as uppity as Burton when she chose to, but I never figured it would work to my advantage. "It might interest you to know that Cal is insisting Kat was murdered."

"So we're listening to Cal now?" Burton tried to push his way past Jessica and me. I blocked him. He jabbed a hand in the air. "Come on. I wouldn't be surprised if it turns out he rigged that machine to harm her. They aren't exactly a happy family, if you hadn't noticed."

"Give me the package, Burton." *Your family's a mess, too*, I thought as I thrust out my hand. I was still having trouble reconciling the sad, hurt man I'd seen in Mom's office with the arrogant heir to the Windham empire I saw now and had seen everywhere else. What on earth had Kat seen in him?

I expected another pompous comeback, but instead Burton tossed the package at my feet and stalked around me to his car without another word.

"I still can't see how those two were together." Jessica sighed.

I picked up the package as Burton's shiny sports car sped off down the street. I almost didn't need to open it to know what was inside. "Is it stealing if you give it back?"

"It's guilty-looking, I'll tell you that." Jessica stared down the street after Burton's car. "Leydon couldn't have known about those two. He would have had a fit if he knew. Put a stop to it any way he could." She hesitated a bit on those last words, recognizing the weight they carried. "Would he have?" she asked. She didn't have to elaborate—our thoughts had both gone in the same direction.

"Properly provoked, I suppose anyone is capable of anything." I turned back toward Kat's door, still open behind us. "And if Kat was good at anything, it was provoking people."

"She excelled at that." Jessica followed me inside.

"You know," I mused, "I wouldn't put it past Kat to use the secret of her relationship with Burton—depending on how it ended—to wound or threaten Leydon and the store." I paused. "And I wouldn't put it past Burton—or even Leydon—to do anything to keep it quiet."

If only all the tourist types who find Gwen Lake so quaint should see our town's dark underbelly today. It would make Mayor Rose cringe. Maybe that's why she fought so hard to keep up the shiny, happy image.

Jessica turned to look at me as we stood in Kat's hallway. "Either one of them could have done it. Or Cal. The whole B thing could just be a red herring."

I raised an eyebrow at the mystery term.

"Hey, I read books," she said in her defense. "I read people pretty good, too. And Burton was scared. All that arrogant nonsense was just fear."

I thought again of the letters. The person who couldn't find out about Kat and B didn't need to be a spouse. It could be a domineering father. And Jessica was right—maybe B wasn't the murderer. Maybe B was the motive. I made the decision right there to take what I knew to Tallen and brave whatever consequences came from it.

Jessica walked into the living room and wrinkled her nose in disgust. "Did Burton trash the place? It's a mess."

"No," I replied, setting down the crate I was holding. "It looked this way last time."

I suppose to Jessica's pristine housekeeping eyes, the place did look ransacked. To me, it just looked like the haphazard chaos of most creative people. Most of the artists at Batterson hadn't kept organized desks. They had been continually cluttered with art supplies, photos, sketches, and a baffling amount of toys. The large room that housed the collection of cubicles and was known as our art department had looked more like Santa's workshop than any corporate office.

"What are we looking for?" my sister asked.

That was the million-dollar question. "I don't really know.

Something that will tell us if B is Burton or someone else. Anything, I suppose, that points to someone who would want to harm Kat."

We wandered around the apartment, looking for . . . well, whatever. While Jessica attacked the task with gusto, opening drawers, sorting through closets and cabinets, my skin prickled from the reluctance I felt snooping in a dead woman's home. I was snooping on her behalf, yes, but I was still poking around in a place Chief Tallen would not be happy to find me.

But to be honest, I was getting frustrated with Tallen. He should be treating Kat's death as a murder. Why wasn't he interrogating suspects, following clues? And the van. Why hadn't he treated it like a crime scene before Cal stole it? The chief seemed like an upright guy. What could possibly be blinding him to the facts of this case?

I got my answer when I walked into Kat's bedroom and my eyes landed on a shiny object hanging from a blue ribbon on her dresser mirror.

A police whistle exactly like the one on Tallen's desk. *Bobby.*

CHAPTER 24

Things were getting very complicated in Gwen Lake. Every day I felt like I had to tread more carefully, as though I had more secrets to carry. The whistle on Kat's mirror made me doubt everything I thought I knew about her murder. Tallen had to be connected with Kat somehow—it was the only explanation for how he was handling the case. Only how do you confront a police chief with something like that? He'd already warned me off multiple times. If I handled it wrong, if the chief really had somehow played a role in Kat's life and death, then he would shut me out of information faster than Burton's snazzy sports car.

I found myself unable to make the next move. Mostly because I had no idea what that next move should be.

The one thing that helped my sorry state, surprisingly, was spending time with Jessica. And her boys. Complex as they were, my nephews' little lives seemed a refreshing break from all the adult intrigue filling my life lately.

So when Jessica invited me over for dinner on Wednesday, I readily accepted. Which is how I found myself lingering in Chaz and Taylor's room, enjoying how their personalities were all over the space.

The twins' room looked exactly as it always had—artfully decorated, neatly arranged, and brimming with sports memorabilia. From the moment Jessica knew she was having twin boys, she had devised a perfectly coordinated set of furniture and decor in complimentary shades of blue and green. Chaz had always been the blue; Taylor the green.

I admit, part of me had always wondered if Chaz's fiercely competitive nature was a gift from his father or if his desire for the blue ribbon first prize stemmed from the color blue of his surroundings. I loved both boys, but Taylor had always occupied a softer spot in my heart. I knew what it was like to have a sibling who seemed effortlessly perfect at everything. Whether those things mattered to me or not, Jessica's superiority was my constant companion. As, I suspect, Chaz's was to Taylor.

What struck me now, however, was the collection of wonderful drawings that joined all those sports posters on the wall on Taylor's side of the room. I'm no art critic and certainly no childhood expert, but the boy had real talent. His drawings went beyond the crude figures we associate with children's drawings and showed real movement, a keen sense of color, and even a hint of perspective. I recognized Jessica, Hal, and Chaz in several drawings—he'd managed to capture them, even at his age.

Taylor bounded into the room behind me, laughing at something his brother had said in the hallway. He rolled onto his bed, still giggling. "Hey, Aunt Shelby. Whatcha doing in here?"

I sat down next to him, drinking in his sweet, easy smile. "I'm looking at all your cool drawings. You're really good at it."

He turned over to view the wall. "I like it. I draw stuff all the time. I put the ones I like best up here."

I noticed none of the drawings were about sports. Even his pictures of Chaz and Hal had them doing other things. That felt important. My heart twisted at the thought that this kid's attention and talents were off the sports field, no matter how hard his father and brother might drag him back onto it. Somebody had to encourage the natural talent Taylor had before it got squashed. And I knew, just by the drawings, that it would be a true shame if that happened.

A perfect, genius idea struck me. I swiveled around on the

bed so that Taylor and I were perched on our elbows, facing the wall. "They're all good," I said. "Have you got a favorite?"

He scrunched up his face in thought. An artist is always his own worst critic. "Nope. I like 'em all."

"What about your mom? Does she have a favorite?" My idea was forming fast and furious, humming inside my chest.

He thought again. "She likes the purple bird."

I took a moment to admire the big, bold bird with wide eyes and crazy, colorful wings. "I love that it's purple. Real birds never get to be purple." I had always thought the best artists took our real world and layered something new and wonderful onto it. Kat certainly did.

Taylor flopped onto his back and frowned. "Dad says it's silly."

The humming in my chest heated up to a low burn. How could a father call his son's artwork silly? To his face? Mom might have been dangerously close to a helicopter parent before that was a thing, and super-judgmental of my choice in boyfriends, but she never ever belittled anything I created or any ideas I had. Gave suggestions or helped me evaluate, yes, but always with a supportive hand.

"I don't think art is ever silly. I think art is important." I waded carefully into these waters. "You know my work is with art, don't you?"

"I thought you worked in an office. Well, before Granny's store, I mean."

How do you explain an involuntary corporate layoff to a nine-year-old? "Well, I did, but then they changed things, and it was time to get a new job. But what I did was help the artists at my company make stuff for other companies. People do art for work. You could grow up and go to school for art or do art for work, too. If you want."

To my deep regret, Taylor looked like that was a completely foreign idea. As if I'd just told him there were zebra-striped frogs on Mars.

"Yep," I continued. "You could."

"Hmmm." Taylor rolled that idea around in his brain. I could practically see his vision of the world shift a bit. Now my idea blazed with a "Got to do it" urgency I felt to my fingertips.

"Could I hire you?" I asked as if it were a wonderful secret.

His eyes popped. "Huh?"

"Could I buy a piece of your art to make something special for your mom? I need a gift for her birthday coming up. We'd have to keep it a secret, but I want to buy your purple bird painting and get it made into a needlepoint canvas for her. It's her favorite, right? And you know how much she loves to stitch. It could be a present from both of us."

He turned his gaze back to the bird. "I'd give it to you."

"I know you would, but I want to be the first person to pay you for your art. Would you let me?"

His smile was far more payment to me than I could ever give to him. "Okay."

"We can't tell your mom yet, though. I want it to be a surprise." *And I don't want your dad to squash the joy of it.* Yes, it felt a tad meddling, but I knew deep down this was one chance— maybe my only chance—to plant an artistic seed in my talented nephew.

Plus, I was pretty sure Jessica would love it. It wouldn't be hard for me to reproduce the drawing on a needlepoint canvas, pull the corresponding colored threads, and box the whole thing up like a one-of-a-kind kit. Way better than any birthday trinket I could buy at Windham's. And, truth be told, I found my fondness for my sister growing lately. A win-win-win all around. Even if Hal might not agree.

"What's a fair price for this, you think?" I was curious to see what he'd say. I'd probably give him whatever he asked for.

"A million dollars?"

I cracked up. The only thing better than an artist is an artist with great business sense. "You think I have a million dollars?"

"Okay, maybe not. Ten dollars and a milkshake from Mister Scoops?"

Mister Scoops made great milkshakes. I held out a hand. "You got a deal, mister."

He shook it with pint-sized pride. "Mom'll like this."

"She will." I looked around the room. I needed some way to get the drawing back to the shop without folding it and placing it in my handbag. "You got a book around here that's big enough to put that drawing in?"

Taylor jumped off his bed to scan his bookshelf and selected an old picture book about dinosaurs. "This one?"

We pulled the drawing from the wall, slid it into the book, and grinned at each other. "We'll tell them you're lending me this book for something at Granny's shop, okay?"

"Got it."

Chaz appeared in the doorway. "Mom says it's time for dinner."

Dinner that night was good, as was everything Jessica made. And dessert was a fabulous cheesecake. But those few moments with Taylor? Those were definitely the sweetest part of my night. Definitely the cure for all the tension and trouble brewing around me.

Thursday was the final needlepoint night, and I was glad not only for the chance to finish up the project on time, but also for the opportunity to sort through the new information and figure out what to do next. Since Cherie couldn't make it, I could freely update my small but mighty squad of stitchers/investigators and figure out a next step.

Officially, Jake, Deb, Jessica, Mark, and I were gluing the cork backs to the sets of coasters. They looked fabulous. Not at all the work of beginners. I was proud of all of us. Unofficially, we were examining the baffling number of possibilities that had arisen in the case.

"Kat can't have had a thing with Tallen," Mark pronounced

after I updated the group on everything I'd learned since our last meeting.

Deb shot him a sideways glance. "Why not? He's not my type, but he's not an unattractive man, and he wouldn't be the first married man to have a thing on the side with a younger woman. And like Shelby said, it would explain a lot."

"Yeah, but *Kat*?"

She narrowed her eyes at him. "You were thinking maybe along the lines of a flight attendant?"

"What a bomb that would be if it got out," Mark said. "The chief of police cheating on the mayor? People would go nuts. If Kat had some reason to take it public . . ."

"It could have been just a platonic, father-figure thing," Jessica offered. "We don't know that it was a romance."

I shook my head. "Not based on the letters I read. This was a romance."

"But not necessarily a romance that resulted in murder," Jake added.

"Someone killed Kat," I reiterated. "This is a murder." Saying it aloud still made me a bit queasy. Kat hadn't just died; she'd been *killed*. Rather brutally. That doubled the unfairness of it all.

"Okay, if we're talking crime of passion, doesn't that put Burton in the spotlight?" Jake asked. "We already know they were together."

"Burton wanted some of Kat's work bad enough to try and steal it," I added.

"Yeah," Mark sneered. "Like he didn't have the cash to pay you what it was worth. That's low."

"Don't forget, the letters talk about someone finding out. Not necessarily a spouse," Deb said. "It could be Leydon they were worried about. He'd blow a gasket if he knew his son was getting it on with the store's biggest enemy."

Jessica began tying the *A* trio of coasters together with a colored ribbon. "And we know he has a temper." She used some fancy knot, which made the set look like something you'd find in a gift store. Again, my chest filled with pride. We'd done the Needle proud, and we hadn't even started gathering the handwriting samples that would help our investigation.

"Stop that!" Jessica snapped as Nabbit tried, again, to make off with a section of ribbon. He'd been attempting to steal some every second since we sat down. His persistence was entertaining, if annoying.

"Did you manage to see the sharpening machine at Windham's?" Deb asked.

"Wouldn't let me near it," I replied.

Deb handed the fateful *B* coasters to Jessica to get their gift ribbon wrapping. "And since we can't get access to the one in the van anymore, it'll be hard to figure out how somebody might have sabotaged it."

Mark sat back. "While I'll admit someone might have messed with it to get it turning the wrong way, I can't come up with a good reason why Kat would have had it rotating toward her to sharpen a knife. I don't think that matters. As far as I'm concerned, the machine couldn't have done it."

"I'm with you," I agreed. "So why didn't Tallen jump on that possibility?"

"Well, he wouldn't if he's guilty, would he?" Jake replied. "I work on the squad cars, and I know the guy who handles the fleet. He'll do the evidence work on the van when they bring it here. I didn't let on about anything, but I asked him to keep an eye out."

"I can't believe Cal thought he'd get away with taking it," Jake said. "You can't hide in that thing no matter where you go."

I remembered Cal's searing glare and the booming thunk his punch to the van's side had made. "He thought it belonged to him. He thought he should have had it all along."

"Which is a pretty solid motive to murder your sister," Mark said. He shook his head as he wiped a bead of glue from the cork square he was applying to an *L* coaster. "Geez, my sister bugs me, but I'd never sink a knife into her chest."

For a surprising glimmer of a moment, I realized how much the friction between my sister and me had died down. I was proud of that, too.

"If the letters and the coins don't have anything to do with her death, then Cal or Leydon really are the prime suspects," Mark continued.

My eyes widened with a new thought. "The doubloons. They are silver."

"So?" Jake asked.

"So they couldn't have come from anyone who was a yacht club commodore, right? Because theirs are gold?" I touched the gold one around my neck at the same moment Jessica touched the one around hers. It was poignant how both of us had worn them daily since Dad had left town.

Jake looked around the room. "Does anyone remember if Tallen or Windham was a commodore?"

"Burton isn't old enough to have been a commodore," I replied.

"No, but he'd have a gold one if his father was," Jessica explained.

I caught on to her line of thinking. "And Burton could have given it to Kat. Especially if her own father denied her one of his." The whole thing seemed like such a tangle of family dysfunction.

"Were they? Either one of them?" Jake asked again.

Most of this yacht club stuff had happened while I was away. Jessica looked like she was racking her brain unsuccessfully. "There's got to be a plaque or something at the clubhouse by the dock," I suggested. "Should we go look?"

"We shouldn't have to," Deb said as she dug out her phone and began tapping on the screen. "I bet I can find it."

The room fell silent as Deb swiped through multiple web pages and images. Despite Tallen's warnings, I felt as if we were hot on the trail of the killer. I'd made a promise of sorts to Kat that we'd get justice for her, and I was starting to feel we might actually make good on that promise. The image of that crisscross motif scattered throughout her canvases and decorating her scissors ran through my mind. Every artist puts their life into their work, but I'd never felt it quite so sharply—pun intended—as I did at that moment.

"Here it is." Deb read the list of Gwen Lake Yacht Club commodores aloud. They were familiar names, my father's among them. Also among them were the names Leydon Windham and Evan Tallen.

Mark ran his hands through his hair. "So Chief Tallen probably gave Kat the whistle—although who knows why—but not the doubloon."

"And not Windham," Jake added. "So then, who?" He looked at Deb. "Run through that list again. Who's not on it?"

She did, which resulted only in blank stares between us.

"Maybe it really is a red herring." I sighed. "So we still can't link what was in Kat's box to the murder."

"They've got to be connected," Deb said as she set down her phone.

"But we don't know how," I lamented. "Unless the handwriting samples we get from these give us a new clue."

Jake's phone dinged with a text.

Deb gave me a supportive look. "Those raffle tickets could very well give us something to go on. And Tallen has to interrogate Cal now, so maybe we'll find out what Cal knows that has him convinced his sister was murdered."

"Or maybe not," Jake said, still staring at his phone.

"What do you mean by that?" I asked.

He looked up. "That's my friend at the station. They brought Cal and the van in an hour ago. And, get this, the guys on the shift say Cal has confessed. Cal killed Kat."

CHAPTER 25

I needn't have been so impressed with Jake's information sources—the news had spread all over town long before the sun came up. A murder in Gwen Lake? A brother confessing to killing his sister?

It didn't matter that Kat and Cal weren't exactly town darlings. This was a scandal of the highest degree. Igniting—as most scandals seem to do—equal parts fascination and horror. Stuff like this just didn't happen in our little town. No one wanted to admit to the possibility of such a dark underbelly lurking under all that quirky quaintness.

Most especially Rose Tallen. As wife of the police chief, as mayor, and as Gwen Lake's chief spokesperson, she must have had quite a restless night. I hadn't had much sleep, either, now that I knew my murder suspicions had been right all along. And that I was, in fact, in a business relationship with the murderer. I was pretty sure no small business handbook covered situations like this.

I had to go to Tallen. Given our last exchange, however, I opted to stop first at Deb's for that wickedly strong Azido coffee and six of the largest donuts she had. The chief probably had a million things to do, but I had immediate, practical questions. Was Kat's work no longer Cal's property? If I could still sell it—and I wasn't sure if I could or even should—where did the proceeds go? Had

Burton tried to steal from Kat, Cal, or the Needle? I needed answers, because I knew it was only a matter of hours before Mom would be awake and calling to check on me.

I half expected to be turned away. Instead, the officer behind the desk glanced up, gave me a resigned look, and said, "Chief's in his office," with a weary nod toward Tallen's door. Maybe coffee and donuts really do go a long way with cops.

The chief was on his phone, looking like he'd been up for hours. Only a faint smile crossed his face when I set the offering down on his desk and sat in the guest chair, waiting for him to finish his conversation.

"I'll have a statement later today. Now, if you'll excuse me, I have someone in my office." He paused while whoever was on the other end tried to keep him on the phone. "No, really, I need to go. You'll hear from me when we have more information to give out. But not before. So this needs to be the last time I hear from you this morning, got it?"

Tallen set the phone down even as I could still hear a voice squeezing in a few last words. "You've heard."

I pushed out a breath. "Anyone who hasn't?"

"Sure seems not." He pulled the lid off the brew and inhaled. "Appreciate this. The office coffee leaves a lot to be desired. I used to say Gwen Lake was a boring place to be chief of police. Not today."

"So, Cal did it?" Abrupt, yes, but it was the question that had kept me up for hours.

"The man's an absolute mess. He hardly speaks, and when he does, it makes almost no sense. Some of it's angry accusations. Some of it's pitiful moaning. But people rarely confess to murders they didn't commit."

I didn't want to take up his time. "I need to know what to do."

"You don't need to do anything. We might want an additional statement from you, but that doesn't have to be today. None of this changes what you saw that morning, and you've already told us those details."

Not all of them. I had planned to tell Tallen about Burton and the letters, but it seemed like the wrong time. They had their killer with Cal's confession. The mystery of Kat's romantic life could wait. Besides, on the wild chance those letters *were* from Tallen, I didn't need to add to his aggravation this morning by telling him I knew about them.

"Does George know?" To wake up to the news that your son had taken the life of your daughter . . . Even for such a shambles of a family, that had to be dreadful.

"That'll go down as one of my least pleasant tasks as chief. But it was better he hear it from me than some stranger."

"Is Rose upset?" While it seemed a childish question, this news would taint the town's upcoming press in ways even Rose's savvy marketing couldn't overcome.

"Upset would be putting it mildly. I'm sure she'd love it if I could sweep this whole thing under the rug, but . . ." He simply sighed and bit into the donut.

A knock came on the doorframe as a uniformed officer poked his head in the door. "DA's office will be here in twenty, Chief."

I fished Kat's apartment keys out of my pocket. "I probably shouldn't keep these now."

He looked surprised. "I didn't know you had them."

"Cal gave them to me to pick up the rest of Kat's work."

He took them from me. "We'll secure her apartment for evidence. I can't let you back in there." He nodded, polishing off the last of the coffee. If I drank one of Deb's Azidos that fast, they'd have to peel me off the ceiling.

I nodded. I should have let it go at that, but I found I just couldn't. "But I do have one more question, Chief Tallen, if you don't mind?"

I thought of the least intrusive way to ask my question as I pointed toward the whistle on his desk. "I found one of those in Kat's apartment. Hanging from her mirror. Did you give it to her?" Too bold, probably, but I was short on time, and now I'd never get another chance to go in her apartment.

Tallen responded by rising and closing his office door. Tension wound my stomach tight. What was I about to learn?

"Kat was a sweet kid," he began. "Awkward. Sensitive. Things were tough at home for her. No mom and all." He sat back down. "There was a time a few years ago when she told me she was afraid. George would get . . . rough. Cal would defend her half the time and take George's side the other half. She was starting not to trust anyone." His fingers strayed to the whistle, his mind picturing a long-ago conversation. "I told her she could trust me. She could come to me, and I'd always take her side. I got the dumb idea to give her the whistle as a sort of reminder that she could call for help and I'd answer." His features grew soft. "I didn't know she'd kept it."

I swallowed the fresh lump in my throat. "Seems like she appreciated it." He really was a nice guy. I felt embarrassed for thinking the worst of him even hours ago, and grateful I'd not confronted him with my suspicions.

The whole business just seemed so sad.

"Anything else you need, Shelby?"

I rose, not wanting to take more of his time. "Not unless you want to fill out a raffle ticket for our prize coasters."

I meant it as a joke—and a poor one at that—but he said, "Why not? The rest of my day will rot, so might as well get one good thing out of it."

Surprised, I pulled a drawing ticket out of the envelope full of them in my handbag. "Just your name, a phone number, and which letter coaster you want to win."

The chief thought about it for a moment, then wrote *R* in the blank space to choose a letter. No *B* for Bobby here. I'd been so far off the mark in my thinking. "Rose is gonna need a pick-me-up, don't you think?" he asked as he handed the ticket back.

We all do, I thought as I put the completed ticket into my envelope. I gave him the most supportive smile I could muster on the few hours of sleep I'd had. "Looks like a lucky winner to me."

"Murder! Cal! I can't believe it!" Mom nearly shouted into the phone from the Nimble Nomad's current position outside Sedona. It was just before 10:00 a.m., which meant it was just before seven in Arizona, but I was surprised Mom had waited this long to call. "You were witness to a family murder. Are you okay?"

"I was witness to a body, not the actual murder." Still pretty traumatic—and perhaps a bit more so given Cal's confession—but nothing had changed on the level Mom was inferring. "I never really believed it was an accident." It felt safe to admit that now.

"George must be beside himself with grief."

"Actually, George has been invisible since the memorial." Normally a man you saw all over town, he'd kept to himself.

"Well, who can blame him? It's just terrible." I'm sure I would hide, as well, under the circumstances. Especially with the rumor circulating that Tallen had brought him in for questioning. I'd had customers ask me the most absurd and intrusive questions, and I was involved only on a minor level:

"Was there a lot of blood?"

"Yes, *of course* there was."

"Do you see her body every time you close your eyes?"

"No. But *now* that you've suggested it . . ."

And my personal favorite, "Could you feel the presence of her soul lingering in the van?" I didn't even have an answer for that one.

Mom's voice drew me back to the present. "How are people treating her merchandise? The canvases? Suddenly the scissors seem a bit . . . morbid . . . under the circumstances."

I had chosen not to tell her about Burton's attempt at theft.

I'd address that with the junior Mr. Windham eventually. Maybe even charge him double if I let him have the canvas at all.

"If you want to pull them from the sales floor, Shelby," Mom went on, "I'll completely support you in that decision. I'm in no hurry to profit from that poor woman's death."

I looked over at the surprisingly small number of Kat's works we had left. "It feels weird, and I'm sure not going to hand over any consignment money to Cal, but I think it's good to have her stuff in the hands of stitchers. I think she'd want that."

Part of me disliked how death was good for business. I had consoled myself by believing that selling Kat's works was not only the best way for Kat's talents to live on but was also a way to support Cal. Now I wanted to yank all those consignment payments back out of his pocket. And who knows? Maybe for legal reasons, he'd have to return the profit he'd made.

"I think you're right," Mom said. "She'd want that." She paused. "What's Rose doing about it?"

I heard Dad's voice from somewhere in the distance. "You know Rose. She'd carry on if half the town burned down."

Rose was, in fact, carrying on. I'd received an email from her twenty minutes ago, filled with motivational language about how "Gwen Lake will rise above our current challenge."

"Everything's still on," I replied. "We've finished all the coasters, and we're getting people to fill out raffle tickets."

I had thought about calling off the raffle, since we now knew the identity of Kat's killer, but I knew Rose would balk at that. I was still wildly curious as to who B was—even if the stakes were no longer so high. I tried to tell myself that if no handwriting match emerged, Cal's confession would allow me to put the whole thing to rest. It didn't completely work.

I remembered Chief Tallen's words. *People rarely confess to murders they didn't commit.* And it was clear Cal hadn't been coerced into his confession—unless you counted the alcohol.

There was no reason to think he hadn't done it. Still, I couldn't rest easy that the case was "solved." Why deny it and skip town, only to fold and confess the minute he was caught?

I suppose he was entitled to be the mess Tallen said he was. His dad had been terrible to him, the van wasn't coming to him, and he wasn't profiting off Kat in the way he had planned. He must have sensed how so many people suspected him of murdering his sister. Now he had no one. And a very bleak future behind bars. Mess, indeed. I suppose greed and lack of love really can make people monsters.

"The coasters came out great," I said in an attempt to switch to a more comfortable subject.

"Oh," Mom cooed, "I've heard such good things about your shopping prize. And the stitchers . . . Getting Jake and Mark involved was a stroke of genius. Cherie brings a whole new generation into the shop, too. I tell you, Shelby, you're a natural at this. Even Jessica said so."

The news that Jessica had been bragging about me to Mom hit home with a gratifying ring. If nothing else ever came from this stint of watching the Needle, I'd still be grateful for the new ease I had found with my sister.

And with Taylor. Mom choked up as I told her about my plan to have one of his drawings made into a canvas Jessica could stitch. "I'm so proud of you, I could bust," she said with weepy maternal joy. "I can't wait to see what you come up with next."

Next. I had no real plans for there to be a next. Still, life felt surprisingly good in Gwen Lake, even with everything that had happened. Not good enough to stay, I thought, but good enough not to allow such a long time to pass before my next visit.

"Welcoming you home is what I come up with next."

There was a long, unnerving pause on the other end of the line. "Yes, well, about that . . ."

CHAPTER 26

Jessica, Leona, and JanLi all dropped their jaws in perfect unison when I told them what Mom had told me. "Two more weeks?" they chorused as we stood in the shop.

I offered a sympathetic smile. "It seems they're really enjoying themselves."

"And you're doing a splendid job running the shop while Nina's gone," Leona said.

I looked for the competitive twitch to show up in Jessica's eyes and found none. Evidently, she really did think I was doing a good job.

"I'm not sure I wouldn't stay away until things die down." Leona cringed at the unfortunate wording. "*Settle* down," she corrected.

JanLi touched Jessica's arm. "I'm sure she'll be home for your birthday. She'd never miss that."

I hadn't thought to confirm that Mom and Dad would be home to celebrate Jessica's birthday. "Mom is doing a lot of new things that aren't like her lately," I said, in case they really would miss Jess's big day. "I mean, come on. She got her ears pierced in Las Vegas." Why on earth did I say that?

Oops. Mom evidently hadn't told Jessica. Now there were two big facts my sister was second to know. The old friction rose up fast. "Mom what?!" she nearly shrieked.

Mom had sworn she'd never pierce her ears. Well, the *old* Mom, at least. "Dad made some offhand remark about buying her diamond studs—I think because he figured nothing would ever come of it—but she called his bluff."

My explanation did little to soothe Jessica's wound. "When did she tell you this?"

"This morning." I admitted. "I thought you knew."

JanLi said something that sounded like the Chinese version of "Who'd have thunk it?" I had to agree.

My sister's chin jutted out. "I most certainly did not know."

"It is a bit more conventional than the NYAG's tattoo," I offered. "And I suppose we can blame Dad."

JanLi offered Jessica a cup of tea, because, of course, the right cup of tea was her answer to just about anything. "I hope your father made good on his promise."

Again, I was a bit unnerved—maybe in a good way—of being the one with the inside information. I'd so often felt like the last to know things in this family. "Half a carat in each ear." I'm not much of an expert in these things, but it seemed to me that the diamond studs that often graced Jessica's ears were bigger. I generally kept to artsy dangles or silver hoops.

Leona grinned. "Our Nina is most definitely enjoying herself. Glad to hear it. I don't blame her one bit for extending the trip. After all, why not if you're here?"

There it was again. Another subtle hint that my stay here could be indefinite. I'd surprised even myself by how easily I had accepted another two weeks of running the Needle. After all, it wasn't as if I had an enormous selection of job offers waiting for me. In fact, I hadn't even really made any effort at looking at all. I know I'd been busy with murder, family drama, and such, but what did that apathy say?

I smiled at JanLi and Leona. "Come on. You both could run the place without me. Easily."

"Nope," Leona shot back instantly. "Not and do the shopping prize the way you did. Stepped right up to the plate and hit a home run."

The coasters were made, yes. And I had dreamed up a window display in which they were set them up like Scrabble tiles, with a STOP ON IN AND SIGN UP TO WIN sign. Clever, if I do say so myself. Still, with twenty-six individual prizes to win, we'd need a lot of entrants. I didn't know if we'd be able to pull that off. Or if those entrants would lead us to B.

"Has anyone heard anything about why Cal did it?" Jessica asked, changing the subject.

"Isn't it obvious?" Leona said. "Those two hated each other. And George just kept pouring gasoline on the fire, if you ask me."

JanLi refilled the electric kettle, which was always on when she was in the shop. "But it's a long way from hate to murder. They haven't gotten along for years. Why now?"

I offered the only explanation I had. "He seemed hard up for money. And he made a big deal about the mobile sharpening business being his idea, so the van should have been his. Maybe things just got to the boiling point between them." It takes a lot of hate to sink a knife into someone's chest.

"What will you do now?" Jessica asked, sipping her tea.

I wasn't sure if she was asking about the shop or my efforts to solve Kat's murder. "I had planned to spend this morning getting raffle entries. Maybe I should still do that." Walking among the Gwen Lake businesses, getting people to fill out raffle tickets felt like the dose of normal I needed. Something without lives at stake. I would say hello to a lot of people I knew—or who knew me—and would be a good Needle manager. Maybe now it wouldn't matter so much if I didn't find a B match.

"Good plan," Jessica agreed as she set down her tea. "I'd help, but I've got a class and two committee meetings."

That's our Jessica. A paragon of involvement and fitness. I tucked a handful of raffle tickets slips into her hand. "Maybe you can talk a few of your classmates and committee mates into entering the raffle? Everybody's got an initial."

"I can do that."

As I left JanLi and Leona to mind the shop while I went to play raffle ambassador, I took a moment to admire—and perhaps remember—the beauty of Gwen Lake. Murder or not, the town was still beautiful. A bit of mist rose off the water in that magical way it does some mornings. The mountains rose in the distance behind the town. Pale green leaves were just beginning to appear on the trees. The air felt clearer here. I suppose it actually was, given Savannah's urban atmosphere, but somehow I had noticed it more lately. The sky was a cloudless, perfect blue.

I loved the colors here, and not just in the fall, when people came from all over to gawk at the leaves (and clog the highways). There hadn't been enough color in my life at Batterson. That sounds ridiculous to say of a graphic arts and design agency, but I had spent too much time gazing at the pale white of a computer screen. I liked having this much art in my life. I treasured the chance to get some more art into Taylor's life—if I could manage it. I would have argued otherwise until my last breath a month ago, but I could no longer ignore how part of me might want to stay in Gwen Lake.

As long as nobody kills anyone else, I thought with a smirk. *At least as long as it does not involve me.*

My little jaunt was a success. I nabbed six entrants with a stop at Deb's for coffee; eight at the bank, where a gray-haired teller said she remembered giving me lollipops as a child when I came to make the deposits with Mom; and nearly a dozen at the grocery store, where I picked up a new bag of cat food for Nabbit. Evidently, I was pretty good at this. I beamed at the compliments on how I'd decorated the store window, and tucked all the "So good to see you back in town" comments away in a corner of my softening heart.

I was still smiling when I turned the corner to duck into the butcher shop, daring to take Mr. Sanders up on his offer of a pork chop or two. I was toying with the idea of inviting Jake over for dinner, and I figured good chops were an excellent incentive.

"Well, hello there, young lady," Sanders said with a wide smile. "Come to take me up on my chops?"

Gwen Lake really was filled with nice people. I shouldn't let one pesky murder skew my opinion of the place. "As a matter of fact, I have. And some entrants for the prize drawing."

"Faye told me I have to get into that drawing. She thinks your coasters are spiffy. I'm not sure if that's because she didn't have to make 'em or if she just wants more things with Ss on 'em. Hand some over, and I'll get the boys in the back to enter, too."

He came out from the back a minute or so later with the raffle tickets and "the most perfect pair of chops a lovely lady can have." He slid the package and the tickets across the counter. *On the house* was written across the butcher paper. I thanked him and placed my items in my bag from the grocery store. A pretty good set of errands accomplished all around.

Back at the apartment, I stowed the chops and spread the tickets out on my table. I hadn't come across anyone who had written B as their letter of choice for the prize coaster. Maybe it was for the best that my scheme to find B wouldn't ever work and the mystery would vanish with Kat.

Until I looked again.

CHAPTER 27

"It can't be," I gasped at Nabbit, who was trying to swat several of the raffle tickets off my table. "Can it?"

I ran and fetched the letters and reread them, wondering if I'd misinterpreted their romantic nature. I reread the last three. There was no mistaking that Kat and B had been more than friends. Only I couldn't picture it. Even in the wildest interpretations of illogical love, I couldn't see it.

Still, the handwriting was an indisputable match. The large, bold *B* in the appeared in the name space on the raffle ticket.

On Chester Sanders's raffle ticket. Because he'd signed it with his nickname: Butch.

B—Kat's secret lover—was Chester "Butch" Sanders.

I held the ticket next to the letters again, sure I was wrong. I only ended up more certain I was right.

He was old enough to be her father. Sure, he was friendly, but not in *that* way. And he was married to Faye Sanders. Proper, righteous, judgy Faye Sanders.

"If I had to pick the one woman in Gwen Lake who was the most opposite of Kat Katsaros, it'd be her." Nabbit sat down, fixed his yellow-green eyes on me, and stared. He looked cool and calm. Nowhere near the wild tumble I felt as my mind reeled from this inconceivable information.

The next question struck me. *What do I do with this?* While sleazy, it was not illegal to cheat on your wife. And with Cal's confession, I was no longer looking for a killer. These clandestine lovers, however, did strike me as a strong enough motivation for murder. I just couldn't connect the dots between Cal and Butch. Were there any dots to connect?

I sank down onto the nearest kitchen chair and stared at the tickets and letters for a long, stunned stretch of time. Knowing this whopping secret—one I surely wasn't supposed to know— squeezed my lungs tight. A sense of isolation swept over me, the exact opposite of the connectedness I'd felt walking around town.

Did Faye know? Of course she couldn't know. For one, the wording in the letters made it clear Butch hadn't revealed this shocking relationship to her. For another, Faye didn't strike me as the kind of woman who would put up with infidelity for a single second. Especially an affair as scandalous as this. Having your husband fooling around with a woman almost universally unliked in town and young enough to be his daughter would drive any woman to extremes. But Faye Sanders?

A horrible thought rattled my brain. Did Faye hire Cal to kill Kat?

I would think assassination comes at a high price. The Sanderses—if Faye's purchases at the Needle were any clue— were comfortable but not well off. Still, Cal was hard up for cash, so maybe his fee was negotiable.

I didn't like dreaming up such horrible motivations for people I'd known since I was in kindergarten. Ridiculous as it sounds, it would feel much easier to contemplate a hit-man scenario from one of the Windhams.

And what if I was wrong? This was the kind of accusation you could never take back. What were my obligations now that I had reason to believe what I'd just seen? It wasn't as if I'd caught them together in a passionate embrace. What if there was someone else out there with handwriting just like Butch's?

Did I have the right to ruin Faye's life—and marriage—on circumstantial evidence like this?

Chief Tallen's warning about turning over the wrong rocks rang nauseatingly true now.

"Curiosity didn't kill you," I remarked to Nabbit, "but it's just made me miserable."

Nabbit wrapped his tail around his front paws with a snide, deliberate flourish. *Better you than me.*

I racked my brain for someone to go to with this bombshell of a revelation. This seemed like the kind of thing you take to the police or a pastor or a best friend. I had no pastor.

All I had was a sister. One whose own marriage seemed to be weathering its own share of challenges. Would that give her insight? Or make her the worst person to know? Still, family seemed the best of all my poor options. If nothing else, Jessica had always been good at keeping secrets. Operating your life on so many authentic and less than authentic levels gave you that skill, evidently.

"I'm not swimming in choices," I told Nabbit as I reached for the phone. "And I'm not going to make it much longer keeping this to myself. We gotta bring Jessica in on this, at least for now."

It takes a lot to shock my sister. I have seen her pick up the end of Hal's finger when he sliced it off with a kitchen mandoline and calmly slip it into a snack baggie with a dose of alcohol while dialing the family physician with the other hand. But when she heard the news in my kitchen half an hour later, her skin went from creamy to a blotchy pale.

"You're sure? I mean, really, really sure?" she asked for the second time.

I spread the tickets and one of B's letters on the table. Just one letter. And just one page of the letter. I fought a mad urge to try to stuff the genie back in the bottle and preserve even a small sense of privacy for Kat. "What do you see?"

Jessica took a moment to read the letter, looking a bit ill as she did. "I think you're right. I just . . . I just can't believe it. He's Dad's friend. He's old enough to be my dad, which means he's more than old enough to be Kat's dad."

I channeled my inner JanLi and put the kettle on for tea. Figuring out what to do next wasn't going to be a short conversation. "I like to think of myself as open-minded, but this is a bit of a stretch. I just can't picture them together."

Jessica frowned. "It's inappropriate. He's thirty years her senior."

"It's inappropriate because he's *married*," I corrected. While the age difference was odd, baffling even, they were two consenting adults. "He was cheating on Faye with Kat." My brain took a second to dwell on the massive absurdity of that statement. "Or at least it sure looks like it."

"Oh," Jessica scoffed, "I don't think there's any doubt." She pressed her lips together. "Faye's going to go to pieces when she finds out."

And that was the big question. "Does she find out? Is it really our place to tell her? We could be wrong."

My sister stared down at the two documents, the large rounded *B*s shouting the butcher's guilt like sirens. She looked back up at me with one of those *Don't give me that* mother glares. "You're not wrong."

I poured tea into two mugs while Nabbit wandered back into the kitchen to nudge up against Jessica's legs. She smiled down at him. Pets were too much hassle and mess to have in her household, but she did seem to enjoy other people's animals.

"Why light the fuse to a giant bomb of pain like this?" I asked. "Kat's dead. We know who killed her. I don't see how this could be related to the murder, so is there any point in revealing this?" Even as I said it, the small buzz that had begun in my stomach went up a notch. While I had no idea how, that prickling buzz kept suggesting there was a connection.

Jessica pushed out a breath. "You have to bring this to Tallen. I don't see any other way. At least then it becomes his problem whether or not to reveal it to Faye. And he can decide if it's related to Kat's murder."

My sister was right. I needed to do what I should have done when I found the letters—bring them to Chief Tallen.

Chief Tallen, as you can imagine, did not take the news well.

"Withholding evidence is obstruction of justice. That can be a felony in North Carolina."

His paternal glare put Jessica's to shame, literally making me gulp. "I didn't consider it evidence."

"That's not up to you," he countered.

"You do have to admit," I said in my defense, "the consequences of this are pretty enormous. Not the kind of thing you do lightly. And I only just now figured out who wrote them."

"You mean who you *think* wrote them. We have experts, who can be more certain." After a second, he gave me a dubious look. "Is that why you asked me about the whistle?"

Just when I thought this conversation couldn't get more uncomfortable. "Bobby starts with a *B*. And I couldn't figure out why you were so sure this wasn't a murder."

He sat back in his chair, exasperated. "I *was* considering the possibility of murder. Just not publicly." After an annoyed pause, he continued, "You actually considered the possibility I was dragging my feet on her death investigation because I was cheating on Rose with her?"

It didn't seem wise to lie. "Well . . . maybe?"

His expression changed. "You'd make a good detective. The best ones never rule out even the *most implausible* possibilities." He pinched the bridge of his nose. "Allow me to set the record straight. My relationship with Kat was purely one of a concerned friend. One who knew—more than most—how her father and brother could get out of hand."

So far out of hand that it became murder. "So why did Cal

do it? How? Because Mark, Jake, and I tried to see if we could get a machine to do that, and we couldn't."

Tallen's brows lowered at the news I'd been testing theories. "You, Mark, and Jake? The three of you tried to see if you could get a sharpening machine to throw a lethal knife? And you didn't think it appropriate to tell me any of this?" He glared at me. "This has to stop. Now. We have our suspect in custody. Leave the rest to us. Unless you have any other evidence you might like to bring forward?"

It was more of a warning than a question. "No, sir. But . . ."

I didn't think his look could get darker. "But what?"

"I have questions." When he only pressed his lips together but did not stop me, I went on. "Why in the park? If we couldn't get the machine to do it, how did he? Did he tell you? Was it all his idea, or could someone have put him up to it?"

Evidently, the chief realized he wasn't going to get rid of me without answering a few of my many questions. "Cal isn't giving us consistent information. Half the time he says things that don't make sense. Other times, he brags about how he rigged the machine. Then he dives into remorse. Talks about how he's not who he thought he was, as if being a killer came as a surprise. I think we have a person in a mental crisis here. It's going to take some time to work things out. I've set the forensics people back on it. They'll go over everything again and see if they can determine what happened now that they know what to look for. But again, I won't be discussing the case with you further. Cal has confessed to it. I'm confident the details will become clear soon enough."

"But I'm wondering if—"

Tallen held up a hand and closed his eyes. "I'll take it from here, Shelby. And this time I really mean it."

When he opened his eyes to glare at me again, I had no doubt that he did.

CHAPTER 28

Because the next day was the first Saturday of the month, we had another trunk show at the shop. Mom had arranged it, thinking she'd be back, but it was a low-key thing with a kit producer from Baltimore who specialized in small goods, like pouches and key chains. Customers showed up and purchased a few things. I bought a belt kit to stitch up and give to Dad. Mostly, it felt more obligatory than celebratory. There was no event or artist appearance attached to it, which was good, because no one's heart was really in it. We were all still reeling from the events of the past month.

The NYAGs attended, of course, as did Jake, Mark, Cherie, and Deb. I appreciated their show of support and went out of my way to introduce my corps of stitchers to the NYAGs.

It was fun to put the two groups together, and the NYAGs gushed with compliments about the monogrammed coaster project. As proud as I was of that success, I had trouble celebrating. I found I could barely make conversation with Faye, knowing what I knew. The continual rain of the day seemed to fit my mood. May had come in with a dark and stormy feeling to it, despite it usually being one of North Carolina's more spectacular months.

Weary, I went straight home once the shop closed, and attempted to distract my unsettled mind by tackling one of the trickier stitches on my Kat canvas. I was more than halfway through it now but had trouble feeling proud of my progress.

A knock on my door came late into the evening. The rain hadn't let up, so I was surprised anyone would come calling. Most people I knew at least sent a text before showing up on your doorstep. Or just sent a text.

I tucked my needlework into the clear plastic project tote I used to keep Nabbit from getting into it and hauled myself up off the couch to answer the door.

"Jessica?"

The woman at my door only vaguely resembled my sister. No makeup, mismatched sweats, and hair in a messy ponytail. I suddenly remembered she hadn't shown up at the shop for the trunk show—unusual for her. In fact, the last time I saw her like this, she had had pneumonia.

I pulled her in out of the rain. She hadn't even bothered with an umbrella. "Are you okay?"

"You have to tell Faye," she blurted out. "She deserves to know." Pain cut sharp edges into her words and her eyes. And yet she had an odd resigned stupor about her. As if she'd wrestled with something and lost.

"Yesterday you said it wasn't my place to tell her," I countered, confused.

Something snapped to attention in her expression. "Well, I changed my mind." She walked into the kitchen and I followed her. "I mean, would you want the chief of police telling you your husband was fooling around? Would you? No, you would want to hear that kind of awful news from a friend."

Faye Sanders was not my friend. She was Mom's. But that didn't explain the distraught look on my sister's face. "I guess so," I said gently. "I wouldn't know."

There was a long, heavy pause before Jessica said, "I would."

The weight of that admission pushed me back against the kitchen counter. "Jess." I didn't know what else to say. Parenting disagreements were one thing, but this? Hal cheating?

Who cheats on a woman as beautiful and elegant as Jessica? "I'm . . . wow. That's . . ." I grabbed her hand and was heartsick over how cold it was.

"We're over it. Now," she declared, straightening her back. As if it were a tough stain she had managed to get out in the wash. Almost. "But . . . well, we worked through it."

Having a boyfriend dump you is one thing. I'd "worked through" that. But having your husband, the father of your children, violate the vows of your marriage? It burned a hole in my chest to know Hal had done that to Jessica. I know we live in a world where infidelity happens, where divorces are common, but for some reason, Jess's admission, piled on Butch Sanders's actions, made the world seem like a very broken place.

"How? When? I mean, you don't have to tell me, but . . ."

Jessica sat down on a kitchen chair and smoothed her hair back. "The twins were toddlers. Life was chaos. I was running on no sleep, and the house was a tornado of diapers and laundry. In other words, not much of a wife to come home to—"

"Don't talk like it was your fault," I cut in, with an instant surge of anger and loyalty. "Don't defend him like that."

She didn't acknowledge my comment but went on. "It took a lot of work. And change. And more forgiveness than I ever thought I was capable of showing. But that's how marriage works. Staying married is really hard." Her voice broke a bit on that last word. "But it's worth it. I mean, look at Mom and Dad."

I have often marveled at how I had the privilege of growing up with a model of a great marriage. It was half of what made this absurd business with Kat and Butch so hard to fathom. And while I knew Jessica and Hal's outward perfection came with some hidden strains, I would never have guessed an affair was included.

The relevant question came to me. "How did you find out?" Clearly, the experience had driven her here to my door tonight.

"Mom told me."

"Mom?"

"She was at one of those big craft shows in Charlotte and managed to walk past a restaurant window where Hal was sitting with . . . her." She pulled in a deep "Try not to cry" breath. "Imagine the odds. She waited around, out of his view, until she saw Hal kiss her hand."

Hal was always kissing Jessica's hand. It was part of the gallant charm everyone knew he possessed. For him to do that to another woman felt especially cruel.

"Mom got in her car and drove straight home. She paid for a babysitter, took me out to the park by the bridge, to a back corner, where no one would see us, and told me. Mom let me cry and yell and talk it out until I knew what I was going to do next. And whether or not I wanted to fight for my marriage and family."

She stared fiercely into my eyes. "Would you want Chief Tallen giving you news like that? Pushing you off a cliff like that, without being the kind of person to catch you?"

There was only one answer. "No."

I did not relish the idea of bringing this news to Faye Sanders. "Who should tell her?"

"Well, my first thought was Mom. But I don't think we can wait two more weeks, and I certainly don't want to bring Mom back. This isn't a phone call."

"One of the NYAGs?" Surely, they were closer friends.

"Every single person who knows about this is like a knife in your side. We can't tell anyone else. It's got to be us. We have to be the ones to tell her."

My sister, who had just recently told me not to bring hearsay from Cherie to Chief Tallen, was offering to come with me and bring Faye Sanders the worst of news. So many situations had flipped upside down in the past month that I was wondering if my balance would ever return.

"It's possible she already knows, isn't it?"

"There's only one way to find out. And that's for her to find out. We have to tell her, Shelby. I'm sorry you got mixed up in all this, but you are. You're a strong person, and you're kind. You can do this."

For a moment, the unexpected compliment warmed me. But it was quickly replaced by a chill skittering down my spine as a new, horrible thought rose up. "What if Faye is somehow involved with Kat's death? If she does know, she has a huge motive."

Jessica shook her head. "Faye? She's not a killer. And Cal's confessed."

"Well, no, I can't imagine Faye doing something like that, but I can almost picture her putting someone up to it. Maybe she only meant to hurt Kat or scare her. Maybe she wanted Kat out of the way of her marriage and away from the Needle. What if George put him up to it? Or Leydon Windham promised Cal a bunch of money to get Kat away from Burton? What if Cal is protecting someone? Chief Tallen says he's in some kind of mental crisis. I don't know." The possibilities swam inside my head, making me slightly ill.

Jessica sighed at my long list of theories, putting her hand over one of mine. "Cal's confessed."

"That doesn't mean he really did it. Something feels way off about this, Jess."

My sister squeezed my hand in a gesture so maternal, it tightened my throat. "Let it go, Shelby. Kat has her justice. It's just this last thing that needs to be done. For everyone's sake."

I agreed it had to be done; I just didn't want to be the one to do it. "One of the NYAGs should do this," I argued. "Not us."

The smallest of smiles crossed my sister's face. "We're the new NYAGs, remember?"

Much as I dreaded admitting it, Jessica was right. "Maybe, but we have got to come up with a better name than that."

Jessica straightened her shoulders. "The boys have a base-ball thing tomorrow afternoon after church. I'll ask Faye if we can come see her then. We should do this at her house."

"Okay," I said, even though it didn't feel one bit okay at all.

* * *

I paced the house for what felt like hours after Jessica left.

I had a million questions and no answers. I wanted to talk everything through with Mom—especially since she had found herself in my shoes with Jessica—but my sister and I both knew bringing Mom into this would result in the Nimble Nomad heading straight back home. I had dozens of questions for Cal and Tallen, but, of course, I could not talk to either of them.

No, everything was stuck in neutral until we broke the disturbing news to Faye on Sunday afternoon. And while it felt like a massive case of meddling, Jessica was right: we had to tell Faye what we knew. If it were me, I would have wanted to know. Sharing a painful truth is always a better choice than hiding behind a lie.

Worry and anxiety pushed sleep aside. I kept thinking of all the messed-up families involved in this tangle. George, Cal, and Kat. Faye and Butch. Even Burton and Leydon seemed to be part of all the things that had worked against Kat's happiness. Did Butch truly love Kat? The letters certainly made it seem as if he did, despite what an unlikely couple they made. Did he make her happy? I suppose we'll never know.

Way past when I ought to have been in bed, I stumbled across the book I'd taken from Jessica's house, the one with Taylor's drawing inside. Jessica had managed—and was still managing—to hold her family together. Still, I was coming to see what a massive effort it took. A new admiration for her, and for my own parents, grew in my heart. I remembered when I used to think it was such a simple thing to be happy. When the world could be filled with bright purple birds. A world I still hoped Taylor inhabited.

Staring at his drawing, I suddenly knew no one else but me could make this canvas for him. It had been too long since I'd set aside my artistic side to live only amid the business of art. I'd traded my paintbrushes for a spreadsheet without even realizing it. Maybe part of my restlessness at Batterson had been just that—I had stopped making art and had spent my time making art possible for other people. Basking in the colors of the Nimble Needle had reawakened that side of me. I saw that craving to create in my nephew's eyes. I saw it behind the desire to be accepted in Kat's eyes. I didn't need to facilitate art happening in the world; I needed to be one of the people putting it there.

Without even realizing why I'd done it, I had taken the box of acrylic paints and brushes Kat had in her workshop and had brought it back to my apartment. I had meant to find a good home for it, not yet recognizing that the home might well be with me.

It took me all of fifteen minutes to go down to the shop, cut and tape a square of canvas the right size for Taylor's purple bird, tack it onto a board, and return to my apartment. Wide awake, I spread Kat's art supplies out on my kitchen table, earning some very strange stares from Nabbit. I didn't need a full night's sleep to face the challenge of talking to Faye. I needed this. I needed to create for Taylor, so Taylor could create for his mom.

Taylor's bold design made it easy to paint. My pencil re-creation of his drawing took shape quickly, and then I filled it with all his wonderful, whimsical colors. As I painted, I imagined how much Jessica would love to stitch her son's imagination into life. Would he want to stitch some of it himself? Follow Jake and Mark into the realm of "guys who stitch"? These questions were much more gratifying to ponder than the darker ones of earlier today.

Painting finished, I crawled off to bed close to 3:00 a.m., feeling as if I'd need only a few hours of sleep to face the day's challenge.

CHAPTER 29

"I have to say, I was a bit surprised when you asked to come visit." Faye looked curious as she escorted us to her beautifully appointed sunroom at the back of her house on Sunday afternoon. The rain had finally broken, bathing the room in sunlight. "Why don't we sit and chat out here." It was a bright, cheerful place full of colored cushions—both needlework and otherwise—lush plants and breezy furnishings. The decor was at complete odds with the nature of our coming conversation, but maybe that was for the best. The room seemed a soft place for Faye to land after her fall from the marital cliff from which we were about to throw her.

"I know you're Mom's friend," Jessica began as Faye poured coffee for the three of us from a beautiful service set out on the coffee table. "But Shelby and I find ourselves needing to talk with you."

Faye's expression grew alarmed as she sat down opposite Jessica and me. "What's wrong with Nina? Has something happened?"

"No, not at all. They're having a great time," I replied. "I think the extra pair of weeks will be even better for her."

The alarm faded from Faye's face, and she smiled. "Well, good. She's earned it."

"She has," I went on. "But that's not to say it hasn't been a challenge at the store while she's been gone."

Faye shook her head. "That dreadful business with that dreadful girl." She looked at me. "She would have been all wrong for the Needle. Thank goodness your mother saw that. Who knows what kind of store that girl might have turned the Needle into?"

That woman might have run a pretty amazing business based on what I've seen, I thought, stifling the urge to remind Faye that most women my age didn't care much for being referred to as "that girl."

"She did have a very . . . unique personality," Jessica offered. "One might even say compelling."

"Good heavens, no. She was extreme and irritating," Faye pronounced, waving her hand as if the mention of Kat was an offensive odor. "Not that one should speak ill of the dead."

"I know you didn't care for Kat, but there is something Shelby and I think you need to know about her." Jessica folded her hands in her lap. "Something that might be very . . . difficult to hear."

Faye's spine stiffened. "What on earth are you talking about?"

"Believe me, we're very sorry to have to deliver this news," I began, feeling as if I were falling off that metaphorical cliff myself. "And I would feel so much better if we were wrong, but I'm afraid I don't think we are."

Jessica reached out and took Faye's hand, which only made the woman stiffen more. "Faye, we have reason to believe Butch and Kat were . . . in a relationship."

Faye pulled her hand away. "Relationship? What do you mean by that? What in heaven's name do you mean by that?" Her voice grew sharp and high.

"I found letters in her apartment," I explained. "Letters from him. To her. Very . . . romantic letters. He only signed them B, but I matched the handwriting from his raffle ticket in the shop giveaway."

Faye went very quiet and very still. "You're wrong."

All I could do was shake my head. Some part of me wanted her to have already known. For her just to be embarrassed that we knew, rather than us having to prove to her what we'd discovered. I'd never been especially fond of Faye, but my heart still broke for her at this moment. I'd hoped to spare her the pain of actually seeing what Butch wrote. But it was clear to me she wouldn't believe me without seeing it. I pulled out the raffle ticket and set it on the table.

"Is this Butch's handwriting?" I asked.

"Of course it is."

I swallowed hard as I pulled out a page from the letters and the doubloons from the pouch in which I'd found them at Kat's. I had brought the coins, guessing she might know if they had come from Butch, as well. I set everything beside the raffle ticket. "Is this Butch's handwriting?" I pointed to the page from the letter.

Faye stared at it. She shifted in her seat while she drew her mouth into a tight line. I felt Jessica flinch beside me, perhaps remembering the moment Mom had confronted her with the same devastating news. I watched Faye's eyes take in the passionate words—declarations of devotion for another woman. Another, much younger woman, whom Faye already disliked.

"This means nothing. Anyone could have written this . . . this garbage." Her words came out short and sharp, almost as a hiss. She drew her hands into small, delicate fists.

"I don't think you really believe that," Jessica said gently. "I'm so sorry."

At that last word, something broke loose in Faye. Her gaze snapped up to meet Jessica's, and I swear the air in the room went cold. "He told me he lost those doubloons. One was supposed to be for our son's fiancée. Not for some . . . hussy." The fury began to erupt out of her, hot and dangerous, like lava from a volcano. "Extra hours at the shop? Did he think I really believed him? That I didn't *notice*?"

Jessica and I kept silent, letting her spew what must have been boiling up inside her for who knows how long. "It's never really a surprise," Jessica had told me. "I knew something was off, was wrong, but I wouldn't face it and didn't have the strength to know how to fix it until I had to."

Now Faye had to face it. And I wondered if she and Butch would fix it or if this would be the end for them. Faye Sanders was not the kind of woman to suffer a scandal. She was just as likely to swear us to silence and never speak of it again.

"That ill-mannered, vulgar girl. Her clothes," she spat out with a sneer. "That hair. I was sick when I figured out it was her. Humiliated. To think my own husband would—" Faye clamped her mouth shut, as if fearful she'd fall apart if she said more.

But she did. "Did he think I didn't see how sad he was? When she died? Would he have been that sad for me?" She turned to glare at me. "I'm not sorry she's dead. Do you hear me? I'm glad she's gone."

Even for Faye, that seemed vicious.

"No one would have ever known. Not if you"—she jabbed a finger at me—"hadn't insisted on selling her trash. On letting people buy it. All of this would have gone away. She would never get her hands on my Chester or on the shop, no matter how hard she tried. She can't have it. I won't stand for it. I had to do something. I had to do whatever it took. I had the means, and I used it."

A slow, horrible realization began to run cold under my skin. "What did you do, Faye?" It seemed both impossible and inevitable at the same time.

She'd gone quiet and methodical in front of us, the fury having transformed into an eerie calm. "Cal told me it would be easy to do. That stupid machine. Just a matter of loosening a few bolts and then giving her a batch of dulled knives and telling her they had to be extra sharp." She looked at me as if she were explaining it to a child. "I rather liked the idea of it being Chester's knives. It has a certain justice to it, yes? And he has so many of them. I wanted it to hurt. I wanted it to hurt both of them."

"You had Cal show you how to sabotage Kat's sharpening machine?" I couldn't believe I was asking that question. Out of the corner of my eye, I saw Jessica draw back in revulsion.

Faye looked at me as if it were all so obvious. "Of course not. I got him to do it. Maybe that's why I knew what I knew— it made it so easy to convince Cal. Actually, I think he'd been toying with the idea long before I asked him to. Oh, it took a bit of convincing at first. But my father always said it is astounding what you can get someone to do with the right leverage and enough money."

"You hired Cal to kill his own sister?" I didn't bother to keep the shock from my voice.

"It's not as if they loved each other. They hated each other. And when I told Cal that they're not actual siblings, well, that just put him over the edge."

I think my jaw fell open at her revelation, because she looked almost victorious.

"George isn't Cal's father. Even George doesn't know that, but I was friends with Elena before she died. I'm the only one who knew." Faye shifted her gaze to look out the window. "Elena would be heartbroken to see how Gina turned out. Tasteless. Awkward. I do wonder if George ever figured it out, the way he treated those two."

Stunned, I was still trying to take in the ghastliness of this woman's scheme. "You used the threat of that secret to convince Cal to kill his sister." The words came out slow.

"Why do you think Cal is such a mess? He's always been a

mess, though, hasn't he? I was surprised how easy it was to convince the boy." She turned to Jessica. "You should be happy you have such a good marriage. They're so very rare."

Jessica went pale, and my heart twisted at the painful irony of Faye's compliment.

"You know Cal's confessed to Kat's murder," I said. "He'll tell Chief Tallen what you've done, if he hasn't already."

She almost laughed. "Of course he won't. He knows what I'll do if he does."

But now we know, too, I thought but opted to keep my mouth shut for now. I was silently scrambling for a way to get Chief Tallen over here. In all my investigating, I had never actually thought about what I would do if I found the killer. Or, now, the person who had ordered the murder.

"He thinks he killed her. And why on earth would I stop him from thinking it? I paid him enough to get a good lawyer. If he's lucky, he can keep the van and run away again. But he does seem to mess everything up, so who knows?" Faye sighed and waved her hand again, as if the subject was becoming tiresome. "I find I don't really care, to be honest."

"He murdered Kat." Jessica finally broke her silence. "Cal killed her."

Jessica hadn't registered what Faye had just said. Cal only *thought* he had killed Kat. Which meant . . .

"Oh, hon," Faye replied with an eerie civility. "You can't trust people like that with the really important things."

"What are you saying?" I began to feel ill myself. Mark was right. The machine wasn't capable of sinking a knife into someone like that.

But Faye was.

She almost seemed proud to explain it. "He was supposed to rig the machine, tell her to sharpen all those knives extra sharp, and then disappear. We would both get what we wanted. She put him off, saying she had to get ready for her little stint at the Needle. I couldn't have that. I told him to tell her I absolutely wanted those knives done before she went to the Needle."

"That's why she was sharpening in the parking lot when she was supposed to be at the shop," I noted. The gruesome details began falling into place in my brain. "The machine would malfunction there, where it would take people a while to find her." Kat might have even let Faye into the van, thinking she was checking up on her husband's knives. The whole thing was horridly, calculatedly evil.

Faye went on. "Leave it to Cal Katsaros to have a *malfunction* malfunction. I had to verify. You always have to verify. To think I had to go down there and do what he couldn't. You can't just assume with people on things like that. You have to make sure things have gotten done. If he had just stayed the course, he could have gotten his van and taken off. But then he didn't have the spine to live with it, did he?"

"The machine didn't stab her, so you did." My gaze wandered to Faye's elegant hands, and I struggled to picture them doing such a terrible thing.

"If you know what you are doing, it isn't hard." Something hideously close to a smile crossed her face. "And surely a butcher's wife knows what she's doing. It was so easy to make sure it still looked like the accident Cal had set up—or had tried to."

"And you are going to let Cal take the blame for Kat's murder for you." Any sympathetic kindness that had been in Jessica's voice was long gone.

Faye blinked at her. "Wouldn't you?"

CHAPTER 30

How, exactly, do you extract yourself from an unexpected murder confession long enough to call the police?

Stumped in my search for a better option, I blurted out, "I need to use your washroom . . . I think I might be sick," to Faye and Jessica. I didn't wait around for Faye's reply, just clamped my hand over my mouth, gave a silent thanks that my cell phone was in my pocket rather than where I usually kept it, in my handbag, and ran from the room. It wasn't much of a lie. The current conversation had caused a wave of nausea to rise up in me that was stronger than any from the rockiest boat.

My hands were shaking as I tried to dial Chief Tallen on my cell phone from Faye's potpourri-scented powder room. He'd given me his direct line. If he didn't pick up, I was going to dial 911. Faye seemed too calm for what had just happened, and part of me didn't want to find out what would happen when the anger boiled over again. We were, after all, talking about someone who'd sunk a knife into Kat's chest. I didn't even like the idea of leaving Jessica alone with Faye, but what else could I do?

"Tallen," came the chief's voice over the line.

"It's Faye!" I yelled in a whisper. "I'm at Faye's house, and she just confessed to murdering Kat. Get over here!"

"Shelby?"

"Yes. I'll explain when you get here, but she just told Jessica and me that she stabbed Kat after hiring Cal to mess with Kat's sharpening machine. She let Cal think it's him, but it's not. It's her!" I cracked open the powder-room door for a second to make sure Faye was not heading down the hall to do me in.

"What? How?"

"I don't have time. She thinks I'm getting sick in her powder room. Come now!"

I could hear the chair scraping back from his desk. "Keep her talking. I'll be there as fast as I can. You're sure?"

"Absolutely!"

I clicked off the call, flushed the toilet, which I hadn't used, and splashed water on my face. Opening the door, I called, "Faye, could I trouble you for a glass of water?" Maybe my tapping into her hospitality would keep her occupied.

"Of course, dear," she called from the sunroom, as if nothing was out of the ordinary. I wondered if a confession like this brought on a sort of shock, a disassociation that allowed her to act this way. Then again, I'd just sent her to the kitchen— where she kept her cutlery.

I went to dash back toward the sunroom and Jessica only to run headlong into Faye. "Calm down. It's not as if I'm going to hurt you next." Her eerily polite tone of voice almost sent me back to the powder room for real.

"Sorry," I gasped for no real reason other than blind fear.

"I'll bring you a cold washcloth with that water," Faye said. She touched my arm, and it was all I could do not to flinch. Faye. Butch. Kat. Cal. All the players in this gruesome drama kept spinning around me.

I found Jessica standing in the sunroom, looking exactly like I felt. I mouthed, "I called Tallen," while miming holding a phone to my ear. We clutched each other's hands as we both sat down. My ears strained for the sound of Tallen's squad car siren until I realized he probably wouldn't alert Faye to his arrival.

It felt like an hour before Faye returned with a glass of water for each of us and a washcloth on a saucer for me. "Now," she said, the civility beginning to drain from her voice, "what are we going to do about what you know?" Her eyes narrowed. "We're going to have to do something."

I heard Jessica gulp next to me. Images of every true-crime show hostage tied up in the basement burst into my head.

"We won't tell anyone," I lied. What a foolish thing to say.

She cocked her head to one side. "You don't really expect me to believe that, do you?"

It was like watching someone transform from Martha Stewart into the evil witch from *Snow White* right in front of your face. My brain kept shouting, *This isn't happening. This can't be happening.* "No, ma'am." My voice sounded like I was five. Jessica's hand tightened on mine.

Faye walked past Jessica and me to the sunroom doors, and I heard the click of the lock being thrown. *Maybe she won't murder us here. It'd be too hard to get the stains out. Where is Tallen?*

Out of nowhere I blurted, "I called Mom from your bathroom. She knows." Jessica's head whipped around to face me with wide eyes. "Don't make this worse by hurting us," I continued, my hands up in a pleading gesture. "You're upset. You have every right to be."

"Upset?" Faye shouted. "I am not upset. I am *livid*. You told Nina? Who else have you told? Do you want the whole town to know what that fool husband of mine has done?"

She wasn't making sense. What Butch had done, while questionable, paled in comparison to what Faye had done. While Faye's calm had been eerie, I realized it was much less dangerous than the rage taking shape in front of us. And we all now knew what Faye's rage was capable of.

I heard Tallen's voice in my head. *Keep her talking.* "What can we do?" I asked. "How can we help?" Again, ridiculous questions, but I was grasping at straws here.

"Help?" she snapped. "I think you young ladies have helped quite enough." She pressed her lips together and shut her eyes for a moment. "I'm going to have to do something." She turned her back on us to look out the sunroom windows. Her hand went up to press against her temple. "I need time to think."

"Take all the time you need," Jessica said, her voice a squeak. "Just please remember we're Nina's daughters, and I have two sons of my own. There's no need to hurt us."

I began looking around the room for something—anything—to use against her. Could I bash the coffeepot over her head? Throw hot coffee in her face? There was nothing else nearby. The room was all soft yellow floral cushions and curvy rattan. And the only way out of the sunroom was through the locked doors behind us.

Ah, but we were now between Faye and the doors. If we were quick, we could get to the doors and burst through them before Faye caught up to us. I caught Jessica's gaze and nodded toward the doors, cuing her to make a run for it.

"The glass reflects," Faye warned in a low voice that didn't sound like any Faye Sanders I'd ever known. "I can see you." A second later she whirled around. "And him!"

The French doors burst open in a splinter of wood and groaning hardware to reveal Chief Tallen, gun drawn, with two officers behind him.

As real as I knew it was, my brain refused to process the image of Faye Sanders being led away in handcuffs from her lovely house. As much as I had hoped to solve the mystery of Kat's murder, I hadn't counted on it feeling like this. As if the whole world had tumbled off its axis and nothing made sense.

I hadn't let go of Jessica's hand in the past half hour. We clung to each other, companions on this wild, dramatic journey. My body drooped with exhaustion, as if I'd spent weeks held hostage in Faye's sunroom instead of the mere hour it had been.

Chief Tallen walked over to stand in front of me. "You two okay?"

"No," I replied as Jessica shook her head. Okay felt miles from possible at the moment.

"I've got an officer heading over to the butcher shop to get a statement from Butch. Did Faye say anything to give you any indication he was involved?"

I wondered what was ahead for Mr. Sanders. To know that your affair with a far younger woman was about to become public knowledge and, more so, that your wife had murdered her . . . He'd lost both women, now that I thought about it. I'd never condone what he did, but I did feel a small surge of sympathy for the man, who'd been so nice to me. His life was about to come undone. In ways I wasn't sure he could ever put back together again.

"Is Cal still guilty?" I asked, amazed I could process a fact at all, much less formulate a question like that.

"Attempted murder is still murder. He meant to kill her. The fact that he didn't succeed doesn't change much." The chief shook his head. "I can't believe he agreed to this scheme. His own sister. And now George will know the paternity issue, if he doesn't already. Whatever Cal thought he would gain, he's about to lose everything."

In a way, George had now lost his whole family, too. I didn't see any way back for George and Cal, and Kat and Elena were dead. I stared back at the perfectly tended shrubs on Faye's front lawn. "Faye. *Faye*." Maybe I thought if I said it enough times, the total absurdity of it would somehow ring true.

An officer pulled Tallen aside for some procedural business.

I turned to stare at Jessica. She looked as dumbfounded as I felt.

"I'm so glad you're here," she said shakily. "If either of us had done this alone—"

"Hey," I cut in, even though tears threatened my voice. "If you can't count on a sister to see you through a murder confession, who can you count on?"

She pulled me into a hug so tight I nearly squeaked. I hugged her right back. I could feel both of us fighting off tears. I felt as if I could both sleep for a week and never sleep again. For the second time in a month. I had been in Gwen Lake for a month and a day. Who could have guessed all that would happen in so short a span of time?

Jessica straightened up, applying her "Pull it together" face. "I need to go home and hug my boys for an hour straight." She laughed, even though I saw a tear or two steal down her cheeks. "They'll put up a fight, but I don't care."

"They're precious," I said, meaning it. Faye wasn't wrong when she said what Jessica had was rare. Not perfect—not as flawless as my sister would have liked everyone to believe—but rare and precious just the same.

"Do you want to come over?" Jessica asked.

This seemed like time she ought to spend alone with her family. "I'm okay. I think I just want to go home, be alone, and make some sense of all this. And someone needs to call Mom."

"Do you think we should? This sounds like the kind of thing to make Dad drive all night to get back here."

"We should. The Needle needs its Nina. The NYAGs are going to need some help figuring out what to do." I swallowed hard. "And so do I. This is way beyond what I signed up for." I squeezed Jessica's hand again. "Besides," I added, "that way she'll be home for your birthday."

"I'd like that." After a second, she grabbed my hand again. "You sure?"

You know I was. Things were tumbling in all directions, but underneath all the chaos was a calm base of control I knew I had. I could handle this.

Jessica touched my face as if we were children. "You call if you need me. I mean it."

She did. And that meant everything.

I didn't, in fact, go home.

I called Mom from the park because I needed to do this someplace where I could see the sun and the sky. Even surrounded by the lake and the natural beauty, I struggled to find words to convey what her daughters had just been through.

She cried. She gasped. She ordered Dad to "get this van on the road to Gwen Lake this minute," after which I heard Dad's instant agreement and the sound of the van's ignition.

Then I went to CHNO. To my endless relief, Deb and Jake were both there.

"What happened to you?" Jake asked, rising from his place in the booth when I walked in the door.

I held up a *Hang on* finger and turned to Deb. "I need the strongest, calmest source of caffeine you've got."

Deb lowered one eyebrow. "That's a contradiction in terms."

"Make it, anyway."

She gave me a quizzical look, then reached for a mug.

Jake walked up to me and put a hand on my arm. "You do not look okay. What's going on?"

"Sit down," I said, glad for the warmth of his hand against my skin. "You'll never believe it."

EPILOGUE

"Happy Birthday to you," we all sang as Jessica blew out the candles on a perfectly frosted cream-cheese carrot cake. I had tried to get her to let me buy one from the bakery, but Jessica had insisted on making her own. Hers is probably far better, anyway.

And when Chaz bumped into it and put a big dent in one side, she laughed, tousled her son's hair, and told him it looked better with the addition. That's a new side of my sister, one I hadn't seen before.

"Chaz-dented cakes surely have to taste better," Mom teased. While the reason for her quick return to Gwen Lake saddened me, my thankfulness for having her here filled me with a warm glow. After seeing one family and one marriage destroyed, I had new gratitude for my own family.

Birthday dinners at our house always featured presents before we got to eat cake. While Taylor and I were eager for cake, we were both more eager to give Jessica her present. The canvas had come out perfectly. I was as proud of my rendition of Taylor's design as I was of the talented boy who had made it.

We saved what Taylor and I secretly called "the bird" for last. Chaz gifted his mom with a pretty scarf, Hal gave Jessica a hefty bracelet sparkling with diamonds, and Mom and Dad had brought her a gorgeous vase from Santa Fe. I caught Taylor's eye and gave him an encouraging nod right before he presented the gift bag to her.

A long pause filled the air as she caught sight of what lay inside the purple tissue paper. Jessica gave a little gasp, one hand going to her chest, and I knew she loved it.

Mom practically squealed when Jessica held it up. I watched Hal's reaction, hoping he would recognize the gift for the gesture it was. He didn't look pleased, but he didn't look annoyed, either. I suppose neutral acceptance was a good outcome— at least for now.

"You know how much I love the purple bird," Jessica exclaimed. "And now I can stitch it!"

"It was Aunt Shelby's idea," Taylor said, looking a bit embarrassed at being outed for the artist he was.

Jessica and Mom both grinned at me. "Your aunt Shelby has some pretty good ideas, doesn't she?" asked Mom. I wasn't quite sure if she was asking Taylor or Hal.

"Good thing, too," Dad interjected. "We're going to need another dose of those good ideas soon."

The look Mom and Dad exchanged made my stomach give a flip. "Why?" I asked.

"Your mother's been invited to teach a series of needlepoint classes at a retreat in Sedona." It was half boast, half invitation. The boast part aimed at the whole family, the invitation directed at me. And it didn't take a nanosecond of investigation to figure out why.

"Arizona?" Jessica asked. "When? For how long?"

"Six months, starting in September," Mom replied. "Six months fully paid at a fancy resort. It's amazing, isn't it?"

Dad wrapped his arm around Mom. "Nice to see your mother's talents getting the recognition they deserve, isn't it?"

Taylor gave Mom a fist bump. "Way to go, Grandma!"

"Sounds like quite an opportunity," Hal said.

"Well," Mom declared, grinning at me, "since we have some-one who can handle the shop while I'm gone . . ." She smiled at Jessica, as well. "Two someones—two daughters—who can tackle anything that comes their way. I just couldn't say no, now, could I?"

I might have preferred to be asked in private. Then again, it took me only a second to realize it wouldn't have changed my answer. As we'd doled out the prize coasters to all the winners last week, I'd known part of me was embracing Gwen Lake's quirky wonderfulness with all the enthusiasm of Mayor Rose. True to the mayor's call, we were indeed rising to the challenge of getting past the scandalous tale of Kat Katsaros's murder.

"No, Mom," I replied. "You couldn't say no. I'll be glad to watch the shop for you."

"Watch? Oh, hon, I'm going to make you manager."

That sounded alarmingly permanent. Another round of shop sitting was one thing, but being installed as manager? Was I ready for that? "Acting manager?" I suggested, thinking I might want to keep some options open for the time being.

Dad merely winked. "We'll see."

AUTHOR'S NOTE

Writing murder mysteries—or any books, for that matter—means you often send your imagination to new places. For me, that also included adding needlepoint to my longtime knitting craft skill set. I was fortunate to have three shops ready and willing to help me delve into the craft: Stitchers Garden in Naperville, Illinois, and two lovely Charlotte-area shops, Two's Company Needlepoint of South Carolina and Po's Point in North Carolina. The American Needlepoint Guild and its Queen Charlotte chapter welcomed this novice with open arms and loads of encouragement.

Needles aside, crafting a mystery takes a good deal of help, as well. I owe thanks to my husband, Jeff, who endures no end of odd research trips and obscure data hunts. My dynamic duo of Spencerhill agents, Karen Solem and Sandy Harding, continue to offer valuable guidance (and the occasional talk off a ledge . . .). I am delighted to join the Kensington family and am grateful for the editorial support of John Scognamiglio and the publicity prowess of Larissa Ackerman. Mike Rabinowitz was kind enough to review law enforcement details. If I've made procedural goofs, the fault belongs squarely on my shoulders and not his generous assistance.

Thanks, of course, to you, dear reader. I hope you'll join me soon for Shelby's further adventures in Gwen Lake and the Nimble Needle.

—Allie

PATTERN NOTES

If you'd like to make your own monogrammed coasters, I've included Jean Farish's simple and easily adaptable cross-stitch patterns for initials. In this instance, consider each "X" to represent the intersection of vertical and horizontal threads you'll cover in your canvas.

The average coaster is a 4-inch square, so find the center of each letter as well as the center of your canvas to line things up. I find a 10-count canvas (meaning there are 10 stitches per inch) quick and easy for projects like this, and I think it lends itself well to bold designs.

These patterns are simple enough to count them out, but you may find it easier to trace the design onto your canvas using a strong light source (like a sunny window). A quick Internet search will turn up several good video tutorials on how to do this, or your local needlepoint shop will be happy to walk you through the process.

Add a border design if you like, or just let the colors do the talking. You can either send your completed canvases to a finisher or purchase coaster frames and glue the canvases in yourself.

Follow these steps and you'll have your own set of monogrammed coasters. Hopefully, yours will not lead you to any lethal clues. . . .

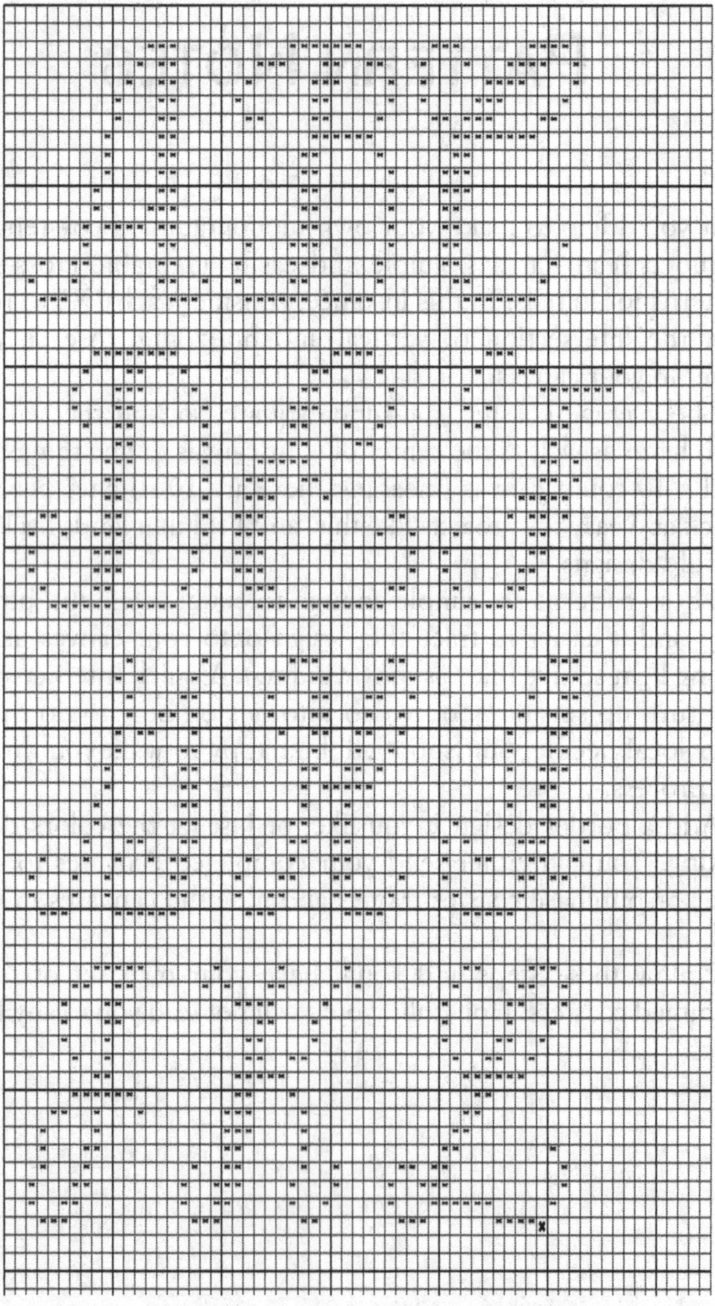

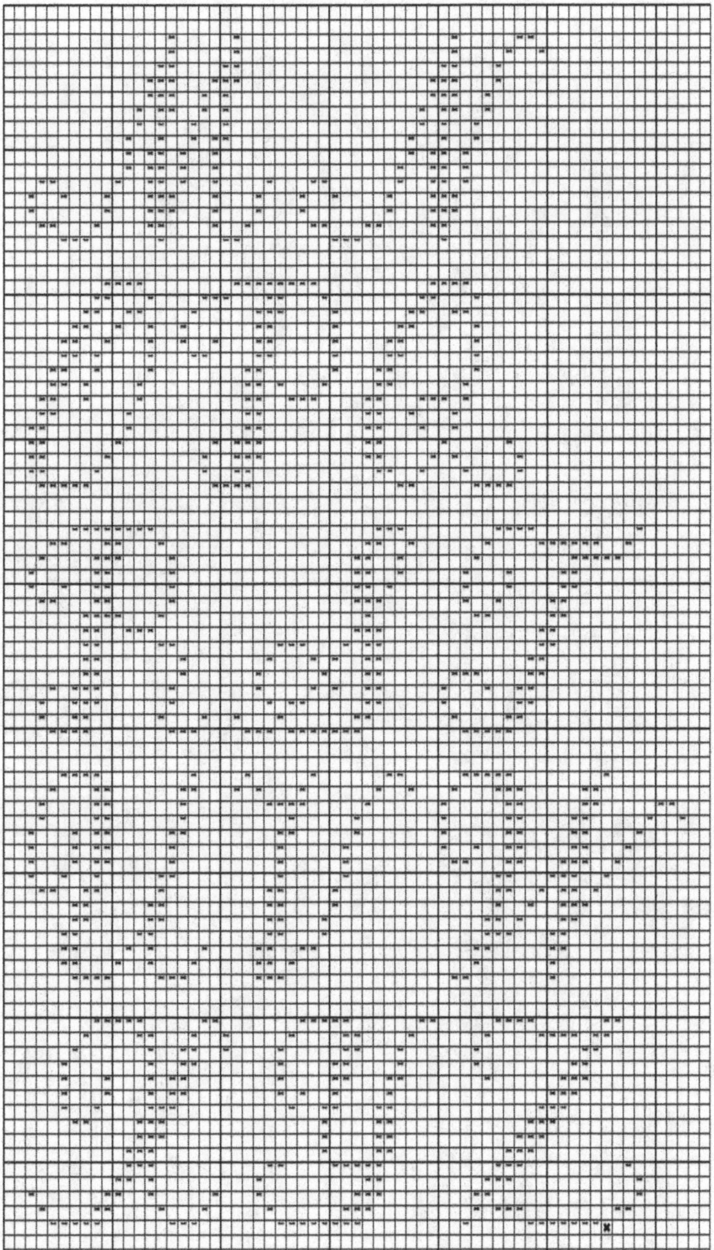

Please turn the page for a sneak peek at the next

Nimble Needle mystery

TWO PURLOINED PILLOWS

coming soon!

CHAPTER 1

I stared in disbelief at my mother. "We are talking about *grown adults* here, aren't we?"

Mom offered me one of her more dubious looks. "I guess that depends. Behavior or chronology?"

Based on the series of warnings Mom had just given me about the two supposed grown adults in question, it was a valid distinction. We were discussing an upcoming event at Nina's Nimble Needle, the needlepoint shop my mother owned and I'd taken over as manager. Event? Maybe. Circus of clashing egos? More likely. "Can't we expect grown adult behavior from actual adults?"

"With those two? Not a chance!" came a declaration from an outlandish older woman named Dot, seated at the large gathering table in the back of Nina's Nimble Needle. All the rest of the NYAGs—the Not Your Average Grannies, who have been shop fixtures for as long as I can remember—nodded in agreement. These women gathered nearly every day at the shop to work on their needlepoint and flex their considerable gossip skills. The NYAGs knew about all the goings-on in town and had opinions on most of them. They were some of our best customers, staunchest allies, sources of endless amusement, and some of Mom's closest friends. I adored them as much as they frustrated me. And I knew enough to take their warnings to heart as much as Mom's.

Evidently my worry showed on my face, because Dot consoled, "Don't worry, hon," with a dismissive wave. "You're up for it. The trick will be to keep 'em apart."

"*Far* apart," added Tilly, another NYAG, as she looked up from the Christmas stocking she was working on for her fifth grandchild. It's not at all uncommon to see people working on Christmas stockings in June here at the store. Or baby items the minute a pregnancy is announced (if even before). Needlepoint takes time to accomplish. Lots of it.

"Dot's right. You can handle 'em," cheered Livvy, another NYAG, in her musical Charleston accent.

I welcomed the consensus of NYAG support. After all, I'd been taking time to accomplish my work here, too. I'd been stepping farther and farther into my role as the permanent replacement for my mother, Nina. I'd been back in my hometown of Gwen Lake, North Carolina, and running the shop for just over a year now, and almost everyone considered me in charge.

Almost everyone.

In many ways Mom was the irreplaceable Nina of Nina's Nimble Needle, and I respected that. I honored what she'd built here. I had no plans—ever—to make it Shelby's Nimble Needle. But enough time had passed that I was now embracing the delicate task of adding my own touches to the enterprise. My role in the upcoming Gwen Lake Arts Festival was feeling like a major milestone in that transition.

The two-week arts festival was a big deal. Mom and Dad had been gone for a large portion of the past year, enjoying a spiffy artist-in-residence gig Mom had secured in Sedona. Mom insisted she'd returned to Gwen Lake "just to enjoy the festival," but no one really believed her. The long lecture she'd just given me on how to keep rival needlepoint canvas designers Laura Bitters and Paul Bardo from making scenes told me otherwise. I gave Mom points for declaring she wouldn't meddle, and I believe she was trying not to meddle, but the honest truth was Mom wasn't particularly succeeding. She'd catch herself telling me how to do something, apologize, and back off, only to reinsert herself again on some new subject.

It had to be hard. The store was deeply connected to who she was and how she'd spent her time for so many years. Most days I gave her a compassionate benefit of the doubt and lots of understanding. And in this case, I genuinely needed her backup. The trouble everyone else seemed to be sure was headed our way was going to need all hands—and all wisdom—on deck.

"They wouldn't really go at each other in public, would they?" I asked. These people were supposed to be seasoned professionals. Celebrities in the dignified sphere of needlework. Surely we could count on them to have better public manners than hotel-wrecking rock stars.

Evidently not.

All the NYAGs and Mom nodded a silent "They certainly would." Even Leona, one of our two staff working behind the counter, tsked and made a face.

"Seriously?" I questioned, trying to imagine what a needlepoint smackdown might look like. Even with all my experience with ill-tempered artists from my former job at a Savannah graphic arts firm, I couldn't believe the level of warnings coming my way. Based on my recent list of "don'ts," it seemed dangerous even to put Laura and Paul in the same county, much less in the same room at the charity auction event taking place tomorrow night.

Mom drew my attention back to her notes. She'd come into the shop this morning with a typed list of warnings—not exactly a confidence-boosting maneuver. "Paul is set to come by in about an hour. Laura isn't due until after three. Mayor Rose put Laura up at Kathy's inn with all the other artists."

"And Paul?" I asked, wanting to know just how much distance was between these two artists.

"He wouldn't stay in town. While it's usually Laura who needs lots of privacy, Paul now claims he needs *seclusion*." Mom gave the last word a *You've got to be kidding me* emphasis. Mom and Gwen Lake's Mayor Rose had come up with the idea to bring the two artists together in the hopes of spurring a charity auction bidding war. "Their appearances here at the shop are at least two hours apart tomorrow. I hope that's enough."

I'd followed Mom's entire detailed list of instructions for setting up the shop's role in selling each artist's canvases and hosting some activities. Still, as the dueling pair arrived today, I felt like Mom should be drawing me a battle map.

I allowed myself one tiny complaint. "I wish you'd set it up so I could greet Laura first." Laura Bitters was one of the first people to encourage me as an artist. In many ways, the camp summer I'd spent with her launched my career. Before Laura, I'd seen creativity only as something my mother possessed. Laura somehow saw the spark of creativity in me and nurtured it until I felt like maybe, just maybe, I was an artist, too. I had never really thanked her enough for that and was looking forward to a long-overdue catch-up during her visit here.

"You know Paul," Mom said with a sigh. "He always has to be first."

"Does he?" I pushed back, wishing I'd been a bit more forceful in voicing my opinion. I would have met with Laura first, even if Paul tried to throw his weight around. I told myself, for what felt like the hundredth time, to swallow my pride and be grateful for her strategic assistance.

"Paul's pillow will have to be auctioned off first, too," Mom warned. "Otherwise, he'll make a scene." Paul Bardo was a highly regarded canvas painter who specialized in architectural designs. We were counting on his rendition of Gwen Lake's famous "Blossoming Bridge" to be one of the most highly bid on items at the charity auction. The stone bridge, with flowering plants blooming in containers built all along its expanse, was the town's chief landmark. Everybody knew us by it and the charming beauty it brought to our lakeshore. So the fact that this landmark was depicted on a canvas not only designed by Paul but also stitched by the man himself made it hugely valuable.

Given that the auction was supporting arts programming in town, I took the view that if Paul and his work could bring in the big bucks, he was worth the coddling. Surely I could put up with a massive ego and a testy temperament for a few days if it sent funds to one of my favorite causes, right? How awful could the man be and still have such a loyal following?

Leona gave a soft laugh from behind the register. "He'll make a scene no matter what you do. But Nina's right. It will be *less* of a scene if he goes first."

"But if Paul goes first, doesn't that give Laura the advantage of knowing what high bid to beat if she wants to come out on top?" In courtroom cases, the defense always gets the final word, so it must be the stronger position.

Mom gave a small harrumph. "He won't even consider the possibility that Laura could bring a higher bid. Paul has to be first in everything. If he weren't so dang talented, I'd have dropped him as a vendor long ago." She closed her notebook. "Laura will still make a scene about not being first, but she's mostly all bark and no bite."

"Full of sound and fury, signifying nothing," Tilly quoted.

"Isn't that from *Macbeth*?" I asked. "Maybe we shouldn't be quoting from a play where so many people end up killing each other."

"Laura's far from nothing," Mom chided gently. "She's the best floral canvas designer there is, in my opinion. And while

I'll never say this in front of Paul, she deserves all the success she's seen."

"He's a great talent, too," Dot admitted. "He's just a top-flight jerk. How anybody with that prickly a personality makes all that gorgeous art is beyond me. Laura is a shy thing, but she's so much nicer."

"Artists are complicated people," I appeased. I certainly knew that to be true. I'd spent several years refereeing artistic personalities at the design firm. In fact, it had been my experience that the more talent any artist had, the more difficult they were to deal with. Only graphic designers, while artists, didn't have customers the way canvas design artists did. Many needle-pointers were fiercely devoted to their favorite designers. They flocked to trunk shows and events where they could meet them. They paid high prices for their work. How could you be a topflight jerk and still keep that kind of following?

If there was a mark I could make on the needlework world in my time managing the Needle, I hoped to create a world that gathered artists who could be vastly talented *and* nice.

It's always good to have lofty goals.

I just wouldn't see that goal come to fruition with this up-coming pair of guest artists. In this case, it was sounding like "no blood spilled" was closer to reasonable.

"I know it's a bit of a challenge," Mom said, in the under-statement of the day. "But it will work in our favor. Both of them will be bent on having their pillow outearn the other's."

"I know that." We all knew that.

Mom leaned in. "I wouldn't be surprised to learn either of them has planted bidders in the audience to drive the prices up." She smirked. "Higher bids mean more money to the school art programs."

"Sure, but is it worth the risk of such a drama fest?" I asked.

Mom nodded toward the shopwindow, where we all could

see a short, dark-haired man strutting toward the shop door. "I guess we're about to find out."

What had to be the great Paul Bardo strode into the shop carrying a portfolio case and a *Take notice* smirk. In terms of ego per inch, the man packed a high ratio.

"I'm here," he announced.

No doubt about that.

CHAPTER 2

I merely smiled, mustered all the reverence I could, and replied, "So you are, Mr. Bardo. And what a privilege it is to be hosting you."

He looked at me as if he couldn't quite understand why I had replied. "I was talking to Nina." The man had a voice that reminded me of steel wool—sharp, scratchy, and weirdly squishy around the edges.

"Paul," Mom said, grandly ignoring the snub and extending her hand. "What a thrill it is to see you again."

"Nina darling. Still as beautiful as ever." He somehow managed to make the compliment sound like she ought to be thrilled to have been graced with it. There was something not quite sincere behind his eyes. *I bet you say that to all the girls.*

I'd wrangled enough massive egos in my day to know now was not the time to back down. I stepped forward and extended my hand for a shake, as well. "I'm Shelby Phillips, her daughter. I'm running the Nimble Needle these days."

Paul did not look pleased to be dealing with what he considered the B team. "Is this no longer *Nina's* Nimble Needle?" The situation clearly did not meet with his approval. He glared at Mom with an expression that roughly translated to *You're not really going to make me work with her, are you?*

Mom gave an uncomfortable cough. "Now, Paul . . ."

I swallowed hard and applied a smile, as if I hadn't heard the condescension in his voice. "The store name has not changed, Mr. Bardo. But I'll be handling your appearance here." Since he hadn't accepted my offer of a shake, I held out the same hand toward the portfolio he'd brought into the shop. He was delivering canvases so we could hang them for display and sale.

He practically sneered as he clutched the case closer to his chest. "Not if I can help it."

We were off to a stellar start. With no reason to think it wouldn't just go straight downhill from there. Mom had warned me, but I had thought she was exaggerating. From behind me, I heard murmurs of disbelief and disapproval from the NYAGs. Mom was oddly silent. Shocked, I hoped, by the blatant condescension of our guest.

"Now, Paul . . . ," she said again after a wildly uncomfortable pause during which everybody stared at everybody else.

"Let's just move things along, shall we?" I offered. "I will need to get started on these if you want them displayed to your high standards." I tried—and failed—to take the case of canvases out of Paul's hands.

Paul blinked at Mom, slightly stunned that I'd even attempted to yank the portfolio's handle from his thick, short fingers. "Does she know the proper way to hang these?"

"Of course she does," Mom replied. "Come on now, don't be so difficult."

I wondered if he caught the small snort I heard from the table of NYAGs behind me. Technically, Paul had asked a rather insulting question. Hanging canvases is an essential skill in running a needlepoint shop. And, I might add, not a particularly complicated one. The open-holed mesh on which Paul's masterpieces were painted was quite stiff and durable. The edges were taped to keep them from any fraying, and there were no frames around these canvases. The process mostly involved carefully tacking them to a vertical surface so they could be seen by customers. Needlepointers never manhandled them and usually treated them like the art pieces they were.

Still, it was clear Paul viewed this as a test of my credentials. I wouldn't be surprised if he thought anyone other than Nina would toss them in a shoebox on a table. I was more than ready to prove him wrong. Ready, in fact, to show off the ingenious display tactic I'd created exclusively for Paul's and Laura's visit.

The Nimble Needle was a long rectangular space dotted with two tables and a sales counter. At the back was the large oval table, where the NYAGs were currently giving Paul a combination of admiration for his well-known talent and side-eye for his condescension.

Closer to the front was a smaller table, reserved for specialty displays like seasonal items. Currently, it held an after-season sale of Easter designs. On the long wall on our left hung a series of large boards, vertically hinged like pages in a giant book. Normally, they held the many canvases in stock at the store so that customers could easily browse the large selection. Flipping those boards was always an inspiring experience—so much color and art ready to be stitched. It was a rare Needle customer who didn't flip through those boards and discover three or four things they wanted to take home.

Yesterday I'd spent hours emptying those boards, so now they stood bare and waiting for one of our two featured guests. A front-and-center focus worthy of a needlework celebrity.

The shop's other long wall, opposite, on the right, usually held the fibers. It was a carnival of color—the endless variety of colored threads, floss, wools, and silks used to stitch the canvases. Customers were always darting back and forth between the canvases and the fibers, choosing and combining to create their projects. Needlepointers call it "pulling colors," and it is one of my favorite activities to watch. So much excitement and possibility!

That wall still held some of the fibers, but many of them had been moved to the back wall, so there was a large clear space on the right-side wall. It had taken a bit of ingenuity and planning, but I knew it was necessary considering our rival artists. Now there was a clear space on each opposite wall for Paul's and Laura's canvases. I'd guessed neither of them would consent to having their work displayed anywhere near the other's—and boy, was I right. This bit of rearranging meant Paul's and Laura's art would be as far away from each other as we could physically manage.

I thought of it as the display version of the game of "keep them away from each other," which we'd be playing all week. The whole strategy gave me a new appreciation for the high-tension act some of my married friends had bemoaned in needing to keep feuding family members apart at weddings and such.

The need for this unique display tactic struck me as ridiculous and territorial. A level of coddling that professional adults shouldn't need. It was clear from Paul's glare, however, that he took the whole display dynamic quite seriously. I had no doubt Laura would, as well.

I continued in my best *I'm here to meet your needs* voice from my design firm days. "Your designs will be exclusively featured on one of these walls. The pillow with your bridge design, of course, will be in the window at town hall." His pillow and a pillow with one of Laura Bitters's acclaimed botanical designs—both stitched by the artist themselves—would be featured. I didn't mention that dual display at the moment.

"Your pillow is a one of a kind, after all. But the limited-edition canvases of the same design will be right here for sale. As well as all the other outstanding original designs you've brought with you. Our customers are eager to see them, I promise you." Paul had hand-painted a limited edition of twenty-five of the same canvas featuring the Blossoming Bridge that appeared on the auction pillow. We were all sure they'd go fast, despite a hefty price tag.

Non-stitchers will occasionally ask me why needlepoint canvases come at such a high price. The simple answer is, because you are buying art. Yes, you embellish that design with your stitches, but a well-painted canvas gives you the artistic foundation. An elaborate version of coloring within the lines, if you will, only here you are adding fiber color atop the colors a talented artist painted on the mesh canvas.

It is 100 percent art, and a unique partnership between designer and stitcher. That's one of the things I like most about needlepoint: it's art and craft. You can spend less money for manufactured canvas—the needlepoint equivalent of an art print—but it's always worth the higher price to get actual art painted by an actual artist. It's not hard to see why they sign their work, as any painter would.

It was clear Paul thought of himself as a venerated artist. He was, but I didn't think he needed to get quite so high-and-mighty about it. The man's thick black eyebrows lowered as he glanced back and forth between the shop walls. "Which wall?" He said the two words so sharply they almost weren't a question.

Here was the beauty of my scheme. "Your choice."

It worked. It was clear this choice made the man very happy. He'd get to decide which wall was his and which would be relegated—because I'm sure that's how he would view it—to Laura.

To my great satisfaction, Paul loosened his death grip on the portfolio and handed it off to me. Mom shot me a proud look. From behind Paul, Leona gave me a thumbs-up of victory.

Paul turned, steepled his hands, and walked slowly between the walls. He looked like a general choosing battle tactics. The man went back and forth no less than three times before selecting the spot on the wall with the threads. I could have guessed it: this meant no other canvases would be near his. He probably also had some theory as to why the wall on the right held more gravitas than the wall on the left, but I certainly wasn't going to ask him the reason behind his choice.

"Excellent," I said, trying to sound as if I found his choice brilliant.

"Show us what you've brought," Mom said, walking back to where I'd set down the portfolio. "We've all been dying to see."

Paul walked over and unzipped the case as if unveiling a statue. "The one," he said with an *And you all know which one I mean* tone, "is already in the window at town hall." He opened the case and took out one of the limited-edition unstitched canvases of the same design. Complete, unsurprisingly, with a huge signature in one corner. "But what do you think? So much better in person, yes?"

Gasps went up around the room. It was undeniably beautiful. I had seen a photo of Paul's stitched canvas, made into a pillow, which evidently had been placed in the town hall window before his arrival here. In person, it really was stunning. Part of the reason Paul got away with such a monumental ego was that he was a monumental talent. He had gained some notoriety just from the fact that he was a man—the majority of designers and stitchers were women—but that just seemed to add to his well-nurtured mystique.

Mom put her hand to her chest. "It's just gorgeous. Our little bridge, an exclusive Paul Bardo design."

Paul leaned in. "Better than hers, don't you think?"

Again, I'm sure no one in the room missed the derisive snort from the NYAG table. I could only muse about the irony of it all. They might take all the potshots they wanted at Paul Bardo, but I knew at least two of them would pay the hefty price for one of those limited-edition canvases. And, while I wouldn't point it out at the moment, they'd do the same for Laura's.

Mom applied her "customer service" voice, the melodic, appeasing tone of which she was a master and I'd become an eager student. "Paul, you promised me you wouldn't get like that."

"Whose idea was it to invite both of us, anyway?" Paul sneered.

"Mine," came a commanding voice from behind us. I hadn't noticed Mayor Rose Tallen come in the door.

She did not look happy.

Nor did Laura Bitters, who stood behind her.